BELOVED BRIDE

M JAMES

Copyright © 2022 by M. James.

All rights reserved.

No part of this book may be reproduced in any form or by any electronic or mechanical means, including information storage and retrieval systems, without written permission from the author, except for the use of brief quotations in a book review.

This is a work of fiction. Names, characters, businesses, places, events and incidents are either the products of the author's imagination or used in a fictitious manner. Any resemblance to actual persons, living or dead, or actual events is purely coincidental.

AUTHOR'S NOTE AND CONTENT
WARNING FOR READERS:

Beloved Bride contains several scenes of assault and physical violence, including scenes of children in danger, violence and assault involving female characters and discussion of the emotional impact of these events. Readers who are sensitive to this material or who have experienced assault themselves may want to proceed with caution.

The road to Viktor and Caterina's happily ever after has been a difficult one, but I hope that you find it satisfying and cathartic in the end.

This will be one of those books you have to discuss! Join my Facebook group to connect with other readers and a lot of other cool and fun stuff here!

CATERINA

For a minute, all I can hear is the screaming.

Anika. Anika. Anika.

Her name repeats over and over in my head as I fling myself to the carpet next to Viktor, reaching for the tiny hand outstretched on the bloodied rug. In that moment, I forget about Viktor, our argument, the conversation we just had, everything that happened out in the gardens. The world narrows down to the small, still body in front of me, her skin waxy pale and her eyes shuttered closed, fringed lashes on her cheeks.

Viktor is already reaching for her, scooping her up into his arms. Luca reaches out, a hand on his shoulder as he tries to stop him, but Viktor flings it away.

"Viktor—it might not be good to move her—"

"Get out of my way!" he roars, rising to his feet with his daughter clasped in his arms. "Get the fucking doctor," he adds to no one in particular, and I see Levin already in motion, reaching for his phone. I almost wonder if I should do it myself, but Viktor is already heading for the stairs, and I want to be with Anika. I don't want to let her out of my sight for even a moment.

And I want to be with my husband right now, too. Everything else fades into the background, faced with the terrible possibility that we could lose Anika.

We can't. That can't happen. I won't let it.

I think that over and over as I follow Viktor upstairs, as if there's really anything I could truly do about it. "Where's Yelena?" I ask breathlessly as we reach the hallway, and he turns to walk towards Anika's room.

"She was in the playroom when the shooting started," he says curtly. "Some of our security is there, keeping her safe."

"Should I check on her—"

"Do what you want." His voice is clipped, all of his focus on the child in his arms. "I'm staying with Anika."

I follow him into the bedroom, watching as he lays her down on one side of the bed. Even the full-sized bed in her room makes her look small in her current state, her blond hair tangled and matted around her face, the blood on her shirt an ugly, terrifying stain.

It's impossible to tell what is hers and what could be from someone else. I press one hand to my chest as I step closer, willing it to slow down, for my panic to recede, so that I can think. So that I can be there for Viktor, who is pale as death, kneeling next to the bed as he reaches for his daughter's hand. It's very small in his, her arm limp, and I swallow hard, fighting back the tears. Crying won't help anything right now. Truthfully, I could probably be of more help watching Yelena or going downstairs to help Sofia and Ana. But I can't pull myself away from this spot.

There's a brisk knock at the door, and Levin steps inside. "The doctor is on his way," he says briskly. "I told him that the first priority is Anika."

"Send him up as soon as he gets here." Viktor reaches out, touching the little girl's stomach. "She's still bleeding. Caterina, get something—"

I nearly shove past Levin in my haste, looking for the first bathroom or closet that I see. There's a linen closet a few steps away, and I grab a handful of washcloths, hurrying back into the room and handing one to Viktor. He shakes his head, still gripping Anika's hand.

"You do it," he says firmly. "The wound is in her belly. Hold the cloth there. I can't—"

He breaks off, but I know what he's not saying. He doesn't want to let go of her hand, because he's not sure that she's going to make it. I'm not sure either—can a child as small as Anika survive a wound like that? She's still breathing, but shallowly, her skin waxy and pale. I press the cloth to her stomach, feeling another twist of nausea at the sight of blood blooming over the cloth, but I don't let go. I've never been particularly good with this kind of thing, which I suppose is a shortcoming, being in a mafia family and married to the Bratva leader. Blood and violence are a part of our lives.

Especially lately, it's become more and more clear that being squeamish isn't something I can afford.

"Where the fuck is that fucking doctor?" Viktor growls under his breath, his lips pressed tightly together. "If she dies because he took his fucking time—"

"He's coming as fast as he can, I'm sure of it," I say softly. "She'll live, Viktor. She has to—"

"You don't know that." He looks up at me then, and I can see the naked pain in his eyes. I'm not sure I've ever seen that level of emotion from him without something tempering it, concealing the true depth of it from me. I know why now, of course—why he'd wanted a wife to fuck and give him an heir and nothing more. There's more to that conversation that I know we need to have, too—but not now.

"She's a fighter," I say gently, taking the bloody cloth away from her belly and replacing it with a clean one. It's slower to stain this time, which I hope is a good sign—and not a sign that we're losing her. "It's Anika, Viktor. She's stubborn as hell, you know that. She's not going to go out like this."

Viktor laughs at that, a startling sound, as if he hadn't expected it. "You're right," he grunts, rubbing his thumb over Anika's fragile, pale knuckles. "Out of the two of them, she is our little fighter. She won't give up so easily."

I give him a startled look, wondering if he realized what he just said. *Our little fighter.* Something warm and soft blooms inside of my chest, because when I think of reasons to stay with Viktor, beyond obligation and my own reluctant desire, I think of his daughters. Of Anika and Yelena, who needs a mother, someone who can raise them to think for themselves, to see beyond the world that they'll grow up in. Someone who can do better for them than my own mother did.

I know Viktor married me to be a stepmother to them. But for him to say that, to call Anika ours, means something to me.

Why can't he just do something different? My heart aches in my chest, looking at my handsome husband as he holds his daughter's hand, his face taut, his eyes begging her to make it, to survive. I know if Anika dies, his loss will be incalculable. I can't understand why he can't apply that to the women who pass through his warehouse, why he can't think of the parents who have lost their children, grown as they are. *I'll talk to him about it again*, I think to myself, glancing nervously at the door as we wait for the doctor. *Maybe this will make him see things differently. Maybe there's some way to convince him.*

I've tried not to think of how things *could* be, because that seems like a recipe for disappointment and misery. Sofia learned to live with her husband's position and obligations, to turn a blind eye to the things she might disagree with, and to exist in a world that she might not have chosen for herself. It should be *easier* for me because I was born for this, raised for it. I was born into a world of violent men who did evil things, and I'd always known I'd have to turn a blind eye to what my husband did.

So why is it so hard with Viktor? Is it because what he does feels so much different from moving weapons or selling drugs? Is it because I can't stop seeing his daughters' faces every time I look at Sasha? Is it because I'm a woman with stepdaughters, who can't see how what he does has any moral value at all, despite his arguments?

Or is it simply because I want him, because my feelings for him are greater than just obligation, no matter how much I want to pretend otherwise—and I can't justify that to myself unless he changes?

My train of thought is cut off abruptly by the door opening as the doctor strides in, his face tightening instantly at the sight of Anika on the bed. I'm sure he must know that Viktor won't take his daughter's death lightly, and the man must be quaking in his shoes, knowing that the responsibility of saving Anika rests on him

"What's happened?" he asks briskly, taking in the scene in front of him—Anika's still body, her hand in Viktor's, the cloth I have pressed to her stomach.

"There was an attack." Viktor's tone is taut and brittle. "Gunshots. Anika got caught somewhere in the middle of it. I'm not sure what her injuries are, exactly—"

"Excuse me." The doctor nudges me aside, leaving me with a bloody cloth in my hands and my heart beating rapidly again, my anxiety rising at the look on his face. "This would be difficult for a healthy adult to survive," he says tersely, looking at Viktor. "For a child of her age—"

"She can't die," Viktor says sharply. "I'm relying on you to—"

"I'll do all I can, *pakhan*," the doctor says, inclining his head respectfully. I'm momentarily startled by the address, but after a moment's thought, it makes sense. Of course, here, near his safe house, in Russia, Viktor would have a doctor who is loyal to him and aware of his position. *No wonder the man was practically shaking when he walked in.* He knows well enough who Viktor is and his reputation.

"She is a small child," the doctor continues in his calm, thickly accented voice. "I cannot work magic. But if she can be saved, I assure you that I will—"

"Do whatever you have to," Viktor says sharply.

"I will. But for now, I need you both to step away so that I can do my work and examine her."

For a moment, I think Viktor is going to refuse. His jaw tightens, and I can see how difficult it is for him to let go of Anika's hand, setting it gently on the bed as he pushes himself to his feet.

I come around to the side he's standing on, and I half expect him to push me away or ignore me. All of his focus has been on the small girl lying on the bed, which is no surprise. But what *is* a surprise is when he reaches out for *my* hand, his broad, rough palm wrapping around mine as he clutches it tightly. When I look up at him, he's still staring straight at the bed, watching the doctor like a hawk as he examines Anika. His face is drawn tight, years older in a matter of minutes, though he's still as coldly, cruelly handsome as ever. But in this moment, my brutal Bratva husband isn't pushing me away, punishing me, or shutting me out.

At this moment, he *needs* me. And though I have so many reasons to pull away myself, to shut down and step away, leaving him to his worry and his grief, I don't. I can't find it in myself to let him suffer alone.

After all, at the very least, he cared for me when I was most in need of him. He helped me, fed me, bathed me, did all he could to make sure I survived. And now that it's not me lying on a bed, in pain and close to death, I know he needs me to return that care.

I feel almost guilty for my suspicions now, thinking he was behind my kidnapping. In retrospect, thinking over everything he told me in the garden, it feels like ridiculous paranoia. The only thing keeping me from feeling entirely ashamed is the fact that every man in my life so far, including Viktor, has treated me in a way to make me think that such a horrific thing could be possible.

The punishments haven't helped, I think grimly. Even now, I feel sore and stiff from the last one he meted out, not to mention what we did up against that tree in the garden. But even those I feel conflicted about, because as much as I resent my husband "punishing" me, the methods he uses, make me feel as if I'm melting from the inside out, as if some deep, primal part of me has always needed exactly that. As if I want it, whether it's deserved or not.

The doctor clears his throat, breaking me out of my thoughts, and I feel Viktor tense next to me.

"She'll need surgery to remove the bullet," the doctor says. "There's no time to take her to the nearest hospital; she wouldn't make the trip. I'll have to find a way to create a sterile environment here and have your man send for assistance. She's stable for now, but I'll need to operate as soon as possible."

"Do what you need to," Viktor says curtly. "Levin will make certain that you have everything you require."

"Thank you, *pakhan*." The doctor eyes me. "This is your wife?"

"Caterina Andreyva," Viktor says. "My wife and my daughter's stepmother."

"She'll need close care, if she survives the surgery," the doctor says. "Is your wife up to the task?"

"I'm standing right here," I say crisply, my annoyance with the peculiarities of mob men and their associates just about at its breaking point. "You can speak directly to me."

The doctor looks at Viktor, as if confirming that, and I see Viktor's mouth twitch with an unusual hint of humor, especially under the circumstances. I'd forgotten that, at times, he likes my feistier side.

Just not always when it's aimed at him.

"You heard my wife," Viktor says coolly.

"I'm sorry, Mrs. Andreyva," the doctor says, paling slightly. "What I meant to ask was, are *you* up to the task? I know not everyone can handle medical—"

"I'll be fine," I tell him firmly. "Anika is my daughter too, as far as I'm concerned. Whatever she needs, I'll assist with."

"Very good." The doctor seems relieved that the conversation hadn't exploded as it could have. "Please have your man make the arrangements as quickly as possible."

"Stay here," Viktor says to me, still holding my hand. "I'll go speak with Levin and return directly."

He didn't say *please*, though I hardly expected it from him. Still, it sounded more like a request than an order, the closest I've ever heard from him. "Alright," I say softly. "Hurry back."

Viktor looks at me, surprised. "I will," he promises. And then, wonder of wonders, he raises my hand to his lips, kissing it gently before turning sharply towards the door to go and find Levin.

I look back at the bed and the small girl lying there, her shallow breaths very visible.

Fight, Anika, I think quietly, wrapping my arms around myself as I watch her, my heart in my throat. *For all of us, fight.*

VIKTOR

It feels like hours before we know the outcome of Anika's surgery. The doctor emerges, looking drawn and exhausted, but without the fear that I would have expected if it had gone poorly.

"She's stable," he tells Caterina and me. "I can't say for sure which way it will go. I have her on fluids and antibiotics to fight infection. All of her vitals look remarkably good for such trauma. But I can't make promises, nor would I, *pakhan*. The coming days will tell us what the outcome will be."

I nod, feeling tenser than I've ever been. I can feel the anger bubbling just beneath the surface, but my more rational side reminds me that there's no reason to take it out on this man. He's done his best, and I can't deny that. He's not the one responsible for what's happened to my daughter.

I intend to make sure that those who are, pay with their lives.

"Let's go to bed, Viktor," Caterina says gently, resting a hand on my arm. "We can't do anything more tonight, and you need rest. Someone will come to get us if anything changes in the night."

"As much as you might want to sit up with her," the doctor

agrees, "it isn't wise. You'll need your own strength. Your wife is right."

There's a small, twitching smile on Caterina's lips at that. "Can he check on the others?" she asks softly. "Sofia didn't look well—"

"Yes." I glance at the doctor. "I'd appreciate it if you would examine the others here. Luca Romano's wife is pregnant, and the shock may have been difficult for her. She should take priority, but everyone here should be checked to ensure their health."

"Of course, *pakhan*."

I stand up slowly, feeling Caterina at my elbow. She stays there as we walk towards the stairs, and it's all I can do not to turn to go to Anika's bedroom. "Let's check on her once," I say, pausing. "Before we go to our rooms."

"Alright." The worry in Caterina's eyes is clear. "It'll make us both feel better to see her, I think. I hope."

Very little looks as if it's changed, when we open the door to look in on her. A nurse is sitting at her bedside, monitoring her vitals and waiting to change the fluids when need be. Anika herself is sleeping quietly, changed into clean pajamas, with the edge of her bandages visible where the blanket is pushed aside. Seeing us at the door, the nurse quickly adjusts the blanket, covering her up entirely.

"She's sleeping well," the nurse says quietly, a flicker of nervousness in her eyes as she looks at me, and I nod.

"There's nothing else we can do for tonight," Caterina says quietly, and I know she's right. Sitting up at Anika's side will only make me exhausted and groggy when what I need is to be clearheaded in the days to come, to make sure that Alexei and his men meet a bloody end to their jumped-up mutiny. "You need rest, Viktor."

I nod, following her to our suite of rooms. I can feel the exhaustion down to my bones, the flood of adrenaline beginning with our encounter in the garden through the firefight in the house all the way through my daughter's surgery finally ebbing and leaving me entirely drained. It's hard to remember why I was angry with her or what animosity there was between us. Right now, all I know is that I desperately need her, my wife, to be someone I can lean on. And despite what I know are her misgivings about me—about *us*—she's done exactly that.

Caterina pushes the door to our room open, and I see that there's already a fire roaring, thanks to the maids. I sink into one of the chairs in front of it, undoing one of the top buttons of my shirt. Behind me, I can hear the rustling of her clothing as she starts to change, and I feel a sudden deep throb of desire for her—but not the kind I'm accustomed to feeling.

She often makes me feel almost mad with the need to possess her, brutal in my need, nearly crazed with the desire to make her submit to me, to own her, to make her mine in such a way that she could never think of being separate from me. *One flesh*, I think often, and how I can make her physically mine so thoroughly that she could never exist apart from me. It feels hungry, primal, but tonight that's not what I feel.

Tonight, all I want is to hold her close, to lose myself in the sweetness of her body, to feel the pleasure that could wipe away some of the grief that I can feel aching in my bones. I want to forget briefly, have some respite from it, to feel wanted. To feel the warm comfort of another person surrounding me, just for a little while. Long enough for me to fall asleep afterward and hopefully not dream.

"Come here," I say gruffly, but I hope that she can hear in my voice that it's a request, not an order.

I can *feel* her hesitation even from behind where I'm sitting, but then her footsteps come closer, and I see her come around to the front of the wing chair, her expression wary. She's in nothing but her bra and a pair of lavender panties that cling to her hipbones, and I suddenly want her with an intensity that makes my mouth feel dry.

She's my wife. I don't need an excuse to want her, yet I feel myself trying to justify it. *I need to forget for a little while. I need comfort. I need* her—that last thought is almost frightening in its intensity, because since Vera died, I've been resolute that I wouldn't *need* another woman, not in a specific way. Not beyond the ordinary needs of my body. But something about Caterina's particular mixture of strength and fragility makes me want to protect and possess her all at once, keep her safe and break her all at the same time.

Caterina shifts her weight, looking down at me, and then suddenly, with a sharp breath as if she's made up her mind about something, she sinks to her knees in front of me.

"Is this what you need?" she asks softly, sliding her hands up my thighs. "A distraction?"

I nod, speechless at how quickly she picked up on what I was thinking, on what I needed. *She's a good wife,* I think, as her hands slide up my thighs, her body moving in between my legs. *She could be a better one, if you could be the man she needs. If you could change the things that hurt her.*

Another woman had needed those same things from me. She had needed change, for me to be a better man, a different one, and I hadn't been able to do that for her. I don't know that I can do it for Caterina. I don't know that I can be more than I was made to be, more than what I was taught. I don't know who else *to* be. But looking at the woman kneeling between my legs, her beautiful face soft and open as her dark hair tumbles around her shoulders and she reaches for my belt buckle, I wonder if there's some other choice besides the one that I thought I'd irrevocably made.

Could I be better for her? I hadn't been able to, for Vera. The thought that I might make changes for Caterina, when I couldn't for my first wife, who died as a result of my neglect, makes me feel a wave of guilt so deep and overwhelming that I nearly push Caterina away, my desire briefly ebbing. But her hands are on my buckle, pulling down my zipper, and when her fingers slip inside to brush against my naked flesh, it comes roaring back.

I'm nothing if not a man who can put aside his moral quandaries, I think grimly as she wraps her hand around me, slipping my cock out and running her hand along the length of it. She looks so beautiful, her ripe, luscious lips parting as she leans forward to trail her tongue over me, sliding up my length to the tip, and in an instant, I'm fully hard, my cock throbbing in her grasp as she slides her lips over the head of it.

"Oh *god*, Caterina—*bladya*—" I curse under my breath as she takes more of it in her mouth, her soft hair tumbling over my thighs as her warm, wet mouth suctions around my length, sliding down inch by inch as her tongue tangles around it and her head bobs. Her tongue lashes over the tip, and then she slips down further, taking me into her throat as she goes all the way down, the muscles of her throat squeezing pleasurably around my cock as I grip the arms of the chair.

"*Fuck*, that feels good," I murmur as she slides up and back down again, but I want more. I don't want an emotionless blowjob, however, arousing it is to see my beautiful wife kneeling for me of her own volition in front of the fireplace as I lean back and watch my cock slide between her lips. I want *her*, the softness of her body, the warmth of her, the comfort of another human holding me. A person who, for all our conflicts and difficulties, is bound to me and my life.

I reach for her, pulling her off of my cock as I stand up, and I see the surprise in Caterina's face as I turn her towards the bed. "Go and lay down," I tell her, but again, there's no cruelty in my voice, no hint of order. That might be why she goes without hesitation, the sight of her ass in the lavender material stretched tightly over it, arousing me even more. I can see the hints of welts left from her most recent spanking, and my cock throbs at the sight, remembering the pleasure of punishing her, of hearing her beg for me despite the spanking she received.

But that isn't what I want from her tonight. I follow her to the bed, stripping off as I go. I swallow hard with desire when I see Caterina slide her panties down her hips, one hand going up to unhook her bra as she tosses it aside. She turns to face me, slender and nude, and I can see the flicker of worry in her eyes. Her wounds are beginning to heal, showing where they'll leave scars behind, and I know she's afraid I won't want her, that I won't desire her any longer when her pale flesh is covered in scars.

I know that I won't care. If anything, the scars on her body remind me of her strength, that she survived something that I've known grown men to cripple under the weight of, that she fought back and refused to die. She's all the more beautiful to me for that, even if I'm still angry at her for trying to run.

At least now, I understand why she did, even if I can't comprehend how she could have imagined I'd do something so terrible. I can understand the fear that would have driven her to try to run.

All I can hope is that there's a way for us to move forward from this, that the miscommunications between us, the secrets and the lies, and the ways that we've both hidden a great deal from each other haven't prevented us from having any sort of marriage at all. I don't know what I want from Caterina any longer—my own feelings are as muddled and confused as hers, and I can hardly sort through it with my daughter downstairs clinging to life.

What I do know is that right now, tonight, she's all that I want. She's what I *need;* the only thing I can think of that can give me the comfort I crave. And so, when she slides naked onto the bed, I follow her, reaching to pull her into my arms as I lean over her slender body, kissing her full lips slowly and unhurriedly, wanting to savor her mouth.

She always tastes so sweet. I suck her lower lip between mine, licking along the edge of it, and I hear her soft gasp. She twitches beneath me, her hands coming up to press against my shoulders. I slide one arm underneath her, moving her up to brace against the pillows as I deepen the kiss, my tongue sliding into her mouth.

Caterina moans softly, arching against me, and I feel my cock harden against her thigh, aching with the need to be inside of her. I want her, but I want the distraction most of all, and I want to make this last as long as possible for exactly that reason. I want to draw it out, to lose myself in the pleasure of her body for as long as I can, and I keep kissing her, running my hand down her side as I savor the taste of her lips.

"Viktor—" she whispers my name, and I can hear the hesitancy there, the confusion. I know this isn't what she's used to, not the man that she's become accustomed to having in bed. I don't know if I've *ever* touched her this gently, but I don't want to be rough with her tonight. I want to seduce her, to make her give herself over to me willingly, to beg for me because she wants more of the pleasure I can give her, not despite the pain.

My hand brushes over her flat belly, down to the space between her legs, over the naked flesh there. I can feel that she's faintly wet, her lips warm and soft against my fingers. When I slip them in between, my fingertips brushing against her clit, she cries out against my mouth, her body arching again as her hips twitch against my hand.

"Viktor—" when she whispers my name again, this time, it's more of a plea.

I want to give her what she's asking for, what she's *begging* me for. I rub my fingers against her, circling that hard nub; I can feel her soften against me, the rush of her arousal coating my fingers as I stroke her between our tangled bodies, and I close my eyes, losing myself in the feeling of her against me.

She feels so fucking *good*, her soft skin and small breasts, the warmth of her sinking into me as she tilts her chin up to kiss me again, and the brush of her tongue against mine nearly takes my breath away with how badly I want her.

At this moment, I feel as if I'd do anything, be anyone, if it meant keeping her by my side. If it meant Caterina would be *mine*, in every possible way.

Her body tenses, her hips arching tightly against my fingers, and I can feel the tremor that passes through her as her arms tighten around my neck, her mouth opening in a soft gasp. I know her well enough now to know the signs that mean she's coming for me, and it feels good to know she's giving in to it, that she *wants* it, that she's not fighting it. This isn't despite herself. This is her wanting me, wanting the pleasure that I can give her, and the rush of need that washes over me at that thought is enough to make me want to plunge my cock into her now. I'm throbbing painfully against her thigh, my entire body rigid with the effort. I want to feel her coming against me for a moment more, the way her body shudders as she arches her back and moans against my lips.

And then, just as I feel her start to relax, her body sinking back into the mattress, her clit pulsing against my fingertips, I reach for my cock, angling it so that I can slip between her folds, and the feeling of my aching cockhead slipping into the tight, wet heat of her pussy is so good that I groan aloud, kissing her hard and fierce as I thrust into her.

Caterina's legs tighten around me, wrapping around mine as she arches into the thrust, gasping with pleasure. I can still feel her fluttering from her orgasm, a sensation that makes my back arch, my fingers digging into the mattress as I start to fuck her harder, wanting more. As much as I want to go slowly, I can't stop myself from thrusting hard and deep, wanting to feel all of her wrapped around me, wanting more of her small, eager cries as she arches up against me, her legs wrapped around my hips.

"Viktor–" she gasps my name again, and I feel a shudder of pleasure at the sound of it, my body reacting instantly to the sound of her voice, wanting more.

"Cat," I whisper it softly in her ear, and I feel the tremble that ripples through her. I've heard Sofia call her the nickname before, but I've never called her anything so familiar. I don't even know if she wants that, but in this particular moment, it feels right.

I want that familiarity with her. I want *us*, beyond just the arrangement that I made with Luca. I don't even know if that's possible, after everything that's happened between us. But all I know right now is that I don't want to let her go.

I can feel her trembling around me, her muscles tightening with the oncoming rush of pleasure, and I know that I can't hold mine back much longer either. "I'm–" the intensity of it is too much, I can barely speak, and I feel Caterina lean up, her lips brushing over mine.

"Me too," she whispers, and then I feel her let go.

There's no chance that I can last a second longer. She feels too good, every inch of her pressed against me, and my cock feels as if it's about to burst. I thrust into her hard, reveling in the feeling of her clenching around me as her head drops back against the pillows, a long moan slipping from her lips as her arms tighten around my neck. I feel her come hard, my orgasm following close behind.

For that one blissful moment, everything slips away–all of my fears and worries and anger, everything that crowds together in my head all day, every day. There's nothing but her, soft and warm and wanting, clasped in my arms, and I forget everything else.

"Caterina!" I groan out her name against her mouth as I come, filling her as I thrust into her as deeply as I can and stay there, my hips rocking against hers as I feel the hot rush of my orgasm, the ecstasy of it rippling along my spine and lighting every nerve in my body on fire, a pleasure like nothing I've felt with any other woman.

Life with Caterina isn't easy. She's far from being the compliant bride that I'd expected. But being with her is like nothing else I've ever experienced.

I know, beyond a shadow of a doubt, that I don't want to lose her.

CATERINA

I wake the next morning to a soft rapping at the bedroom door, which wakes me up and not Viktor. He's snoring next to me, still passed out as hard as he'd been last night not long after we'd slept together–which is in and of itself something that I'm still coming to terms with.

I'd been caught off guard in the garden, but I'm not sure what my excuse was for giving in to him last night. He'd needed me, but more than that–I'd wanted to be there for him. And I don't know how to feel about that. I should hate him, but after what he shared with me, I can't feel the same bitterness and suspicion that I did before. And after Anika–

The knocking at the door comes again, and I swing my legs out of bed, grabbing for my robe and wrapping it around me as I pad across the room. I crack the door open to see Sasha standing there, her face scrunched with worry, and I feel a flare of panic.

"Is it Anika?"

"No, ma'am." She shakes her head. "It's Yelena. She's been having panic attacks all night. Olga said she'd cry it out, but she won't stop, and now she's asking for you. Can you come downstairs? We can't get her to calm down, and I'm afraid she's going to hurt herself at this point."

"Of course. Give me just a second." I shut the door, quickly grabbing a pair of leggings and a top and throwing them on. I know I probably look like a mess—my hair is in a complete tangle, but I don't have time to look any more presentable than that. Sasha won't care, and Yelena certainly won't.

I can hear Yelena crying before we even get to her room. Sasha pushes open the door, her face a mask of worry as I step inside in front of her, only to see the small blonde seven-year-old in a ball on the rug. What I can see of her face is pink and swollen from crying.

"Yelena," I murmur her name softly, sinking down onto the rug next to her. "Yelena, it's Cat. Can you look at me?"

It takes her a minute to gather herself enough to do that. She peeks up from her arms, sniffling. She looks like a mess, her face tear-stained and strings of snot dripping from her nose, and I look around desperately for something to clean her up a bit with.

"Here." Sasha hands me a box of tissues, and I reach for Yelena gently, touching her face as I wipe her nose with my other hand.

"You'll feel better when I'm done," I tell her gently as she tries to pull away. "It's no fun crying, I know. I've been there plenty of times."

Yelena peers at me, her expression dubious. "You have?" she manages through tears, and I nod, wiping away the last of the snot and taking another tissue to dab at her cheeks.

"I definitely have," I tell her firmly. "Trust me, more often than I'd like to."

"Why?" Yelena purses her lips at me, but her sobs have slowed, the distraction of the person she wanted to talk to enough to calm her down a little.

I debate how much to say to her. She's only seven, and I don't want to make things worse. But she's also not an ordinary seven-year-old. She's the daughter of the Bratva *pakhan*, and she's in the middle of a panic attack because yesterday, while she was in an unfamiliar place, strangers came and started shooting.

Her life has never been, and will never be, ordinary, any more than mine was or ever will be. I certainly would never say anything to traumatize her. Still, I can't see how my mother overly sheltered me, treating me with kid gloves helped either.

I reach for her, pulling her into the circle of my arms, and she lets me easily, nestling against me as I stroke the tangle of her hair. "I lost my parents a few months ago," I tell her quietly, looking down at the little girl as I soothe her. "My mom, and then not too long after that, my dad."

Yelena tenses in my arms. "Is something going to happen to my dad?" she asks in a small voice, tears threatening again, and I bite my lip, realizing I might not have said the right thing. *Being a parent of any kind is really hard,* I think ruefully, bending to gently kiss the top of her head. *I've got to somehow keep these two girls from being totally fucked up, living this life. Not to mention the child I might have–if I even can anymore–*

That last thought makes my chest constrict, and I push it away, focusing on Yelena. "Your dad is going to be just fine," I tell her firmly, hoping that it's true and I'm not lying to her. "He's a tough man. It would be hard for anyone to hurt him. Lots of people respect him. He's going to be fine."

"And my sister?" Her face screws up tightly, her eyes squeezing shut as she starts to cry again, and I know that's the root of all this. "I heard that she might die–she's mean to me sometimes, but I don't want her to *die*–"

I take a breath, trying to think of how to comfort her without lying. "Anika is really badly hurt," I tell Yelena finally, holding her a little tighter. "There was a fight downstairs–some bad men got in, and they caused problems. Anika got in the middle of it by accident. But the doctor did all he could, and he's optimistic–"

"I don't know what op–opt–op–means," Yelena says in a small voice.

"He has hope it'll be okay," I tell her gently. "And that's his whole job, so if he's hopeful, then your dad and I are too."

Yelena nods, burrowing into my chest again. "Don't leave me," she whispers in her small voice, her other hand coming up to make a fist in my shirt. "I miss my mama. Papa said you were going to be our mama now–"

"And I am," I promise her.

"But you left."

I wince. I *definitely* am not about to share the details of my kidnapping and everything that happened afterward with a seven-year-old. "Your dad and I had to go on a business trip, and it took longer than we thought it would. But we definitely didn't want to leave you or your sister. We brought you here because we missed you so much–"

"You brought us here because there was danger. Papa said so, he said home was dangerous, there's a bad man –"

Oh, Viktor. From all I've seen, Viktor is an excellent father, especially in terms of men in the various crime families. But telling Yelena that there was danger at home and she was being brought here because of it, might not have been the best choice. I know he meant it to ensure that she knew the seriousness of the situation. She's *seven*, I think to myself as I hold her close, letting her sniffle and cry against my shirt as I rub her back and soothe her.

"She's already calmed down a lot," Sasha mouths, nodding at the little girl. "Since you came in."

I feel a flush of warmth at that, only adding to the feeling that I've had since Yelena crawled into my arms. I've always loved children, wanted to nurture and teach and care for them, others as well as my own. I love both of these girls, even if Anika has an unmatched attitude, and I want to keep them safe. The fact that Yelena trusts me means more to me than I can say.

I also know that it means I can't leave, no matter what happens between Viktor and me. These girls have lost one mother already, and I can tell just from Yelena's reaction to me leaving for the business trip with Viktor that she, at the very least, would be devastated if I left for good. And I think that Anika might be too, as well as she would hide it.

Viktor and I will have to work something out. I'd always known I would have a marriage of convenience, and I knew I might not like my husband. This should be no different. Even if it makes things more difficult that I *do* desire him, that's my own burden to shoulder. In time, I'm sure it will fade.

I glance up at Sasha, who is kneeling on the carpet now, watching Yelena concernedly as she sniffles and hiccups against my chest. The girl is astonishingly beautiful, with that rich strawberry blonde hair and bright green eyes, slender and elegant like a dancer. I think of everything that Viktor told me that happened to her, and I can't help but be astonished that she's still as composed as she is, considering. I think of everything that's happened to me, Franco, my kidnapping, my torture, and how close to the edge of collapse I came. And Sasha wasn't raised in this life like I was. She didn't grow up with the knowledge of violence, even if I was sheltered from a great deal of it.

Or maybe she did. I remember what Viktor said–*she was on the verge of aging out of the foster care system*–and I wonder how bad that is, exactly, in Russia. Maybe her life, even before Viktor picked her up, was much worse than I, someone who has been pampered for most of my life, can imagine.

Regardless, I can't help but be impressed by her ability to adapt to her circumstances and remain at least outwardly positive, despite everything. She's looking at Yelena with genuine care and affection, even though Yelena's father is directly responsible for a great deal of what happened to Sasha. And she treats me with a sort of kind respect, without any resentment, even though I'm Viktor's wife. It's not fear, either–I've never seen anything to indicate that she's afraid of me.

Yelena has fallen asleep on my chest by that point, and I slowly get to my feet, carrying her over to her bed and laying her gently on top of it. Sasha hands me a knitted throw blanket, and I put it over her, tucking the edges in around her shoulders as the small girl curls into a ball, still fast asleep.

"If she wakes up and needs me, come and get me," I whisper as Sasha and I step outside. She nods, and I hesitate, wanting to ask her questions and unsure if I should.

"Mrs. Andreyev? Is there something else?"

I hesitate, looking at her. "I–" I take a breath, wondering how to say what I want to ask. "How do you feel about my husband, Sasha? I know what happened to you, why you're here. You don't have to mince words with me. I won't be angry with you."

There's a flicker of fear in Sasha's eyes anyway, and that alone tells me I won't get an entirely truthful answer–but it's hard to blame her. "I'm very appreciative of the place he's given me here," she says quietly. "And that he took revenge for me."

"You don't hate him?" I look at her, wishing more than anything that I could get her to speak plainly to me. "He's the reason you're here, that all of that happened to you."

Sasha hesitates, licking her lips nervously. "Your husband is a man who does evil things," she says finally, looking away. "But I don't think that he, in and of himself, is an evil man. I think that he believes he is making do with the choices that were given to him, as we all do."

"That's very generous, especially when he's brought you back here, to your home, but you're still a part of his household."

"My choices here were not good either," she says quietly. "That doesn't mean that I wouldn't have liked the opportunity to make them for myself. But that's not the way life worked for me, is it? And it's better now than it could have been."

"So you wouldn't have liked what he had intended for you? A place in a prince's harem?"

Sasha shrugs, her mouth twitching slightly. "How should I know? I've never been a prince's mistress, and now I never will. But I do know that my place in Mr. Andreyev's household is better than what I might have had. I just wish I had chosen it for myself." She shrugs again, looking shyly up at me. "Does that answer your questions, Mrs. Andreyva?"

"You can call me Caterina," I tell her gently. "We don't need to be so formal–"

"I don't think that would be appropriate," she says firmly. "But I'm glad to know that you care." She pauses. "Maybe one day it will have an influence on your husband." She takes a step back then, her shoulders tensing as if she's afraid she's said too much. "I'll let you know if Yelena needs you again."

"Okay," I say quietly. "Thank you."

I glance towards the door as Sasha disappears down the hall, thinking of the small girl sleeping inside and the one down the hall, fighting for her life.

I can't help but continue to hope that I could somehow have an influence on Viktor–if only for them. If only so they don't grow up and one day have to come to terms with the same thing that I did–that my father was a man who I loved…and also a man who did evil things.

CATERINA

On the way back towards the stairs, I almost run directly into Max. He stops short, his handsome face flushing a little. "I'm sorry, Mrs. Andreyva," he says. "I was just going to check on Anika. I know that your husband is not of the same faith as you are, but I think a little prayer could help anyone, especially that poor child." He glances past me in the direction that Sasha left. "Was that Sasha?"

I blink at him. "Yes? She was helping me with Yelena. Did you need her for something?"

He flushes deeper at that, and my eyes widen slightly. "No," he says quickly. "I just–I had spoken with her the other day, told her that if she was ever in need of someone to talk to about her–trials–that I would be there to listen. If she needed spiritual guidance, or–"

I press my lips together, trying hard not to laugh. From the brief time I'd spent with Max, I'd gotten the impression that he was earnest in his beliefs, even if he, for whatever reason, was no longer a priest. My suspicions, from what Viktor had briefly told me about him, were that he still stuck to the rules of *being* a priest, even if he'd been defrocked. Which means that if he was, for instance, nursing a crush on Sasha, it would be very distressing for him.

That's all we need, I think wryly. *A former priest fighting his vows over one of Viktor's girls.* Looking at his reddened face, I think it's fairly clear that he wouldn't go through with it. It's on the tip of my tongue to tell him to give Sasha a wide berth, but then I stop myself. *Could it really hurt if a handsome former priest had a crush on her? It might make her feel good, and it's harmless. He's not going to* act *on it.*

Besides, I have two children already. I can't worry too much about Sasha, who is a grown woman, if very young.

"I'm going upstairs to check on my husband," I tell him. "But if there's any change with Anika, please come get us. We'll be down to look in on her before too much longer."

He clears his throat, obviously grateful for the change in subject. "Of course, Mrs. Andreyva."

When I make it back upstairs to our room, Viktor is just starting to wake up, sitting up in bed. He looks over at me as I walk in, and the smile on his face almost undoes me. He looks kinder, softer, handsome in a different way than I'm used to. Nothing like the husband that I've grown accustomed to.

"Where did you go off to so early?" he asks almost teasingly, and I blink at him. It's been a long time, if ever, since I've heard him talk to me that way, and it's startling. It's also not entirely unpleasant, and that makes me flinch back because I know that *more* affection between us is only going to make it that much harder to keep my walls up. And they have to stay up if there's never going to be any changes, if I'm going to stay for Yelena and Anika. *They're what really matters,* I remind myself. Nothing else–not Viktor, or my own happiness, or any future that I could have foreseen matters as much as making sure that those girls don't lose someone else that they love. And I hope, with everything in me, that Yelena isn't about to lose a sister.

"I went downstairs," I tell him, walking towards the dresser to get a fresh change of clothes. My top is a mess after Yelena cried on me for so long. "Yelena was having a panic attack and asked for me. She's worried about Anika."

"We all are." Viktor runs a hand through his hair. "We should go check on her."

"Max is with her right now. Let me change, and we'll go."

Viktor frowns. "That's kind of him. Max has never been all that fond of children."

"Well, maybe he makes an exception for Anika." I shrug. "A child on the verge of dying is probably a different story." My chest tightens just saying it out loud, and I grab the dress I'd planned to change into, walking towards the bathroom. I suddenly feel as if I can't wait another minute to go and check on my other stepdaughter, my worries for her overtaking everything else.

Everything except what Sasha had said to me, which is still in the back of my head, echoing. *Maybe you can be an influence on him.*

If that's true, then I could change things. But I don't believe that, not really.

The door opens, and Viktor joins me, his own clothes in hand. "You could have knocked," I say crossly, and he looks at me, amused.

"I've been inside of every part of your body, wife," he says wryly. "I've done things to you that I know no other man has. And you think I'm concerned that I might walk in on you–what? Peeing?"

I flush. "I just might have liked a little privacy, that's all."

"Perhaps I was hoping I'd catch you half-dressed, so I could kiss you again while feeling your body under my hands." He reaches for me, his hands cupping my breasts through my thin top.

"Viktor, that shirt is a mess–"

"I don't care. I've never cared. Children are messy. Vera worried about the same things, but something so trivial won't stop me from wanting my wife–"

The mention of Vera stops me short. "Viktor–" I step away, pulling off my top and turning my back to him so that the sight of my breasts in only my bra won't encourage him more–although I'm well aware by now that what my husband wants, he gets. Turning my back won't stop him if he's insistent on taking me again.

"We need to talk more about what you told me in the garden," I tell him insistently, stepping out of my leggings and reaching for the dress. "About Vera and what happened to her. About–" *About the baby that she would have had,* I want to say, but it's too hard to say the words out loud. I'm still astonished by that part of the story, that Vera killed herself knowing she was pregnant. She must have been so horrified by her husband that she couldn't bear the thought of bringing another child into his world.

Haven't I felt the same way? I think back to our wedding night, standing on the balcony and considering the drop down from the penthouse suite to the sidewalk below, calculating the urge to continue living versus the life I'd have to live. Vera may have simply felt that there was no way she could go on, baby or not.

"What else is there to talk about?" Viktor asks, and I can hear the edge returning to his voice. "I had another wife. She gave me two daughters that she didn't want, and then when there was another possibility of a son, she killed herself. What else is there to the story?"

"You didn't think that she was at that point?"

"Are you saying it's my fault?" Viktor turns to look at me. "Because if you are, Caterina, you're not saying anything that I haven't said to myself. I've gone over the possibilities of what I could have done differently, where it could be my fault, a hundred times over. I've thought of what I could have changed, regretted the words I said to her and things I did, wondered if I just hadn't gone on that business trip if she might not have died. But I couldn't stay home forever. I have a business to run. And she did things wrong, too–" he runs his hand through his hair again. "I can't change it, Caterina. I simply can't. All I can do is try to not let it happen again, which is why I've tried to make things as good as I can between us–"

"That's my point," I say quietly. "There is something you can change. Something that might have made things different with Vera, and that could mean a different life for your daughters. It could make our marriage better–"

"What?" Viktor turns to face me, and I can hear the genuine question in his voice. There's no anger or sarcasm in it. "What could I do, Caterina, to make you want to be married to me? To make you–" he stops there, but I know exactly what the words are that he's not speaking.

To make you love me.

That brings me up short. *Can I love him, even if things change?* I wonder, looking at my husband across the arm's length between us, trying to imagine a different life, one where I don't feel guilty for wanting him, desiring him. If I didn't have that guilt, would I want other things, too? Would I find a possibility for love in his arms, something that I've long since given up on? Could we have a marriage in every possible sense, not just one of convenience, meant for the children?

"You could find some other business to run," I say quietly, forcing the words out past the lump in my throat, my racing pulse. "You could stop trafficking in women and do something else. Something like–"

"Something like Luca does? Or your father?" Viktor lets out a sharp, frustrated breath. "We've talked about this before, Caterina, I–"

"I know your reasons!" I say quickly. "I know your justifications. But it doesn't matter. Someone like Sasha–she's grateful for what she has now, but it still wasn't her *choice*. Viktor–people are stronger than you think. *Women* are. We can live through so much if we choose it. If we live our lives based on our own will, no matter how bad or good it is." I shake my head, swallowing hard. "Nothing that's ever happened to me has been because of my own choice, and that has made it all so much harder–"

"You did choose, though." Viktor frowns. "You could have refused to marry Franco or me."

"But the consequences–"

"It was still your choice!" His expression is clearly frustrated. "You just chose the route that would prevent you from losing the things you wanted or from feeling guilty because of blood that would be shed."

"People dying because I refused to marry you isn't a choice!"

"It is," he insists. "It just wasn't the choice you could live with. That's why you stayed, why you came back. And when you tried to run, it was simply because you could no longer live with the choice you made."

I let out a long breath, feeling deflated, defeated. He isn't wrong. And I don't know how to make him see that the consequences of *his* choices are so much worse than he realizes.

"Viktor—your daughters—do you want them to grow up and find out what you do? Do you think they'll agree with your justifications? Or will they, like me, just see other daughters that you thought were less important, other families that you were fine with tearing apart? Will a small part of them hate you, just like a part of me hates my father?"

He looks at me for a long moment, and I can see the pain in the back of his eyes. It tells me, in that instant, that he's thought of this too. That I'm not saying anything new to him—which makes me wonder, how has he decided that it's not worth changing for?

"I want my daughters to be proud of me," Viktor says quietly. "I want them, always, to love me. I've tried my best to be a good father. And if there was potential for our marriage to be more, Caterina, I would want that too. But Cat—"

"Don't call me that," I say softly. "Not while things are like this."

He clears his throat. "Caterina. This is all I know. This is the business that my grandfather and father built from scratch. This is how we came to hold the power we have, how I've become the man I am, how I'm able to give my daughters and you everything you have. And you want me to turn my back on that, and what? Start from scratch? Rely on other men, on Luca and perhaps Liam, to ensure that I'm successful in the future? Is that the man you want me to be?"

"I want you to be the man that I know you *are*," I say softly. "I know that deep down, there's goodness in you, Viktor. I know that you're conflicted. And I—" I swallow hard, feeling my heart ache at the words I'm about to say. "I don't know if I can ever give you a child now, after what the doctor said. I might never be able to do that. But if I do—and if we had a son—I think you would feel conflicted about passing this legacy on to him. But you don't have to—"

There's a knock at the bedroom door, interrupting me, and I see a flash of relief on Viktor's face that the conversation has been stopped.

He turns, stepping out of the bathroom, and leaves me there, staring after him. I know there was a moment when he wanted things to be different. But also, I don't truly think they'll ever change. And that leaves my heart even heavier than before.

VIKTOR

Few things in my life have made me feel as wounded as my wife standing in front of me, telling me that my daughters might one day grow up to hate me. Telling me that *she* hates her own father in some ways because of the truths she's learned about him over time.

And it doesn't help that nothing she's saying is anything I haven't said to myself already.

I stride downstairs, not bothering to wait for her. I need to see my daughter, and I don't trust what I might say next to Caterina. I want our marriage to work, but she wants to change me–to change my entire life. *Our* whole life, because whether she likes it or not, she's a part of this too. She benefits from it too–*or where does she think the money, her clothes, this safe house, our home, and everything else we have comes from?* I think darkly, a hint of bitterness setting in.

All I can see is a repeat of Vera, the same resentment between us growing. It's not what I want for Caterina and me, but perhaps the only way a man like me *can* be married is to have a distance between himself and his wife. I'd thought Caterina might understand, but clearly, I'd been wrong.

I push open the door to Anika's room to see the doctor checking her vitals, Max sitting on one side of the room. He stands immediately, and I give him a tight smile. "Thank you for looking in on her," I tell him, and he nods, his youthful face calmer than I've seen it in a long time.

"I thought she could use the prayer," he says, and I force myself not to roll my eyes.

"You know I don't put much stock in that, son," I tell him, striding towards Anika's bedside. "But it can't hurt. And what you've done for this family isn't something I'll soon forget."

Max licks his lips nervously, hesitating. "So you'll–look into what I asked?"

I hesitate. "I don't know if I can help you there. I don't have much influence–"

"But you said Luca Romano might."

"He might. I'm hesitant to owe him a favor. But under the circumstances–" I pause, looking at Max's expression, one that's faintly hopeful and afraid to hope all at once. "When things are settled with my daughter and with Alexei, I'll see what I can do."

"Thank you, sir." Max's expression turns to relief. "Even if it's not the outcome I hoped for, if there's a possibility–"

I nod, turning my attention to Anika. I hear his retreat towards the door, but I don't bother looking after him. All of my attention is on my daughter, my breath caught in my throat as I wait to hear what the doctor will say.

"It's good news," he says finally, when he looks up. "She's not out of the woods yet, but everything points to a full recovery. She'll need time here to rest and heal, but from what you said, this is the safest place for her right now. It'll be some time before she can return to New York–"

"That's fine," I say curtly. "Whatever it takes for her to recover, that's what we'll do."

I look down at my daughter, and I can see already that some of her color is returning, her sleep looking peaceful instead of nearly dead. It terrifies me that she still hasn't woken or stirred at all, but I know from what I've been told that that's normal, even desirable. She's in a healing sleep, and if she wakes up from it whole, that's all that matters to me.

There are footsteps behind me, light and soft, and I know that it's Caterina. I can smell her perfume, and something in my chest lightens, knowing that she's here despite myself. I know that I shouldn't take comfort in her presence, that there's nothing that can make our marriage be what I want it to be. But I can't help the feeling of lightness that washes over me knowing that she's here, that she loves my daughter too, that whatever happens next, I won't have to bear it alone.

"How is she?" Caterina asks softly.

"Healing," I tell her, not taking my eyes off of Anika. "The doctor is hopeful that she'll make a full recovery."

"I'll let the two of you have some time with her before I send the nurse in," he says, looking up. "There's nothing particularly concerning that I see right now. It's not certain yet, but everything points to a positive outcome." He nods to me, circling around the bed and leaving Caterina and me there, looking down at the girl I now can't help but think of as *our* daughter and not just mine.

I know that she feels the same.

"When do you think we should let Yelena see her?" Caterina sounds worried. "I know she's afraid her sister is going to die, but I don't know if seeing her like this will help or hurt–"

"If we can wait until Anika wakes up, I think that would be best." I hesitate, glancing over at my wife. Her concern for my children makes me feel all the more for her, and I take a deep breath, forcing the feelings back. I know it will do me–*us*–no good. But I can't help the feeling that if only we could overcome our differences, Caterina could be a wife and mother better than anything I could have possibly hoped for when I asked for her hand from Luca.

"Caterina, I–" I hesitate, and she shakes her head without looking at me.

"Don't, Viktor," she says quietly. "It'll only make things worse. Perhaps it's better if we continue to hate each other."

That brings me up short. "Do you hate me?"

She swallows hard. "I have, sometimes. Not always."

"Do you now?" She won't look at me, and everything in me wants to reach for her, to force her to meet my eyes. But I don't think that will make things better between us.

"Not right now," she says softly. "I'm just sad. For us, for them, for–"

For any baby that there might be in the future. She doesn't have to say it out loud for me to know what she's thinking.

"Do you think you'll hate me again?"

"I don't know." She still won't look at me, and I can feel the need to look into her eyes churning in my gut, the need to *see* her, to see what she's thinking.

"Do you truly think I've hated you?"

Caterina shrugs, and I see a slight tremor in her chin as if she's holding back tears. "I don't know," she says softly. "I think you hated me when I ran. I think you've always disliked me, from the minute you realized that I'm not the woman that you expected to marry."

"I don't dislike you." I look at her, startled. "How could I? You've been difficult to be married to at times, of course. And no, you're not what I expected. But dislike you?" I shake my head. "I've been impressed by your backbone, Caterina. And after your kidnapping–" I take a breath, feeling almost desperate. "Caterina, look at me, please."

For a moment, I think that she's not going to. Her shoulders have stiffened, her gaze fixed squarely on the bed, almost as if she can't bear to look at me. And then slowly, she turns, her dark gaze meeting mine.

"What, Viktor?" she asks softly. "Tell me what you thought of me, after."

I can't stop myself. I reach up to touch her face, my fingers stroking along her cheekbone, down to her jaw. I feel the slight tremor that passes through her at my touch, even as she keeps herself ramrod straight, tension in every line of her body.

"I thought you were brave," I murmur. "As brave as any soldier or brigadier I've ever employed, if not more. I've known men who couldn't endure what you did. I think–" I pause, not wanting to finish, to pull my hand away, to stop touching her. "You're the strongest woman I've ever known, Caterina. And even if you'll never truly love me or want to be my wife, I couldn't have chosen a better woman to be a mother to my daughters."

Caterina's mouth parts slightly, and I can see her indrawn breath, the shimmer in her eyes. I can feel the pull between us, the tension in the air thickening, and I know that she wants me to kiss her as badly as I want to do it. I can already feel what her mouth would feel like underneath mine, the softness, the way she'd tense just before she yielded to me, the struggle within her.

"Things could be different," she whispers, and the tremor passes through her again, her face still cupped in my hand. "They could be so different, Viktor, if only–"

If only you weren't the man that you are. I can hear the words, unspoken, hovering between us. "I've tried to be a good man to you," I murmur. "To you, to my daughters–I cared for you when you were sick, did all I could to nurse you back to health, tried to show you how I feel for you–"

"I know," Caterina whispers. "I know, Viktor. But–"

"But it's not enough." I drop my hand from her cheek, feeling the burning resentment in my chest. "I've never asked you to be anything other than what you are, a stubborn, difficult woman–"

Caterina raises her chin. "I tried to be something other than what I was made to be, Viktor. But first, I was talked into a marriage with you, with the blood of everyone who would have been hurt in a war between your faction and Luca's offered up as the burden that would have been on my shoulders. And then I was dragged back here by you when I tried to run. I *can't* be anything other than what I was made into. If I'm stubborn and difficult, Viktor, it's because I'm trying to keep some part of myself when every man I've ever known has chipped away pieces of me until sometimes I don't know what's left!"

She's speaking in hushed, angry tones, her chest heaving, and I still want to kiss her as much as ever. Her pale face is flushed at the cheekbones, the way it always is when she's angry. In a split second, I realize that I love that I know that about her, the same way that I know the way she'll give in when I kiss her and the way her body tightens just before she comes, the way I want to know everything else about her– the way she looks when she's truly happy, the sound of her laugh, the sound that her voice would make if it whispered the words *I love you.* I want everything from her, more than I wanted even from Vera, because when I loved Vera, I was young and stupid, and now I'm older and wiser. I know what I want, what I *need*, and Caterina is all of those things.

She's everything.

And yet, she thinks that I'm not worthy of her love.

"I've tried to give you everything I can–"

"You know what I need." She shakes her head, taking a step back. "I need you to be the man that I know you can be, Viktor. For me, for your daughters, for every woman that you haven't picked up and snatched out of her life yet into one that she didn't choose. And if you can't do that–" Caterina presses her lips together. "I won't leave, Viktor, because of the children. Because Yelena and Anika need me. But as for the rest–" she turns around, walking away from me towards the door.

It's on the tip of my tongue to call after her, and I nearly physically reach for her, wanting to stop her, to keep her here. But she's already at the door, and when she opens it, I see Levin standing there, his fist poised as if to knock.

"Mrs. Andreyva." He inclines his head, stepping back as Caterina sweeps past him.

I step out, too, closing the door behind me. "What is it, Levin?"

"I have news." He presses his lips together, looking displeased. "We can't find any hint of Alexei. He wasn't among the men who attacked the house, and none of them were ours, which means he contracted them out."

"And?" I demand, feeling my shoulders tense.

"He's gone dark." Levin looks frustrated. "There's absolutely no hint of him anywhere. He's disappeared, like a ghost, and I suspect that we won't see him coming until there's an attack. Which means–"

"We need to beef up security." I rub a hand across my mouth, thinking. "Contract some more men. And keep digging. He can't have disappeared entirely."

"There's more." Levin lets out a breath. "I can't get in touch with Mikhail. From what I know, no one else can either."

"You think he's defected to Alexei's side?"

"I think he's dead," Levin says bluntly. "Or captured, which is worse. It's not looking good, Viktor. Alexei has a good portion of your men. He's building a case to become your rival, and it's going to get bloody. He won't stop at hurting your family, you know that–"

"I know," I say curtly. "But it's going to be him who hurts in the end. I'll see to that. I can protect my family, especially with you at my side. But I need to know where Alexei is."

"I'll do all I can," Levin promises. "You know that I will, *pakhan*."

"I do. You've always been loyal to me, Levin. I trust you above anyone else."

"I'm grateful." He inclines his head. "I'll let you know as soon as there's any other news."

I pinch the bridge of my nose as he walks away, feeling the heaviness that Caterina's arrival had momentarily lifted return. The burden of responsibility feels weightier than ever, and I wish more than anything that she understood that. That she could see how I feel that there are no good choices for me, only the path that I was set on. No matter what I do, it will be wrong because of the choices made for me from the beginning.

This is the life I was given, the legacy I was handed. It seems impossible to me that I could walk away from it.

And yet, that's exactly what she wants me to do.

CATERINA

Deep in my heart, as I walk away from Viktor, I know that nothing will change. I know that he's too far into this life to walk away, too deeply immersed to ever see a different path forward. I know that a part of him *wants* it to be different, but not nearly enough.

I know that any future I have with him will be limited to what I can live with–which, if he continues to be the man that he is, means distance. Means loving only his children, and any child I might give him, but never him. It means going back to the kind of life I'd once expected to have with a husband, which shouldn't hurt. It only does because for a brief moment, I'd had a taste of something different.

Even as dark and depraved as some of the things Viktor has done to me are, it awakened something in me, desires that I didn't know I had. And now I have to let that go–walk away from it. It hurts more than I'd thought it would because I hadn't known I could feel desire so deeply, *want* so much, experience so much pleasure. I want more of it. I've begun to crave it, almost like an addiction.

The thought lingers with me all day, sticking in my brain, making me feel restless and unsettled. The thought of never touching Viktor or being touched with that kind of desperate need, feeling that line between pain and pleasure that he's shown me, letting go and giving myself over to everything that he's taught me to crave, makes me feel like bursting into tears, as if I'm losing something that I didn't know I needed.

And yet–

You can't love a man like him. You can't give yourself to him willingly, night after night, and still feel good about yourself–still feel like yourself at all. It's not possible. If he won't change, then neither can the marriage that you'd thought you'd have.

But when I go upstairs to get ready for bed, I can't stop thinking about it. I can feel the desire shivering through me, like an addict in need of another hit. All I can picture is his cruelly handsome face as he punished me, as he did things to me that I'd never imagined could turn me on or bring me pleasure.

Once more, I think to myself, trying desperately to rationalize it. *One more time,* I tell myself. *One more time, and you can enjoy every second of it without guilt. And then never again.*

My choice. My decision. Deep down, I don't know if it makes it better or worse, what that means for me, and who I am as a person.

All I know is that I need to experience what my husband can do to me, *with* me, completely, of my own volition. Just once. And then I'll put my walls up and never look back. I'll never let him touch me that way again.

So instead of what I normally would wear to bed, I change into a short, cranberry red slip made of silk, with thin straps at my shoulders and eyelash lace feathering over my breasts and along the tops of my thighs. I leave my hair long and loose, and when I hear Viktor's footsteps on the stairs, I sink to my knees in front of the fireplace, feeling my heart race as I keep my eyes lowered, my hands clasped together in my lap. The way I know he would want me, if I planned to submit to him.

This is exactly what I intend on doing–just for tonight.

The door opens, and I hear his footsteps as he walks into the room. I can hear his indrawn breath, the way he goes very still as he stops in front of me, and I know he's looking down at me. I can almost hear the pounding of my own heart, my pulse in my throat as I wait for him to say something.

It hadn't occurred to me until exactly this moment that he might be displeased enough with me after our conversation today to turn me down. To tell me that *he* doesn't want *me*.

I don't know what I'll do if that happens. It's just tonight. After tonight—

After tonight, I can't ever allow myself to do this again. I know that, beyond a shadow of a doubt. Which means this is it.

The last time I'll let myself open up to my husband, let myself desire him before I close that part of myself off completely. Before I let the part of me that *wants*, *desires*, die forever.

I can't have both. That much is clear. And I can't bear to live in this in-between forever.

"Does this mean what I think it does, Caterina?" Viktor's voice comes from above me, deep and gruff, and I can hear the heat in it. The *need*. He wants me, wants what I'm offering him, and the leap of my heart in my chest tells me that for tonight, this was the right decision. When my bed is cold and lonely in the nights to come, I can have this memory, at least when I long for something I can't ever have again. One night where both of us took exactly what we wanted from each other, and I submitted to him completely of my own volition.

"Yes," I whisper, my voice smaller than I meant for it to be. "Yes, it does."

"I'll do what I please to you tonight, if that's so," he says roughly, his accent thickening, and it sends a shiver down my spine. "*Anything* I please, Caterina. Do you understand?"

I nod.

"Say it aloud, *printsessa*."

"Yes, Viktor."

"Yes, *sir*."

"Sir—" I whisper the word aloud, and it hovers between us, making me tremble with need.

"Do you want a word to stop things if it's too much?"

The offer alone gives me pause, because Viktor has never done anything other than taking what he wants before. I consider it, for just a moment, because I know how brutal he can be, how roughly he can take me if it pleases him–and I think it might please him tonight.

But I want to know just how far down this rabbit hole goes–what it would be, with no holds barred between us, with both of us giving and getting exactly what we want.

"No, sir," I whisper, still not looking up. "I don't want that."

Viktor is very quiet for a moment, and then I hear him breathe in deeply. "Stand up then, *printsessa*. You have my permission."

I stand up slowly, my knees feeling weak. I feel as if I can barely breathe, my heart pounding with anticipation, and I still don't raise my eyes to his, waiting for his next instructions.

"Walk to the bed, and place your hands on the mattress."

Oh god. I know a hint of what's coming next, some form of punishment, and I don't know if I'm terrified, aroused, or both. I walk slowly towards the bed, feeling the dampness on my thighs already, the pulse between them telling me just how turned on I am by this. Viktor's roughness has aroused me before, but something about this, about submitting willingly to him, has made me wetter than I've ever been in the past. I can feel the ache there, and all I want is for him to touch me, for his hands or his mouth to graze over my pulsing clit, and give me the pleasure that I'm already craving.

But I know there's still time before that happens. I know he'll draw it out, make me beg, and something about that is even more arousing.

I bend forward, placing my hands on the mattress, and I can feel the silk of my slip ride up the back of my thighs, exposing the bottom curve of my ass cheeks. I hear Viktor's murmur of appreciation as he crosses the room to stand behind me, the warmth of him so close that it almost feels as if he's touching me. I'm more aware of his physical presence than ever before, of how big he is, how powerful. It sends another electric shiver through me, and Viktor chuckles.

"You want me badly, don't you, *printsessa*? You must, to offer yourself up like this." His voice deepens, and I can hear the heat building there. "Reach behind you, and lift that slip up so I can see your ass. I hope for your sake that you're not wearing panties, *printsessa*."

I wince, but I follow his instructions. I reach for the lace hem, tugging it up so that he can see that I am, in fact, wearing the matching thong beneath it.

Viktor makes a *tsking* sound, his hand caressing the curve of my ass. "Naughty girl," he murmurs. "A true submissive would be bare for me. But I can't be angry at another reason to punish my *printsessa*, to show her how to truly submit." He reaches for the string of the panties, and as he pulls them down, his fingers graze over the gusset, eliciting another dark chuckle from him.

"They're soaked through." He grunts, and I can hear the naked desire in his voice. "You're dripping for me already, and I haven't even touched you. Look at me, *printsessa*."

I don't want to. I can feel the flush of heat creeping up my neck and over my cheeks, embarrassment at how wet I am, at how much my body craves him overtaking me. But I'd agreed to this–*asked* for it, even–and I'd foregone any chance of a safe word. All that's left is to obey or face the consequences.

A choice, and one that I've made.

Which is all I wanted–all I want for anyone else.

I turn to look at my husband. His eyes are dark and heated, his face taut with desire, cruelly handsome as always. My panties are balled in his fist, and as I watch, he lifts them to his nose, breathing in my scent deeply. I can feel my face flame at that, burning red, and I can see from his smile that he did it intentionally, that he knows exactly how it would affect me.

"Open your mouth, *printsessa*."

Oh god. Oh god, no. I wince at that, but his expression leaves no room for argument, just as I'd known there wouldn't be. And so I part my lips, opening my mouth only for him to reach out and push the damp silk inside.

"When you moan for me, you can moan through the taste of your own dripping pussy," he growls, his accent thick and rough, the Russian clear. It arouses me in a way that I know it shouldn't. Still, it's so different from anything I've known before Viktor, anything I'd ever expected. Not sophisticated or elegant, like the men I grew up with. My husband, brutal and rough, a Bratva leader, their *pakhan*, their

Ussuri. Bear. A man to respect and fear, or else he'd eat you alive and relish it as he did.

A man that I want, precisely because of his roughness, because of the way he terrifies me and arouses me all at once, the way he's both cruel and gentle by turns.

Viktor runs something over my ass, then with his other hand, something cool and soft, and I turn to look. He holds the implement up, and I gasp softly.

It's a leather flogger, the tails long and soft-looking, but I can only imagine that they won't *feel* soft when he cracks it against my skin. Another shiver goes through me, and Viktor smiles.

"This will be new for you, *printsessa*. But remember, you agreed to let me do as I wish." He touches my hand. "Hold this up and keep your lovely ass bare for me, or I'll punish you twice over."

I nod, swallowing hard, tasting myself on my tongue. He runs one hand over the small of my back, pressing down. "Push that ass out for me, *printsessa*. Show me how much you want to be taught. How much do you want me to punish you for speaking to me as you did earlier? For being defiant. Show me how you want to submit."

I'm nearly shaking with need, and I can feel how wet I am, my thighs sticky with it as I obey, arching my back so that I know he can see all of it, my bare ass, the edges of my pink, swollen pussy, dripping with need for him. My fingers curl around the silk of my slip. I can feel them trembling slightly as Viktor steps behind me, the cool air sweeping over my ass as he brings the flogger down, and the soft leather tails snap over my skin, striking my left ass cheek.

I gasp, the sharp crack of it stinging as he brings it down again, this time on the other side. He whips me with effortless efficiency, the tails striking each side of my ass and working down to the curve of it, grazing the tops of my thighs, again and again as I feel heat blossoming over my skin. It was just pain at first, just the stinging that turned bright and sharp and more painful with each blow, radiating down my thighs. But as it goes on, I feel it start to turn into pleasure, that heat warming my skin, turning into a glow that makes my back arch and my thighs spread wider.

"Ah, yes, *printsessa*," Viktor growls, pausing to drag the flogger over my reddening flesh again. "Push that gorgeous ass out for me. You want it, don't you, *malyshka*?" His voice makes me shudder with desire, rough and full of inescapable need that only intensifies my own. I can tell how aroused he is, and I realize suddenly that this is an exercise in self-control for him, too, drawing out the punishment as he makes himself wait to take me, to revel in his own pleasure.

"More," he murmurs, swishing the flogger over my skin. "Yes, you can take more. Can't you, my princess?"

He says it in English this time, and I nod, my fingers curling into the duvet as I feel myself clench, my dripping pussy aching, needing to be filled.

Needing to be filled by *him*.

But I'm not ready to beg. Not quite yet.

Viktor begins again, the flogger striking my ass in the rhythmic pattern that I know will leave marks tomorrow, a part of me feels a hot, flushed thrill at that, the thought that I won't be able to sit or move or do anything for a day or two without feeling the reminder of his punishment and everything that comes after. I can feel my arousal building, my heart beating wildly in my chest, and I clutch at the bed, gasping as I can feel myself slipping into that place where I almost feel as if I'm floating.

"You can't come yet, *printsessa*," Viktor murmurs. Another thrill rushes through me, realizing that he can see how close I am to the edge, that he's in tune enough with my body to know that I can feel the first tremors running through me, threatening to tip me over into a shuddering climax. "Not until I say."

I moan at that, pressing my face against the duvet as I feel myself clench again, aching for fulfillment that isn't there, for friction that I can't get. I can't even grind against the bed, he's positioned me in such a way that I can't reach it, and I know that's on purpose.

"Are you ready for more, *malyshka*?" he asks. I nod breathlessly, wondering as I do what he's saying. I've never heard him call me that before, and the way he says it is almost tender, not the taunting sarcasm that I hear when he calls me *printsessa*. It seems sweeter, like a real pet name.

I shouldn't like it. I should resist anything that seems like love or tenderness between us, that could bind us closer together instead of giving me the distance that I know I should insist upon. But at this moment, it sends a rush of pleasure through me, my chest tightening at the sound of his voice murmuring the pet name, caressing me.

I hear the swish of the flogger again, but this time it isn't my ass that it hits. Viktor brings it up between my legs, the tails striking me in multiple places at once—my inner thighs, the soft folds of my pussy, nearly grazing over my clit. I almost scream with mingled pain and pleasure, the duvet muffling the sounds as Viktor swings it again.

"Spread your legs, *printsessa*," he orders. "Wider. Let me see how aroused you are for me, that swollen clit. Ahh, yes, *krasivaya*," he groans, and the flogger swings again.

This time, it lands squarely on my pussy, barely grazing my inner thighs as it slaps against my puffy, drenched outer folds, swinging up to strike my clit. I do scream this time, around the panties in my mouth, shoving my face into the blankets as I dig my fingers into the bed. A full-body shudder ripples through me, every muscle I have tensed with the effort not to come.

"No, *printsessa*," Viktor orders. "I want to hear your pleasure and your pain. Don't deny me what I want, or your punishment will go on for much longer before I allow you your release." He reaches down then, turning my head to the side as he grabs the silk in my mouth and yanks it out, leaving nothing at all to muffle the sounds.

Oh god. I can't hold on much longer. I'm trembling with need, my body shaking with the effort, my arousal slick on my inner thighs, dripping from the need to come. "Someone will hear," I whisper, my voice trembling, cheeks flushed with embarrassment at the thought. There's an entire house of staff, not to mention everyone we know staying with us on the floor below. Any of them could hear—

"I don't care," Viktor says gruffly. "Let them hear. What matters is that *I* want to hear it, *malyshka*. Your screams, your moans, your cries of pleasure." His hand strokes over the curve of my ass, down my thigh, so tantalizingly close to where I need it. "Few things make me as hard as the sounds you make when I punish you, *printsessa*." He squeezes a handful of my ass, the flesh stinging in his grip. "Except perhaps the sounds that you make when you come."

Fuck. His deep, growling, and thickly accented voice sends a thrill of pleasure through me that nearly undoes me. I don't know how I can take anymore, how much longer I can go before I come apart, whether he gives me permission or not. When he steps back, and I know what comes next, I take a shuddering breath, telling myself that I can manage a little longer. I can keep myself from orgasming, just a few seconds more.

Surely he'll allow it, if I please him. And I know this pleases him.

I don't muffle my cry this time when the flogger strikes between my thighs. The tails snap against my clit, the burning pleasure radiating between my thighs, and I hear Viktor's grunt of pleasure as he swings it again, and my back arches, another scream spilling from my lips.

"Please!" I gasp, feeling as if I can't bear it a second longer. "Please, Viktor, I can't take anymore—"

"Can't take any more of what?" He drags the tails over my ass, and I can feel that they're wet from my pussy, the leather soaked from how aroused I am. "Tell me, *malyshka,* what do you need?"

"I—oh, Viktor, please—"

"Say it." His voice is deep and threatening. "Say it, or I'll lash your pussy until you can't stop yourself, *printsessa*, and then I'll punish you for coming without permission. It will be a long time before you have the pleasure of my cock, if you earn it at all, unless you beg the way I know that you can."

Oh god. Nothing sounds worse, at this moment, than a hollow orgasm without him touching me, followed by being denied anything else. I *need* to come, but more than anything, I need to come with him filling me, with friction on my clit and his thick cock pounding into me, and I'm willing to say whatever he wants if I can have it.

Besides, didn't I come in here tonight with the intent of exploring this to its limits?

"I need to come," I whisper breathlessly. "I need it so badly, please make me come, Viktor, please let me, I need it—"

I'm gasping, the words tumbling over each other, and I almost sob with relief when I hear the flogger drop to the floor. "Alright, *malyshka*," Viktor croons roughly. "I'll give you what you need. I'll make that pussy come for me—"

"Yes, oh god yes, please—" I press my forehead against the duvet, another shudder rippling through me as I feel my body clench hard, aching for his cock. I expect to hear the sound of his zipper, to feel his swollen tip pressing against me, and the anticipation is more than I can bear.

But to my utter shock, that's not what happens at all.

I gasp as Viktor sinks to his knees behind me, his hands gripping the flushed, stinging backs of my thighs as he leans forward, breathing in. "Ah, you're so wet, *printsessa*," he groans. "So wet for my cock. But not yet. You've taken your punishment so well, I think I'll make you come like this, first."

And then, as he kneels behind me, I feel his hot tongue slide over my clit.

"Viktor!" I cry out his name, a gasp of shocked pleasure escaping my lips as I arch backward, his mouth pressing against the swollen folds of my pussy as he drags his tongue from my clit to my entrance, the tip of his tongue dipping inside for a moment, lapping up my arousal, and then flicking back to my clit, where I'm throbbing for him, desperate for his touch.

I forget any thoughts of embarrassment or holding back. I forget all of it, the pleasure that Viktor is giving me coursing through my body as I arch backward, grinding against his face, desperate for more of his hot, wet, lapping tongue against my clit, driving me towards the climax that I need so badly. It feels so good, his hands squeezing my thighs, pulling me back onto his face as he devours me.

BELOVED BRIDE

I never imagined a man could eat me out like this, hungry and passionate, as if the taste and scent and sounds of me, my pleasure, is driving his own.

"Oh god, Viktor!" I scream as I feel my body tighten, the tight knot of pleasure deep inside of me starting to unfurl, my thighs shaking as he grips them, holding my legs apart, his tongue lashing against my clit as I buck against his face. "Fuck, I'm coming, *Viktor!*"

I moan aloud, a long, helpless sound of pure pleasure that ends on a sound that's almost a shriek as I come hard on his tongue, grinding against him as my arousal floods out over his tongue. I know his face must be soaked in it, drenched, but he only presses his mouth more firmly against me, lapping me up as he licks me in the fast, quick circles that he knows drive me insane, carrying me through the orgasm as I writhe atop the bed.

And then, just as the climax starts to slow, he stands up abruptly, and I hear the sound of him quickly undoing his belt and sliding down his zipper, the knowledge of what he's about to do sending another ripple of pleasure through me. His hand is on my hip, holding me, his fingers pressed into my skin as he slides out his cock, and I have just a moment to register the thick, swollen heat of his cockhead pressing into my folds before he thrusts forward, filling me in one hard stroke that buries him to the very hilt.

"*Bladya!*" Viktor curses aloud, grabbing my hips in both of his hands as he slams into me again. "Fuck, *printsessa*, that fucking pussy—" he growls, thrusting hard and fast as I clench around him, still squeezing and fluttering from the aftershocks of my orgasm. "So tight, so wet, *fuck*, you feel so good." He takes a deep, shuddering breath, slowing his thrusts slightly as his hips rock against me. "The way you grip me when you come, *malyshka*, so fucking *good*."

He presses his hand between my shoulder blades, pushing me down into the mattress, holding me there as he takes me with long, hard strokes that fill me completely with every thrust, sending jolts of pleasure through my body. It feels so good, so *right*, like nothing else I've ever experienced. Viktor knows how to play my body like a fine instrument, how to touch and caress and kiss and lick and punish and fuck me until I'm screaming with pleasure, how to make me want to give everything to him no matter how wrong I feel that it is. He's doing that now, making me question my commitment to make this only one night, to think of ways we could do this again, reasons I could give into him. It's enough to make me almost want him to hurry up and come so that we can be done, so I can put it behind me before I lose my resolve. I can feel that he's close, his hips jerking as he pounds into me, fucking me as thoroughly as I knew he would.

But then, suddenly, he slows, a groan spilling from his lips as his hands sweep down my sides, down to my waist, and I hear him groan.

"Fuck, I'm close." He thrusts once more, dragging his cock out of me inch by inch in a slow slide that makes me cry out and then slamming himself into me to the hilt. "I could flood your sweet pussy with my cum right now—"

"Oh god, Viktor—" I moan against the duvet, feeling myself twitch and shudder at his words, on the verge of another climax too.

"No," he whispers. "I want more."

More? What does he mean, more? For a minute, I think that he's going to fuck me in the ass, and that sends a thrill of adrenaline through me. I don't love the feeling of him in my ass, but the feeling of utter submission turns me on, and I know he can make me come again. He's made me come with his cock in my ass before, and I know he'd do it again if he chose to tonight.

And this is the last night I intend to allow him to get away with it, if he wants it.

Viktor pulls out, and the sudden hollow feeling that he leaves behind makes me moan helplessly, my ass arching upwards, wanting him inside of me again. He grabs my waist, and before I know what's happening, he rolls me over onto my back. I have just a moment to wince at the feeling of the embroidered duvet scratching against the fresh welts on my ass and thighs as he pushes me backward before he grips my calves, spreading my legs apart as he moves me so that my ass is on the very edge of the bed.

BELOVED BRIDE

He looks so handsome that I can hardly stand it. His dark hair is tousled, his blue eyes bright in his chiseled face, taut with pleasure. I can see the muscles of his arms flexing beneath his shirt, his pants open to display the hard, pulsing length of his cock jutting out from the vee of his fly. I have the sudden, desperate urge to see more of him on this, the one night that I'm allowing myself to enjoy my husband however I please.

He's on the verge of thrusting himself into me again, his cock hovering above my drenched, aching pussy. I shove myself up with my hands, sitting up in a crunch as I reach for his shirt.

"What—" Viktor looks down at me, surprise and even a flicker of annoyance at being interrupted on his face, but I ignore it.

"I want something too," I murmur, looking up at him and meeting his bright, lustful gaze for the first time since we started this tonight. "I want to see you."

It's difficult to get the buttons of his shirt undone. My fingers are trembling, but I manage to slip them out, pulling it down over his shoulders so that the shirt falls to the floor and leaves all of his muscled arms and chest bare, down to the hard plane of his abdomen, the dark hair there leading mouth-wateringly down to the cock that's aimed almost threateningly where I need it the most. It's more erotic than him being completely naked, just shirtless with his pants open to reveal his throbbing cock. I look up at him as I reach down, wrapping my hand around his length that's slick with my arousal to stroke him, long and slow.

Viktor groans, tipping his head back as I tighten my grip on his cock, and when he looks down at me again, there's a wicked glint in his eyes.

"Ah, so you want to tease me too, wife? Perhaps you've already forgotten who's in charge here."

I meet his gaze fearlessly, my mouth twitching with a smile that's difficult to hold back as I squeeze his shaft, my palm rubbing over the slick tip and making him suck in his breath with a hiss. "Then remind me, *husband*."

Viktor shoves me backward with one hand on my chest,

planted between my breasts as he looms over me, his cock pushing between my spread thighs. My legs wrap around his hips without a second thought, my back arching as he thrusts into me hard, and I cry out, his cock sinking all the way to the hilt as he leans forward. "You're overdressed now," he murmurs. "And I want to see you, too."

I expect him to take my slip off, pushing it up my body and over my head, but instead, he grabs it at the lacy vee of the neckline, and I gasp.

"Viktor—"

He doesn't say a word, only grips the slip in both of his hands, and as I stare down at him, he yanks in opposite directions as his hips rock forwards, burying his cock inside of me as he rips the garment apart.

The silk opens with a wet tearing sound, all the way down to my belly, the fabric sliding sideways to expose my breasts, my nipples stiffening under Viktor's hot gaze. His hands go immediately to my breasts, squeezing them as he slides his cock in and out of me in long, measured strokes, so that I feel every inch of him.

"Ah yes, that's what I wanted," he murmurs. "I wanted to look at you, *printsessa*, to see my beautiful wife as I fucked her. Your breasts—" His hand slides over them, his palm rubbing over my nipples, down to my stomach. "Your body—your face." His palm comes up, cupping my cheek, and I let out a small sound somewhere between a moan and a cry.

I'd worried so much about Viktor finding me beautiful, healing and scarring as I am. I'd chosen my lingerie tonight with that in mind, covering the worst of the marks on my breasts and stomach, assuming he wouldn't notice the ones on my thighs too much. But he doesn't care. He's touching me like a priceless piece of art, stroking my breasts and stomach and waist and hips, his hands gripping what remains of the silk as he sinks his cock into me again and holds himself there, rocking against me as he tears it open the rest of the way so that nothing is covering me, nothing but my body lying naked in a pool of dark red silk, writhing beneath him as he pleasures me with his cock.

"So beautiful," he murmurs. "*Malyshka krasivaya.*"

The sudden tenderness in his voice sends shivers through my body, tingling sparks over my skin, his hands sliding up my thighs to grip my calves and spread my legs apart, hooking them over his shoulders as he thrusts into me again and again. "Come for me again, *malyshka*," he murmurs, his hand reaching between my legs, spreading my folds so that he can play with my clit. "Watch me fuck you and come for me."

Spread apart the way I am, I can see it, his huge cock splitting me again and again, thrusting powerfully into me as he rolls my clit between his fingers, driving me to the very edge of climax. His other hand is gripping my calf, and I can feel his gaze raking hotly over my body, devouring me with his eyes the way he did with his mouth earlier as he pushes me towards another orgasm.

"Viktor!" I scream his name as it crashes over me, the feeling of his cock filling me and his fingers on my clit too much. I've never seen anything as erotic as my gorgeous husband between my thighs, fucking me to another orgasm as he croons to me in Russian. The shame that I feel at being so aroused by it, at the way my body answers so effortlessly to him, is overcome by the endless, blinding pleasure that engulfs me. It arches my back and makes me claw at the duvet, my head tipping back as I cry out, moaning and gasping his name. I feel him shudder and surge inside of me, his hips jerking as he suddenly lets go of my leg. His hand comes out from between my thighs, his body spilling forwards as he grabs my face in his hands, and his mouth crashes down onto mine in a searing kiss as he shudders against me, swallowing up my cries as I arch against him, the sensation of flesh on flesh only intensifying what's left of my orgasm.

"I'm going to come," he groans against my lips. "*Bladya malyshka*, Caterina, *bladya, malyshka krasivaya—bladya—*"

The words tangle together, slurring into another groan as he kisses me again hard, his muscled body pressed against mine as I feel him throbbing inside of me. I can feel it when he comes, hot and thick, filling me as he thrusts again, his hips rocking hard against me as he erupts. It feels as if it goes on forever, my legs wrapped around his hips as he kisses me, his tongue tangling with mine as he grinds his cock into me, as deeply as he can go as he pulses, his cum filling me until I can feel it already dripping out of me around his shaft, sticky on my skin.

He holds himself there past when I've stopped shuddering around him, as his cock starts to soften, his lips still brushing over mine. I shift beneath him as I feel him go soft, but he kisses me again, his hand sliding down between my thighs where his cock was and covering my entrance. "I want my cum inside of you, *malyshka*," he murmurs, still kissing me, his tongue sliding over my bottom lip. I feel his fingers pressing against my entrance, pushing the cum that threatens to leak out of me back inside. "I want to make a baby with you, *printsessa*, a little prince."

"I—" I look up at him, swallowing hard. "I don't know—"

"Fuck what the doctors said," Viktor growls against my lips, his fingers still pressing against my entrance, pushing inside of me, forcing all of that thick, hot cum deeper inside of me. "I want every drop of my cum inside of you, taking root. I want you full of it." I can feel him thickening against my leg even as he says it, his soft cock swelling. His fingers are moving now, almost fucking me, the heel of his hand pressing against my clit, and I gasp softly.

"Ah, yes, *malyshka*, that feels good, doesn't it?" He croons it against my lips, groaning as he feels me tighten around his fingers, pleasure sparking over my skin. "That's right." His hand moves against me, grinding against my clit as his fingers start to thrust, curling inside of me as he pushes them deeper. "Come for me again, *printsessa*, with all that cum deep inside of you. Yes, *bladya*, you're so fucking tight even now, *yes*." He's harder now, his cock rising as he fingerfucks me to another orgasm, pushing them deeper as my pussy tightens, sucking him and his cum deeper into me as my hips arch upwards, greedy for another climax.

His orgasm should have put an end to it, but I can't tell him to stop. I want more, more of the pleasure, more of him inside me, *more*. It feels so good, and when he presses down harder on my clit, his mouth engulfing mine as he kisses me hot and hard, I can't resist.

I cry out against his lips, my body soft and open and pliable for him, ready for all the pleasure that he's willing to give me. I reach up, my fingers in his hair as he makes me come, pulling his mouth harder to mine, my body rolling to one side to curl against him as I arch against his hand. Viktor growls against my lips, his cock rock-hard against my thigh again.

"You want more, *printsessa?*" He nips at my lower lip, pulling his cum-soaked fingers out of me to roll me onto my back again. "Let me fill you up again, then."

VIKTOR

Caterina is driving me fucking insane.

The last thing in the world that I'd expected when I came upstairs tonight was to see my wife in lingerie, kneeling on the floor for my pleasure, ready and willing to submit to me. I would never have expected it.

Nor would I have expected what came after, for her to submit so completely, to take the flogger and beg for me to let her come. Her sweet pleas nearly undid me, but I'd wanted to taste her, to devour her pussy and make her come on my face. To feel how completely she could give herself over to me when she'd decided to allow herself her pleasure.

I don't know why Caterina decided to give in, why she stopped fighting me. But I can't bring myself to care. My wife on her knees of her own volition, my wife bent over the bed for her punishment, my beautiful Caterina spreading her legs and begging for my tongue and my cock is beyond erotic. It's beyond arousing.

It's the best fucking sex I've had in my life, and it's addictive. The thought of losing her now, of losing *this*, is unthinkable.

I'd planned to take her from behind, to finish in her ass and dominate her completely, to take full advantage of her willingness to submit to me. But somewhere in the middle of it, between her grinding out her orgasm shamelessly on my face and the pleasure of having my cock buried inside of her, I'd lost my fucking mind.

That's the only explanation for the things I'd said, the nickname I'd called her, the way I'd felt as if I needed to see her naked body and her face looking up at me as I fucked her more than I needed to breathe. I'd needed to see her eyes, glazed with pleasure and desperate for me, needed her bare, to kiss her and devour her with every part of me as I fucked her. And when I'd come inside of her, the only thing on my mind had been the possible result of my cum flooding her.

Caterina, pregnant with *my* child. Bound to me, irrevocably, forever. *Mine*.

It hadn't been enough to keep Vera with me. But I know it would be enough to keep Caterina. Even my own children, the ones that aren't hers by blood, are part of what kept her from running as long as she did. I know it.

Our child would make her mine forever.

It felt as if something primal overtook me, something fierce and undeniable. I'd never done anything like what I did with her, holding my cum inside of her, fingering her to another orgasm as I pushed it deeper inside of her, and I'd never been aroused by it. For me, coming inside of a woman has always been a physical pleasure, not a psychological one.

But suddenly, the thought of filling Caterina even more, of flooding her with my cum until she couldn't hold another drop, felt arousing in the deepest, most primal, possessive way. *Mine. Mine, mine, mine*. The thought looped in my head as I drove her to another climax, her arousal, and my cum coating my fingers as I thrust them inside of her, and I was suddenly rock-hard again, almost painfully so.

And as she arches against me, grinding out her pleasure against my palm, I can't breathe with how much I want her. Because she wants *me*. For all of her attempts to deny both of us, to rebuff me and fight me and pretend that she despises me, it's all gone tonight.

The desire on her face and written through every part of her body is as naked as she is.

I have to fuck her again.

Fill her, mark her, until she's so utterly soaked in me that she'll never be free of me again.

"You want more, *printsessa?*" I ask, nipping at her lower lip as she clenches around my fingers, savoring the taste of her mouth. I pull my fingers out of her, soaked in our combined cum, and as I roll her onto her back, I look down at her, flushed and disheveled and more beautiful than I've ever seen her. "Let me fill you up again, then."

She gasps, looking up at me, and I take that opportunity to push my fingers into her mouth, sliding them over her tongue so that she can taste herself and me on them. When her lips close around them, tightening as her tongue licks us off of her, I think I might go crazy with lust.

All my life, I've prided myself on my self-control. In a world filled with brutes and cruel men, men driven by their desires, by violence and lust and rage, I've tried to be a man who sticks to a code. It's not a code that everyone understands, perhaps not even one that's moral, but I've clung to it nonetheless. I've refused to torture men for revenge or pleasure, to kill out of anything but a necessity, to fuck women who weren't willing. I've never cheated on a wife. I made a point of coming home every night, of loving my family, of ruling with respect when possible and fear only when necessary. I *am* feared because everyone who knows the name Viktor Andreyev knows that I am merciful until I am not, and then there's no plea or bargain that can save you.

I am the *pakhan*, the Bear, the ruler of my territory, and a name whispered all across Russia. And now one man is threatening to take it all away, and one woman is making me feel as if I've lost every bit of self-control that I've ever had.

I've trusted all my life that that code could wipe away some of the sins I know I've committed, that it could balance the scales. But Caterina tells me that it's not enough.

Just as I demand her submission to me, she's demanding something else.

She's demanding that I *change*.

And right now, looking down at her with her full lips pursed around my fingers and her dark, pleasure-glazed eyes locked onto mine, with her legs around my hips pulling me into her for a second time, I can't help but wonder what that would look like.

If there's a way to keep her and myself, too.

A child. It hadn't worked with Vera, but Caterina is stronger. I saw the horror in her face when I told her what Vera had done. If I give her a child, she'll stay. And one day, she'll see that the good that I try to do outweighs the sins that she can't bear.

She'll see, even though Vera couldn't.

Her gasp when I push myself into her nearly undoes me. I can see the pleasure written across her face in every line of her straining body as she meets my thrusts, arching upwards. Her hands are clawed in the blankets, her breasts shaking as she wraps herself around me, fucking me as hard as I'm fucking her. I can feel how wet she is, my cock glistening each time I slip out of her with her arousal and my cum, and it turns me on even more, making me harder than I've ever been in my life. I want to fuck her all night, take her over and over again until both of us collapse exhausted. I can't remember the last time I wanted a woman this badly—maybe never before in my life.

Caterina makes me feel things I've never felt, want things I've never wanted. Things that are supposed to be unobtainable for a man like me, unrealistic.

Men like me don't marry for love. We don't look for women to be our *partners*. We look for beautiful women, pliable women, women who can bear our children and raise them, women who can run a house and go to functions on our arms and make us the envy of other men.

I'd believed Caterina was all of those things when I'd married her. And she is all of them—except for pliable.

But she's so much more, too.

She's strong, intelligent, brave, and tenacious. She's the kind of woman who, on her own, would be a formidable match against a man like me. The type of woman you meet once in a lifetime, perhaps. The kind of woman that men in my world do their best to subdue.

And the truth is that I have no idea how to make a life with a woman like Caterina. All I've ever known is to try to make her bend to my will, to bring her to heel and force her to submit.

But I don't want to lose her.

I want this.

Forever.

I kiss her again, hot and fierce, as I pound my cock into her, wanting her sore tomorrow, remembering how this felt with every movement. I want her marked inside and out, and from the way she clings to me, her nails digging into my shoulders as she kisses me back, she wants the same.

"Oh, god, Viktor—" she moans my name against my mouth, her body tensing in my arms as I feel her on the verge of coming again, and I can feel my own climax rising hot and fast, quicker than I've ever come for a second time. I feel her tighten around me, her head tipping back as her back arches, and I could hang onto it, could make it last longer, but the draw of the pleasure is too much, the allure of coming with her. I want to pour myself into her as she convulses around me, and as I feel her start to shudder, I let it go.

It feels as if my soul is coming up through my cock when I drive into her, a torrent of cum bursting from me as I fuck her hard, pressing her down into the blankets as her nails score my back, my name tearing from her mouth as she comes again. We've both lost count of her climaxes, and I hear myself muttering through my own, words spilling from my lips before I can stop them between kisses.

"Caterina—*bladya, Lyubov moya, bladya*—" I thrust into her again, reaching for her wrists and pinning them above her head as I grind my mouth against hers, biting at her lower lip, groaning my pleasure as I fuck her hard enough to break her, wanting every drop of pleasure that I can wring out of this moment between us.

Lyubov moya. I hear it again, my own voice saying it before I can stop myself, and as my sense returns, I thank god that she doesn't speak Russian. I'm a fool to say such things, even in the throes of pleasure, but I can't stop myself. She makes me feel as if I'd throw everything to the wind for another night like this.

When I slip out of her, this time, I roll over onto the bed, pulling her into my arms as I move us both to lie on the pillows. We're both panting, sweaty and exhausted, and Caterina slumps against the stack of pillows on the bed, her eyelashes fluttering closed as she tries to catch her breath.

"Ah, you still look so gorgeous," I murmur, pushing a piece of hair out of her face. "*Krasivaya malyshka.*"

"What does that mean?" Caterina asks softly, her eyes still closed. "You said it, when—"

"Beautiful. Beautiful baby." My fingers are still running through her thick dark hair, her naked body cradled in my arms, and I wonder how long it would be before I could be ready to take her again. It's been a long time since I've fucked more than twice in one night, but I can already feel my desire rising again, just from the feeling of her breasts against my chest and her slender body in my arms.

"Oh." Caterina breathes in, and I wonder if she's going to ask about the other, what I'd said as I came the second time.

I'm prepared to lie because I'm not about to admit to it. But instead, to my surprise, she pulls away. Quickly, almost methodically, she extricates herself from my arms and sits up, moving towards the edge of the bed and reaching for the torn puddle of silk on the duvet.

"Where are you going?" I stretch out, reaching for her arm. "Come lie with me for a bit, *malyshka.*"

"I think I liked *printsessa* better." Caterina tries to pull her elbow away, but I tighten my grip, suddenly irritated.

"You hate that nickname." I frown at her, feeling some of my pleasure in the moment we were sharing start to slip away. "What's wrong? Come lie with me. Maybe in a little while—"

"We're not going to fuck again." Caterina jerks her arm,

harder this time, ripping it from my grasp. "I only meant for us to do it once. I got carried away when you—"

"When I fingered you and made you come again? Yes, I know how quickly your pleasure makes you forget what you *meant* to do." I can hear the sarcasm creeping back into my voice, hear myself getting colder. I'd softened with her tonight, let the way that she'd given herself to me get under my skin. But it's becoming clear that she'd meant something different than I'd thought by it, and that makes me angry.

"I don't like being tricked or deceived," I tell her, my voice low and dark. "Nor do I like being used. Not even my wife will get away with those things, so if you meant tonight to be something other than pleasure, *printsessa*, I suggest you—"

"Ah, there it is." Caterina stands up, still beautifully nude, but her expression is as cold as mine. "The Viktor I know is back. Not the one who whispers sweet nothings to me in Russian. There's the *Ussuri* I married."

I glare at her. "I'll whip your backside again, wife, if you haven't had enough—"

"Oh, I've had enough for tonight," Caterina says. "And all the nights."

"If you think you can tell me—"

Caterina balls the silk up in her fist, her expression darkening, too. "I think I can, Viktor," she says quietly. "Unless you want your family life to be miserable, which I don't think you do. You didn't marry me for lust or for love. You married me for two things. You said so yourself. You married me because you needed a mother for your children and a son to inherit." She takes a deep breath. "Very well. I'll do what you married me for. I'll care for Anika and Yelena and raise them as my own, and I'll give you another child if I can, despite what the doctor said. I'll fuck you until I've given you a son, we'll do it the natural way, just as you desire, but this is the *last* time that it will be intimate."

I narrow my eyes at her. "What do you mean by *intimate*, *printsessa*?"

Caterina swallows hard, and I think I see her hands tremble, but she lifts her chin defiantly. "I mean that there will be no more of this. I won't submit to it, and if you do it anyway, you can forget that part of your moral *code* where you believe you don't hurt or force women because you *will* be forcing me. There will be no more punishments, no more of you making my body respond to you against my will, no more seductions. No more going to bed so that you can comfort yourself with me, no more nights like tonight."

"What are you asking for, wife?" There's a dangerous edge to my tone, and I know she can hear it, but she plunges forward anyway.

"I want my own room," she says firmly. "I won't sleep beside you again. We'll fuck when the time of the month is appropriate—I'll track it and share the results with you so that you know I'm not lying. We'll fuck as quickly and clinically as necessary, and you won't touch me outside of that."

I laugh. I can't help it. A moment ago, I felt on the verge of losing my sanity, ready to throw everything away while I was buried inside of her for the sheer pleasure of what I'd thought we were sharing. Now Caterina is speaking to me as coldly as I ever have to her, laying down rules for me, just as she'd tried to do at the beginning of our marriage.

"I think you've seen already how well trying to outline the rules of our marriage to me does, *printsessa*," I tell her darkly. "What, exactly, makes you think that I—"

"If you force me," she says quietly, interrupting me. "Or if you won't make this compromise, then things will turn out as they did with your first wife. The bargain isn't broken if our marriage doesn't end through my leaving and going back to Luca. If I simply die, there will be no reason for war. No excuse to break the contract."

I stare at her, horrified as her words sink in. Slowly, I sit up, feeling everything inside me go cold and dark. I'd wanted to give her the benefit of the doubt, to believe that she wanted things to change, but this is a threat that I can't abide by.

"You would do that to the girls?" I ask her quietly. "Take another mother from them like that?"

"Don't use them as a weapon," Caterina says, her voice hardening. "Don't do that, Viktor. I'm not asking much. I'm asking you—"

"To fuck my wife like I'm jerking off." I snort, swinging my legs over the edge of the bed and reaching for my robe. Caterina flinches back, and I laugh.

"Don't act like I beat you, *printsessa*. You begged for what I did to you tonight, and you've begged for it before. What was tonight, anyway, if not you wanting me? What did you mean by all of this, if you were only going to—"

"I wanted to know what it was like," Caterina says softly, not quite meeting my eyes. "I wanted to know how it would feel to have that kind of pleasure, just once. To submit to you and feel all of it, however far it could go. Just once, before I—"

"Before you cut me off." I glare at her. "I was willing to be different for you, Caterina, softer—"

"You can't do what I need you to do."

I shake my head, rolling my eyes as I turn away. "This again. We've talked about this—"

"Yes, this again!" Caterina moves so that she's in my line of sight again, her arms crossing over her breasts. She seems to have forgotten that she's naked. Something about her ferocity while she's standing there completely bare, her thighs still glistening with my cum, is so erotic that I almost forget that I'm angry with her. "I talked to Sasha—"

"Yes, I know. We've discussed this. And we've discussed my reasons, too—"

"You should never have taken her. Or any of them. You took away their choice—"

"To what?" I round on her, my voice rising with frustration as I face my beautiful, stubborn, infuriating wife. "To live in the gutter, tossed out by people who are done with them as soon as they age out of the system? To starve? To become whores for the lowest price, just to survive? To marry men out of desperation who will hurt them, beat them, steal their beauty and their youth? To be raped and robbed and treated like garbage? Do you know what happens to children in those orphanages, Caterina? Do you know what happens to them after they grow up and leave?" I shake my head in disgust. "You don't, because you're a pampered, selfish brat who lived with a silver spoon in her mouth from the moment you came squalling out of your mother—"

"Sasha *was* raped!" Caterina is shouting now, too, taking a step forward and then another until she's so close that she's almost yelling in my face, her dark eyes furious and impassioned. "And she wouldn't have been if you hadn't taken her and brought her here for that awful man—"

"I killed him!" I glare at her, my own fury matching hers. "One of *my* men. As punishment, I shot him in the head in front of everyone. I avenged her—"

"It never would have happened if she hadn't been in that warehouse." Caterina doesn't back down, not even an inch. "Maybe it's happened to other girls, and you didn't know it. It certainly happens to at least some of them after you sell them. I guarantee they don't all go to their new *masters* and rollover happily like obedient dogs. You brought Sasha here, and you bear responsibility for what happened to her from the moment your men took her—"

"I know." I hold her gaze steadily. "Caterina, I don't kill men easily. I'm not feared because I'm violent or brutal like others in my world, no matter what you might have heard. I'm feared because I'm merciless when betrayed or crossed. I have killed very few men in my life, and I hope to keep it that way. But I killed him without hesitation."

"Because he stole from you." There's derision in Caterina's voice. "As if he'd stolen money or some other possession—"

"Yes, because he stole from me. But also because he stole from *her*. And he had no right to do either."

The words hang between us, heavy in the air. Caterina looks at me for a long moment, her face suddenly sad and tired.

"So did you," she says quietly. "And you didn't have any right, either."

"Caterina—"

"Stop." She holds up a hand. "Just stop, Viktor. I can't be the wife you want, not unless you change in ways that I see now that you can't. I'll do the things that you bargained for. But intimacy, punishments, pleasure, the things we've done together—I didn't bargain for those. And if I tell Luca, he won't take it lightly. Especially now that I've told you no. No more. You fuck me until I give you a son, only when necessary. Or—"

"Or you take the easy way out." I glare at her. "The coward's way out."

"Or I take the only way out that you've left me. Just like Vera did."

Something snaps inside of me at that, something brittle and painful. I grab her arm, snatching up another robe and throwing it over her shoulders so that it drapes around her, covering most of her nudity. She tries to pull away, but I don't give an inch, my fingers sinking into her flesh as I pull her towards the door.

"Viktor!"

I don't answer. I don't look at her. I march her down the hall, towards one of the empty guest rooms further down, and shove the door open, pushing her inside. She staggers as I let go of her, her arms wrapping around her waist as she clutches the robe to her, her face suddenly pale and frightened.

"Don't look at me like that," I snap at her. "Fine. If this is what you want, enough to make those kinds of threats, if that's the way you feel, I won't touch you at all. I'll never fuck you again. We'll use IVF when this business with Alexei is settled, and we're back home, until you give me an heir, and then we'll speak as little as possible. I'll never fucking touch you again, if it's that horrible for you. If my cock inside of you is a fate worse than death." I glare at her, my chest heaving, a rage like I've rarely felt rising up inside of me. "But I warn you, Caterina, not to push too much further. It's unwise to back a bear into a corner. Alexei will find that out soon. I'd hate for you to find out, as well."

Her mouth drops open, but before she can say another

word, I slam the door shut, leaving her on the other side of it. My hand grips the doorknob hard enough to hurt, a riot of emotions rising up in me so quickly that I can't make sense of any of them. I'm furious beyond belief, but there's something else beneath it, too, something that I don't want to look at too closely.

I'd believed that tonight meant something for Caterina. That it had been a step in our marriage, a turning point. She'd let herself go with me, and I'd done the same, against every instinct I had. Against all of my better judgment. I'd said things that I'd told myself I'd never say to another woman again.

Lyubov moya. My love.

I hadn't said it in a very long time. I'd never planned on it again. I'd told myself that my heart was closed.

Caterina has cracked it open against my will. And as I let go of the doorknob, I feel something other than the cold, black rage filling me.

I feel pain, my chest tightening, that rush of grief that had threatened to swallow me after Vera died, despite how furious I'd been with her, too. A sense of loss that I'd hoped to never feel again.

I can hear her starting to cry on the other side of the door, and I want to open it. To go to her. To hold her in my arms and tell her that I can change.

That I can be a better man for her. That we can make some different life, if it means not having a closed-door between us, my wife crying on one side while I seethe on the other.

But then I remember her threat, and my hand drops to my side.

She'd pulled out the one thing that she knew could hurt me, taken the dagger that I'd trusted her with, and driven it into my chest.

I'm not sure if I can ever forgive her.

So I walk down the hall, her muffled sobs fading into the distance, back down to the room that we had shared.

And I close the door behind me, shutting her out.

Maybe for good.

CATERINA

I'm not sure I've ever felt so miserable.

When Viktor slams the door shut, it feels like a physical blow. At that moment, I wanted to take back everything I said, especially my threat, but it's too late. He's on the other side, more furious with me than I've ever seen, and I'm terrified of what that means.

I wrap my arms around myself, sinking to my knees on the floor. I'm shivering, even in the warm robe, kneeling there in the dark as I start to cry. In a matter of moments, things changed so dramatically, and I feel almost in shock, unable to move.

Just a few minutes ago, he'd been inside of me, crooning to me in Russian, holding me in his arms. He'd said things to me that I didn't understand, but I could understand his tone of voice. *Baby. Beautiful baby.* Sweeter than *printsessa*. More loving.

What else did he say?

It doesn't matter.

I swallow hard, squeezing myself tightly. I don't hear his footsteps move away from the door, and for a moment, I think he might come back in. I don't know if I want that or not, if it terrifies me or if it would make me happy. I suppose it depends on the reason why he came back in—to fight with me more, threaten me, or comfort me.

The last is laughable.

You did this to yourself, I tell myself firmly. He'd wanted to hold me, cuddle me, drift off to sleep together, and maybe fuck again. He'd been soft and gentle, more so than he'd ever been with me before. I'd been the one to pull away, to stick to my resolution and put an end to the night. I'd been the one to tell him my demands.

Don't back a bear into a corner.

I'd done exactly that. I'd taken the one threat that I'd known would cut him to the core and used it against him. I'd known exactly what I was doing, and I can't pretend otherwise. I'd done it to get the distance that I'd said I wanted, and it had worked.

Maybe too well.

When his footsteps start to recede, heading back down the hall, I know that he's not coming back in for any reason. Not to hurt or to comfort, and that leaves a hollow feeling in my chest that makes me gasp, bowing forwards as if something struck me. The pain in my chest feels unmatched, a sense of loss that I hadn't known I could feel when it came to any man, let alone Viktor, and I squeeze my eyes tightly shut.

I'd felt something different in him tonight. But our argument had just proved what I'd already known, that it's not enough. I don't know why I'd ever thought it could be different.

Nor do I know why the loss of that possibility hurts so badly.

This is what I was raised for. To be the bride of a man I wouldn't love or even necessarily like, to take his cock and bear his children, to tend his house and smile on his arm. I wasn't made for love or pleasure or joy or fulfillment. I wasn't meant to have a life that made me happy, only one that kept me safe. One that kept me alive, in a world even more deadly to women than the ordinary, everyday one that most of us live in.

Spoiled brat, born with a silver spoon. His words still sting, burning in my head, and I try to shake them loose. But I know he's not entirely wrong. I was born rich and privileged, with everything I could ever want.

Everything except freedom and choice. The same things Viktor takes away from other women, born into less fortunate circumstances, every day.

Why can't he see that I just want him to give them what I've never had? The one thing I would trade it all for?

Except—I haven't. I never have. I married Franco and Viktor, and I won't leave Viktor, not even now.

To save others. To take care of his children. It's not for yourself—

Except sometimes, it has been. The choice to marry Franco was between the life I knew or one that I didn't belong in. And I'd chosen it happily because I hadn't known what was on the other side of it.

I do now.

And now I know more than ever that I can't leave.

I can see all of the days stretching out in front of me, long and miserable, dragging into each other until there's nothing but a black tunnel in front of me. For a moment, the hopelessness that washes over me is so intense that I can't bear it, that I think I'd rather make good on my threat to Viktor whether he tries to touch me again or not.

I'd meant it as an idle threat, one that I knew he wouldn't test.

But in that moment, in the dark, clutching myself as I cry, I don't know if I can stand to go on.

It feels hopeless. Pointless.

The thought of Anika fighting for her life downstairs, and Yelena begging me not to leave again, are all that puts me back together. I cling to that, forcing myself to stand up, to find a light switch, to walk to the bathroom. They need me, even if no one else does. Even if I have nothing else left.

I turn on the shower, letting the water run as hot as I can stand it, and then I slip underneath it. I scrub every inch of myself, trying to wash away not just his touch, but the memory of how much

I enjoyed it. I scrub hard between my legs, trying to wash his cum off of me, out of me, ignoring the throbbing that I feel at the memory of him cupping me, pushing it back inside of me, murmuring to me as he fingered me to another orgasm. He'd wanted to keep all of himself inside of me, and I know the purpose behind it—to get me pregnant. To keep me here with him, bound to him, as if I already wasn't beyond all hope.

I want him out of me. I don't want to have his child, even if I already can't. I think of the life a son of ours would have, and I'm suddenly glad for the fists I took to the gut, the fact that I might have had my fertility literally beaten out of me.

Glad that I can't give Viktor the thing he wants most from me since he can't give me the thing I want most from him.

When I've scrubbed my skin pink, my thighs, and between my legs raw and clean, I sink to the floor of the shower, letting the hot water run over my hair and my face, washing it all away. His touch, his scent, his words, his lips. The way he'd made me feel, just for a little while.

I have to forget it, or I'll go mad. If I'm going to sleep alone, *be* alone, I have to forget. I'd thought tonight would give me something to remember when I was lonely, but instead, it just hurts, a knife twisting in my chest just like the one I know I left in Viktor's.

Our marriage was supposed to heal a war, but we've started a new one instead.

—

The rest of the night isn't easy.

I lie in bed in the dark for a long time, wrapped up in the robe, crying silently. I don't want anyone to hear me, least of all Viktor, but I can't entirely hold it in either. I'd thought the night with him would make things better for me, but it just made it all so much worse.

I'd always dreaded the idea of a cold, unfeeling marriage, even though I knew that was likely my fate. But this—a marriage where we want each other so desperately but can't find a middle ground, is so much worse. I hadn't known how awful this could feel.

Or how awful Viktor and I could be to each other because I know I'm not blameless in this. We're both at each others' throats, and I regret saying some of the things that I did during that last fight.

But I can't exactly take it back now. And it was all I could think of to keep him from ignoring my wishes and continuing to take what he wanted from me.

I'd gone for the nuclear option, and it's opened a gulf so wide between Viktor and me that I don't see any way that we'll ever bridge it.

When I finally wake up, the morning light starts to grey and peek through my curtains; I lay in bed for longer than I usually would. I don't have any clothes in here, and I don't want to go back into my old bedroom with Viktor still there. I know I'll have to face him at some point, but I can't yet, and definitely not in the room where so much happened between us last night.

It feels excruciating, watching the minutes tick by, thinking of what he's doing. Wondering if he's hurting too, if he missed having my body next to his when he woke up this morning, hating myself for caring at all, or missing him. Wanting things to be so different when they so clearly can't be.

Finally, when I'm sure that it's late enough that Viktor will already be up and going about his day, I slide out of bed, wrapping the robe tightly around myself and stepping out into the hall.

I ache all over, as if I'd run a marathon. Not just the lingering soreness from Viktor's flogger last night, but my muscles, from the sex and adrenaline. It should have been a pleasant reminder of all the pleasure I'd experienced last night. Instead, it just makes my chest ache, in a way that feels worse than anything before this.

I feel empty, hollow, as if Viktor carved something out of me that I can't ever get back. *Or maybe I did it myself when I ruined any chance of us ever having a real marriage. When I threatened—*

Is this what Vera felt? This empty, endless sense that nothing will ever get better? That I'll never be happy again?

I've been through so much in a short time. It feels as if I've lived years since my engagement to Franco, but it's been months. Not even a full year since I'd married one husband, been widowed, and married another—since I'd been kidnapped, brutalized, started to fall for the husband that I was never supposed to be given to in the first place and realized that there's no place for those kinds of feelings in this marriage. There was no room for anything other than the marriage of convenience that it was always supposed to be.

The bedroom is empty, as I'd hoped it would be, empty and as cold as I feel right now. There's no fire in the fireplace, and the lights are off, just the daylight coming through the curtains. Any sign of what Viktor and I did last night is gone—the bed made, the flogger put away somewhere, the scraps of my slip discarded. It's as if it never happened, and I wonder if that's how he feels, too, as if it's forgotten.

Everything except the fight that came after. I know he hasn't forgotten that.

I go through the dresser drawers, scooping out clothing to take back to "my" new room. Once I have an armful from that and the closet, I head back down the hallway, feeling a sense of loss as I close the door to the room that Viktor and I shared. I don't know why, exactly. It's not as if this place was ever even our home. It's just a safe house, a luxurious fortress for us to wait out Alexei's plots and plans until Viktor can put a stop to it. This place shouldn't mean anything to me, but somehow closing the door on that bedroom feels like closing a door on something else, like it's imbued with a finality that I haven't felt at any other point.

Pushing it out of my mind, I walk back down towards the new bedroom I'm staying in, dumping the armful of clothes on the bed. I dig a pair of jeans and a sleeveless silk top out of it, throwing a soft cashmere cardigan over that and then going about the business of putting everything away. I could leave it for the maids to do, but something about that feels wrong. I don't want to leave them needless work, and besides, it feels good to have something to keep my hands busy.

It's almost noon by the time I finally make my way downstairs and force myself to go to the kitchen and find something to eat. I'm in the process of trying to use some leftover roast to make a sandwich when I hear footsteps and look up sharply, my heart skipping a beat in my chest as I imagine that it's Viktor. I don't know if I'm hoping for or dreading that possibility.

It's not, though. It's Sofia, walking into the kitchen and pausing as she catches sight of me. "Caterina!" She sounds surprised. "Are you okay? We noticed you weren't down for breakfast this morning. We thought you might not be feeling well. Or that you might be sitting with Anika—"

"I, um—" I swallow hard, the butterknife that I was using to spread mustard on a piece of bread suddenly shaking in my fingers. "It was just a long night, that's all." I don't know what else to say. I know Sofia would understand if I told her everything, but it feels too intimate, almost embarrassing.

"Something to do with Viktor?" she asks, picking up on it anyway. "Caterina, if you need to talk about anything—"

"I don't know what to say." I set the knife down, gripping the edge of the countertop. It feels cold under my fingertips, made of marble or something ridiculously luxurious like that, fancier even than anything I grew up with. I might have been born with a silver spoon in my mouth, as Viktor so viciously threw in my face last night, Viktor has managed to ascend to heights of wealth that I couldn't have imagined even in my family. Even Luca's astonishingly luxurious, expensive penthouse can't compare to this house, and this isn't even Viktor's primary residence. It isn't even one that he uses all that often. It's an *emergency* residence.

And he's made all that money doing something terrible. Something so awful that I can't bring myself to moralize it in my head in any way, no matter what excuses or justifications he comes up with. I simply *can't*.

"I slept with him last night," I admit finally. "I initiated it because I wanted to. Just once. I wanted to really *enjoy* it, just the one time. I told myself that afterward, I'd put some distance between us. And I tried to. But—"

Sofia leans against the counter, looking at me with curious, worried eyes. "But what? He didn't hurt you, did he?"

I laugh, a small, choked sound in my throat. "No," I say quietly. "Or at least—not in a way that I didn't like. But he was—different."

Sofia cocks her head. "Different how?"

"He said things to me in Russian, during—" I clear my throat, feeling my cheeks flush a little. "Pet names. It sounded—sweet. And afterward, he wanted to *cuddle*."

Sofia laughs. "Oh no. Not your husband wanting to *cuddle* you. Although that doesn't seem to really be Viktor's MO if I'm being honest."

"It's not. He's not gentle or cuddly or any of those things. But last night—"

"So that's why you're in here crying into your roast beef sandwich? Because he was too gentle with you?" Sofia sighs. "I'm not trying to be difficult, Caterina, but I don't know what it is that you want. I want to help you, just like you helped me. But I'm just as confused as you are about what's happening here. And I'd be willing to bet that Viktor is confused, too—"

"We had a fight." I push the sandwich away. My appetite is entirely gone. "Afterwards. I told him that I had just wanted the one night with him, and then I wanted to go back to the way things were before. Separate rooms, only sleeping together when it might result in a baby." I bite back everything else—the fact that I might not even be able to have children now, the threat I'd made, what Viktor's first wife had done that had made my words cut so deeply. I can't tell Sofia all of that—it's not my story to tell, and besides, I can't bring myself to say any of it out loud. "He was angry," I finish lamely.

"I mean—you're giving him a hell of a lot of mixed signals, don't you think, Caterina?" Sofia looks at me, her expression still full of worry. "Cat, I did the same thing to Luca for a long time. And I learned—these aren't men to toy with. They're not men to play games with. I thought you knew that. Viktor especially—he's worse even than the men you grew up with. I get how scared you are of him sometimes. I was the same way with Luca. Luca was like nothing I'd ever experienced or known. And I understand being terrified and wanting him at the same time—that was me with Luca, too. But Cat—remember the things you told me. You have to choose. And once you've chosen, you've got to stick with it. Viktor isn't going to react well to games and you giving and then taking away."

"He's not—" I let out a breath, squeezing the edge of the countertop. "He's not a bad man, deep down. He *tries* not to be. He has this code that he tries to live by."

"They all do." Sofia peers at me as if she's trying to figure me out. "But it's not enough for you."

"It should be. I was raised to turn a blind eye to all sorts of things. To not ask what my husband was doing while he was gone, where he was. But I also wasn't raised to love my husband. To *want* him. You can tolerate all kinds of things when you don't have any feelings towards someone other than duty. But Viktor—"

"You're falling for him."

"In lust? In love? I don't know." I shake my head, a short, desperate laugh escaping my lips. "But whichever it is, I just know I have to put some distance between us. I can't live with myself otherwise. Not unless things change, and I know now that they won't."

"You need to stop torturing yourself," Sofia says quietly. "Haven't enough people done that already? Give yourself some peace, Cat. Are you thinking of leaving Viktor?"

I shake my head. "No. I can't. The bargain with Luca—besides, I can't leave Anika and Yelena. Yelena especially has come to depend on me, and I can't do that to them."

"Then, try not to let your thoughts consume you. Have a little peace." Sofia looks at me sympathetically. "There's enough to worry about right now. Maybe in time, Viktor will come to his senses, with some space between the two of you. You have a lifetime to figure it out. It doesn't have to happen in the midst of all of this."

She reaches for the sandwich that I was half in the middle of making, quickly assembling the pieces and handing it to me. "Here, eat this. You need to eat. I came in here to make some tea for Ana and me. I'll make some for all three of us, and then we'll go outside in the garden and sit for a little while. It's sunny out, even if it is a little cold, and Liam got the fire pit going."

I blink at her. "Liam did what?"

Sofia shrugs. "He came outside a little bit ago and offered to start a fire in the pit so that we'd be warmer." She laughs, setting the kettle on the stove. "He's unusually kind, for the son of an Irish King."

"Are they not?" I frown, taking a bite out of my sandwich. "I never really met any of them until Liam."

Sofia shrugs. "From what Luca says, his father wasn't. Conor Macgregor was a devil, ruthless and vicious. As much as any Bratva man—maybe more, since the Irish always feel they have something to prove. Or at least, that's almost word for word what Luca told me. Conor tried to murder Luca in his hospital bed, so I believe it."

I remember when Luca and Liam arrived, Sofia said that Liam wasn't meant to inherit his father's seat. He took it out of necessity to prevent a civil war among the men when his father was executed, leaving a vacancy without his older brother there to fill it.

"Do you think he's hoping for his brother to come back?" I ask curiously. "To relieve him of the position?"

"No one thinks Connor is coming back." Sofia glances at me. "Luca thinks he's dead. I don't know what Viktor thinks, or the inner whispers in the Irish families are; my understanding is that Luca doesn't expect him to ever return. Which means he's stuck with a position he didn't expect to have, and one that he needs to prove that he's strong enough to hold."

"Much like Luca, when my father died."

"Exactly." Sofia picks the kettle up as it starts to whistle, pouring the boiling water into three cups. "They've been spending a lot of time together recently. Luca sees it as a win-win. He's fostering a bond with Liam that may come in handy in the future. His advice will strengthen Liam's ability to run the Kings while ensuring that they're led by someone less duplicitous and bloodthirsty than Conor Macgregor was."

I take the last bite of my sandwich, watching Sofia as she arranges the tea. "Luca talks to you a lot, doesn't he?" I ask quietly. "He tells you a lot."

"More than he should, probably." Sofia hands me one of the cups. "But it's not as if he has close friends. Everyone he knows now could be a rival if the winds changed. His one best friend turned out to be a traitor. He loathes to let too many too close these days. He wants me to be his confidante, and I'm happy to be. At first, I didn't want to be a part of this life. But Luca knows what I can handle and what I'd rather not hear. And I've come to accept that this is what I was meant for. My father had a reason for promising me to Luca, and I don't regret his choice. It's been painful at times, but it's brought me a great deal of love and joy, too."

Her hand drifts down to the gentle swell of her stomach when she says that last, and I feel a tightness in my chest. I don't want to give Viktor a son, but at the same time, the thought of never having a child of my own hurts. I'd never expected to love my future husband, but I'd always looked forward to having children—to being a mother. I am now, in a way, but there's a part of me that feels hollow at the thought that I might never carry one of my own.

"Let's go outside," Sofia says gently. "I don't want to leave Ana too long. She's struggling more since we've been here. There's nothing to distract her, and she's not eating well or doing any of the things her doctors have suggested. And I can't force her. She's—"

"She's depressed." I follow Sofia towards the back door, feeling very much as if I understand what Ana's feeling. I'm hurtling in the same direction. The need to keep it together for Anika and Yelena is the only thing really keeping me from sinking into the same kind of dark place.

"Yes." Sofia lets out a long breath. "And I don't know what to do for her, except try to distract her. So today we're sitting in the gardens and talking. It's the best I can think of, stuck in this house."

She pushes open the door and then stops in her tracks. For a second, I think something bad has happened, and then I follow her gaze and realize what she's looking at.

Liam is perched on one of the wrought-iron seats surrounding the stone firepit, leaning forward and listening to something that Ana is saying, his green eyes bright. Since he's been here, he's let stubble start to grow on his upper lip and jaw, and it suits him, makes him look older.

Neither of us can hear anything they're saying, but it's clear that he's fixated on it, whatever it is. All of his attention is focused on her, and Ana has a shy smile on her face, her hands knotted together in the cashmere blanket covering her lap.

"I thought for sure he would have left once the fire was started," Sofia whispers. "I guess they've just been out there talking the whole time."

"Ana doesn't seem to mind."

"No, but—" Sofia presses her lips together, her brow furrowing. "She's so different, now. You didn't know her very well before, but you met her a few times. She was never *shy*, never quiet. Especially not with men."

"I definitely gathered that, the few times we all hung out." I watch the two of them, feeling something in the pit of my stomach that's so unfamiliar I can't put a name to it at first. When I finally do, I feel horribly guilty.

It's jealousy. Liam is looking at Ana as if he's savoring every word she says, his attraction to her written over every inch of his face, his green eyes gentle and kind. No man has ever looked at me like that, as if he wants to hear every word that comes out of my mouth as if he wants to cherish me, protect me, adore me. Even in his most possessive moments, there's a brutality in Viktor, a ruthlessness that will never go away.

And I don't know if I would want it to. It turns me on, his brutishness, his roughness. It's different from all the men I've ever known, frightening and thrilling all at once. But I felt a hint of that tenderness last night, heard a glimmer of it in his voice—and seeing the way Liam is looking at Ana makes me crave it all over again.

I want that from my husband. I want it from *Viktor*, and I know I can't ever have it.

Getting a glimpse of it was worse than never seeing it at all. And it hurts more than I could have ever imagined it would.

"She needs to be careful," I say quietly, unable to keep the bitterness out of my voice. "He's no good for her."

"He might be." Sofia is still watching the two of them. There's no jealousy in her face, but why would there be? Luca adores her. He's a vicious man too, but not when it comes to his wife. Not anymore. He would burn the world down to protect her and their child, but he'd never lay a finger in violence on her unless she wanted him to.

I know they play some of the same rough games that Viktor enjoys with me. But Sofia wants it now, without reservation. She's come to understand Luca for the man he is and loves him anyway.

But Luca and Viktor are different in many ways.

"He's the head of a crime family." I shake my head. "As damaged as she is, you really think he'd be right for her? Don't you think you should tell him to stay away?"

"That's not my place. If anyone were to say that, it would be Luca. I could say something to Luca, but—" Sofia gestures to the two of them. "He's not even trying to touch her. It's harmless. And look at her face. That's the happiest I've seen her since—" she breaks off, but I know what she's not saying.

"I can't take that away from her," Sofia says simply. "It's harmless, I'm sure of it. Anyway, Liam will wind up marrying someone that helps his position, just like any other leader of one of the families. Probably the daughter of one of the other high-ranking members in the Kings, to guarantee an ally if anyone ever objects to him having taken his father's seat ahead of his brother. It's not serious."

I remember having the same thoughts when Max had watched Sasha heading down the hall, his face flushed with obvious attraction. *A harmless crush. Something to make her feel better.* But something deep in my gut tells me that the way Liam is looking at Ana is more than that.

Sofia takes that moment to step out into the garden, but I can't bring myself to. "I'm going to go up and check on Anika and Yelena," I say quickly, retreating.

"Are you sure?" Sofia looks at me worriedly. "It's nice out next to the fire, I promise. And maybe you shouldn't be alone—"

"I won't be," I tell her firmly. "I'll be with the girls. Let me know if either of you needs anything." I say that last as brightly as I can, trying to reaffirm my position as the one in charge, in control of running the house. What I should be, as Viktor's wife.

Not weak and afraid, on the verge of bursting into tears at any moment and sinking into a place darker than any I've ever been in before.

That's not the woman I am. Not the woman I was raised to be and not the woman he married. If I'm going to insist that he stick to the limits of our marriage as it was arranged, I need to do exactly that.

Mother his children. Run his household. Go to bed with him only when necessary to give him an heir.

And forget about everything else.

CATERINA

Anika is sleeping when I walk quietly into her room. She still looks small and fragile lying there, but I can see that a good bit of the color has returned to her face. She looks significantly better than when we'd brought her up here, and for the first time since then, I feel as if I don't have to worry about whether or not she'll survive the wound. I know the doctor said that she has plenty of healing left to do, but the relief I feel at seeing the warmth and color in her face is palpable.

I reach out to touch her hand, and she shifts a little, making a small noise. Her fingers curl around mine, and my heart nearly stops in my chest.

Yelena has attached herself to me since day one, but I wasn't sure if Anika would ever really warm up to me. I know that her holding my hand in her sleep doesn't really mean anything, but it makes me feel as if I've unlocked something nonetheless, as if I've been given something special. Something that I really needed today, after everything that I lost last night with Viktor.

These girls are the reason I'm staying, above anything else. So to feel Anika's small fingers curl around mine, as if she subconsciously trusts me and wants me here, feels better than I could possibly have imagined.

She moves again, whimpering a little, and then her eyes flicker, her light lashes fluttering against her cheeks as she slowly opens her eyes. I go very still, my heart beating wildly in my chest, afraid that what I'm seeing isn't real.

It's the first time she's woken up since the break-in, and I know I should call for Viktor. But I can't bring myself to move or speak, afraid that I'll realize I'm imagining things.

She turns her head to look at me, blinking slowly. "Caterina?" Her voice is slurred slightly, probably from the painkillers the doctor gave her, but I can hear my name. "Is that you?"

"It is." I grip her hand a little tighter, blinking back the sudden rush of tears. "I'm here, sweetheart."

"Did you…stay?" The words come out with some difficulty, but she manages it. "Stay with me?"

"As much as I could," I tell her, and I feel the tears start to slip over the edge of my eyelids, dripping down my cheeks. I can't stop it, even though I don't want to cry in front of her, because I'd been so afraid that she'd never wake up again. "I promise."

"Why are you crying?" Anika's voice breaks on the words. "Caterina?"

"I'm just so happy to see you awake." I manage a smile through my tears. "I'm so happy, sweetie."

"I was—scared."

"I know." I bend down, kissing her knuckles gently. "We all were. But you're okay now. You're going to be okay."

"Promise?" Anika squints at me, and I can see a little of that suspicion that's always in her face returning. It makes me feel better, not worse because that's the attitude that I recognize, the spark in the little girl that made me certain she'd fight just as hard to survive as she fights everyone else.

"I promise," I tell her firmly. "The doctor said that if you woke up, it would mean that things were going to be okay. And here you are. You're awake."

Anika nods, trying to swallow. "I want—water—" she manages. "I want daddy."

"I'll get you both," I promise her. "Water, and then I'll go find your father." The thought of seeing Viktor makes my stomach clench with anxiety, but if Anika needs him, then I have to put that aside.

I get a cup of water for Anika from the side table, gently sliding one arm under the little girl's shoulders to help her sit up as she reaches for it. "Slowly," I tell her, sniffing back the last of my tears as I hold her. "Be careful."

"I know how to drink water," she mutters, but there's not her usual animosity in it. She drinks all of it and hands me back the cup, and when she looks at me, her expression is softer than I've ever seen it. "Thank you, Caterina," Anika says quietly, her voice still breaking in spots, and I smile down at her.

"You're welcome. I'm going to go get your father, okay?"

She nods, swallowing as she licks her dry lips and settles back into the pillows as I help her lay back.

"I'll be right back, I promise."

I almost run into Levin the moment I step out into the hall, having to back up to keep from smacking directly into him. "Oh." I clear my throat, flushing despite myself. There's no reason that Levin should know anything about what goes on between Viktor and me. Still, he's the closest person to Viktor in this house. For some reason, I feel as if he's picked up on some of it—or at the very least is aware of his employer's darker—proclivities.

"Are you alright, Mrs. Andreyva?"

No. I'm definitely not alright. Nothing that's happened in the last months has been anything approaching alright.

I don't say any of that. I clear my throat, wiping at my eyes quickly. "I'm trying to find Viktor," I tell him quickly. "Anika is awake and asking for him."

The relief on Levin's face is so real and palpable that it makes me like him even more. He's treated me well in the short time that I've known him, especially at the cabin, and I understand why Viktor trusts him. *I* would trust him if need be. But it's even more clear now that he cares for Viktor and his family in a way that goes beyond just duty, and it makes me soften towards him more than I had already.

"I'll go find him, Mrs. Andreyva," Levin says firmly. "You stay with Anika in case she needs you." He hesitates. "Should I have Sasha or Olga bring Yelena up?"

I hesitate for a moment, but shake my head. "Let's go slowly. Anika only just woke up. I don't want to overtire her. Let her see Viktor this time, and the next time she's awake, we'll bring Yelena up too."

Levin nods. "Of course, Mrs. Andreyva. Whatever you say. I'll go and find Viktor."

I sag against the door as he leaves, my heart still beating hard. Viktor will be up any moment, and that knowledge both makes my stomach twist all over again and sends a tingle of anticipation through me all at once. I shouldn't *want* to see him, and part of me doesn't—part of me is terrified to see him again after what happened last night. But another part, maybe the masochistic part that also enjoys the punishments he inflicts on me, can't wait to see him walk into the room.

Forget it, I tell myself, pushing open the door. *Focus on Anika. Focus on the reason you've decided to stay. Forget* him.

It's easier said than done, though.

"Your father is on his way," I tell Anika as I sit down by the bed again. "He'll be up in a minute, just as soon as Levin finds him."

"Is he angry with me?" Anika's voice is very small as she asks the question, her blue eyes looking up at me. I blink at her, startled.

"Of course not, sweetheart. Why would he be mad at you?"

She swallows, blinking rapidly as if fighting back the tears. "I wasn't supposed to be downstairs. Papa told me to stay upstairs with Yelena, but I was curious. I wanted to know what was happening —and I was scared. So I left her and tried to find him and—" Anika bites her lower lip, her face paling a little as she remembers. "It was so loud, and then there was this burning in my stomach, and everything went woozy—"

"Oh, sweetheart." I move to sit on the edge of the bed, reaching for her, and to my surprise, she leans into my embrace. "Your father isn't angry with you. He wants you to listen to him, and there was a reason for him to tell you that. But he's just going to be happy that you're awake and that you're okay."

"I thought he would blame me for, for—"

"No." I shake my head, stroking her hair. "He's not going to blame you for anything. You're safe now, and that's all that matters."

Anika nods, sniffling. For a moment, I think she's going to stay where she is, letting me hold her. But then the door opens, and Viktor walks in, and all her attention is instantly on her father.

My heart drops the moment he walks into the room, mingled dread and desire filling me until I feel as if I'm vibrating from the inside out with it. He looks as handsome as ever, tall and stern, dressed in tailored black slacks and a dark red button-down shirt open at the collar, as if he were going to the office instead of working from a safe house deep in the Russian mountains. He doesn't look at me, his expression as hard as if it were carved from stone, until the moment he sets eyes on his daughter.

I move away as he makes a beeline for the bed, his face going slack with relief as he drops to his knees next to the bed, reaching for Anika and cradling her in his arms.

"Oh, thank god," he murmurs, his broad hand on her hair as her small arms go around his neck, her face burying against his shoulder as Viktor clutches his daughter to him. "Thank god you're awake, *malen'kiy*. You're okay."

"I'm sorry, papa," Anika cries, her voice muffled against his shirt. "I'm sorry I got in the way."

"No." He shakes his head, and I can hear the tightness in Viktor's voice, the emotion. I realize with a start that he's struggling not to cry, and it shocks me just as much as the first time I heard it, when we thought there was a possibility that Anika might not make it. "You don't need to say you're sorry," he tells her firmly. "But you *must* listen to me in the future, *malen'kiy*. It's very important. Your sister needed you, and you're the eldest. It's important that you protect her and listen to your father." He leans back, smoothing her blonde hair away from her face as he looks into her eyes. "Okay?"

Anika nods, looking tearfully at her father. "I promise, papa," she murmurs, and Viktor nods.

"Just focus on getting better, *malyshka*." He hugs her again and then helps her lie back down, adjusting the covers so that she's tucked in. "You're safe here. Just focus on getting well, and we'll be home soon, I promise."

Anika nods, her eyelids already fluttering tiredly. It's clear that she's exhausted, and Viktor stands up, bending to give her a kiss on the forehead before retreating. He walks past me without so much as a glance, striding out of the door, and I hesitate a moment before turning quickly, giving Anika one more glimpse before following him out as well.

"Viktor!"

He's halfway to the stairs before he stops, his shoulders instantly tensing at the sound of my voice.

"What is it, Caterina?" My voice sounds brittle on his lips, and he doesn't turn around.

"I just—" I take a breath, suddenly feeling shaky and uncertain. "The way we left things last night—"

"I don't want to talk about it." He doesn't turn around, but I can see the tension spreading through him. "There's nothing more to say, Caterina. You made your position clear and left me with no choice but to acquiesce to your wishes. So. If you want distance, I am giving you that."

"If we're going to parent the girls, though—"

"*We* are not parenting anyone." His voice is so cold that it sends chills through me. "I am their father, and you will do your best to act as their mother. There's no need for us to act in tandem."

"I—" I don't know what it is that I'm trying to say. I want to tell him that it's not good for them to see so much tension between us, to never see any affection or warmth, but I can't ask for that after what I'd insisted on and said last night. Sofia's words float back to me, *these aren't men who tolerate games*, and I feel my stomach clench.

"There's nothing left to say, Caterina," Viktor repeats. "We don't need to speak to each other more than necessary. You'll let me know when there's a possibility that my presence in your bed could bear fruit, and any messages you might have for me can pass through Levin. You wanted distance. This is that."

I swallow hard, my hands trembling. A dozen things hover on the tip of my tongue, but I know better than to say any of them. I can't say how desperately I want him to turn around so that I can see the look on his face, so that I can know if it's angry or pained or some mixture of both. I can't say how much I want to reach for him, how it's taking everything in me not to tell him I'm sorry, to beg him to let me take it all back, to tell him that I'm aching for him already—for his touch, his kiss, his body.

I can't tell him that he awakened a need in me that I never knew I had and that I feel as if he tore out a piece of my soul last night when he threw me in that room and walked away.

I can't tell him how desperately I want to say the word stinging my lips, a word that I should never say to a man like him.

I can't love him. I can't. Not a man who does the things that he does.

My heart is as traitorous as my body, but I can never tell him that. Never, never, never.

"Are we done here?" Viktor doesn't move, and my chest clenches, my skin buzzing with the need to not let him walk away from me.

But I don't say anything. He lets out a breath at the silence, his shoulders relaxing a fraction, and then he heads for the stairs without so much as a backward glance.

* * *

My second night alone in the guest bedroom isn't much better than the first. I change into silk shorts and a thin tank top, slipping under the warm sheets and turning out the light. The absence of anyone in the bed beside me feels like a gulf, a reminder of how lonely

I am that makes me feel as if I'm drowning. I roll onto my back, smoothing my hand over the cold space next to me, and I close my eyes.

I shouldn't want Viktor here. But I imagine it anyway, his large, solid body taking up the space, radiating heat. His bare skin brushing against me, the hard muscle of his chest and the ridges of his abdomen occasionally bumping up against my arm or my fingers, sending thrills through me that I tell myself I don't feel and don't want.

Nearly every time we've been together that I can think of, with the exception of the cabin and the garden, has been calculated by one of us, set up to inflict punishment or force desire. I imagine what it might be like to simply slip into bed next to him like one half of a normal married couple, to feel his breath on my shoulder and the heat of his body and for him to reach for me naturally, my body softening into his with awakened desire.

No punishments, no taunting, no fighting it. No resistance. Just easy, soft lovemaking, the kind that other people do. Married people who aren't at war with one another, drawing blood with words instead of knives, killing each other slowly with threats instead of bullets.

A flush of heat washes over me at the thought of Viktor's hand on my breasts, teasing my nipples through the thin silk of my tank top, his mouth at my ear, his warm breath sending shivers over my skin. Without thinking, my hand slides to my stomach, slipping down to the waistband of my shorts, and I suck in a breath, imagining that it's Viktor's fingers instead.

Viktor, touching me gently, his fingers slipping in between my folds, the groan he would make when he finds me wet for him already. I know that sound, deep and anticipatory, eager for what comes next. I imagine his lips on my throat, his tongue on the sensitive flesh of my neck, nipping and sucking, intensifying as he leaves a mark on my flesh while his fingers speed up, rubbing over my clit as I gasp and arch upwards, my thighs spreading easily for him.

I shouldn't fantasize about this. I shouldn't touch myself,

imagining my brutal husband being gentle and loving with me, imagining a future that we can't have. It's just a different kind of torture, a new way of tormenting myself with something I desperately want that can never be a reality. But I also can't bring myself to stop, and I let out a sigh as my fingers circle the hard, slick nub of my clit, feeling it pulse as I lose myself in the fantasy.

"Malyshka—" I hear Viktor whisper as he moves closer to me, his hand reaching up to turn my face to his so that he can kiss me, his lips grazing over mine. His other hand is still inside of my shorts, his fingers teasing my clit, and I slide my hand beneath his arm, reaching for the hard length that I can feel pressing against my hip. He groans when my hand slips inside of the pajama pants he's wearing, skimming over his bare abdomen to wrap around his cock. I feel it throb in my palm as his tongue slides into my mouth, tangling with mine as I stroke him slowly, matching the pace of his fingers circling my clit.

"I want your mouth," Viktor groans. He pushes himself to his knees, the covers sliding back as he pushes his pants down to his hips, his hands leaving me for a moment to hook into his waistband and shove them down, revealing his thick, rigid length to my hungry eyes. I love seeing his cock, hard and ready for me, the tip already pearling with pre-cum as his hips jut forwards, the swollen head seeking out the heat and pleasure of my mouth.

I don't hesitate, as hungry for him as he is for me. I welcome the push of his throbbing cockhead, sliding past my lips so I can taste the salty tang of him on my tongue, the velvet texture.

Viktor groans as I start to suck, his fingers returning to tease my clit as his other hand tangles in my hair, pulling my mouth down the length of him as he pushes me towards a climax.

I can feel my thigh muscles tensing, my back arching as I rub my clit faster, feeling myself start to edge towards an orgasm. But I don't want it to end yet; I don't want to come imagining just that. I want more, more than I can have in reality, and I let the image in my head shift. Viktor suddenly fully naked, his lean, muscular, gorgeous body stretched over mine as he nudges my thighs apart.

"Let me in, malyshka. *Let me inside of you." He murmurs the*

words, thick and accented, his voice rough with desire, and I can't deny him. I want him, the heat and weight of him atop me, his hard cock inside of me, stretching me, filling me up, giving me everything I could ever need.

My legs go around his hips, my arms around his neck, pulling him down to me, inside of me. His lips meet mine at the same moment that his cock starts to slide inside of me, his hips pushing forwards in a steady, slow movement that fills me inch by inch, drawing out the pleasure as his mouth captures mine. His hands are in my hair, his tongue in my mouth, his cock in my body, thrusting forwards until he's inside of me as deeply as he can go, and then Viktor rocks against me, his hands tilting my face up so that he's kissing me harder, deeper, fiercely.

This is love, I think, arching so that I'm pressed against him in every place that my skin can touch his, my breasts against his chest, stomach against his stomach, legs twined around his legs. My forehead presses against his, and I gasp, breathing him in, tasting him, consumed by him.

This is everything I want.

He thrusts harder, faster, groaning against my lips as we both push each other towards the apex of our combined pleasure, wanting to come together, to give each other everything, to hold nothing back. I gasp his name as he gasps mine, and I feel him surge forwards, his body shaking—

"Oh!" I gasp aloud as I feel my thighs starting to tremble. I reach down with my other hand, pushing two fingers into my soaked, clenching entrance as my fingers fly over my clit, pushing me closer and closer to the orgasm that I so desperately need. In my mind, Viktor is thrusting faster, his body shuddering with the force of the pleasure that he's holding back by a fragile thread, and I'm so close, so very close—

I nearly scream his name when I come, stopping myself only by biting my lip hard, turning my face into the pillow to muffle the moan of pleasure that rises to a pitch that I'm afraid Viktor might hear. The thought of him hearing me pleasuring myself alone makes me feel horribly embarrassed. The flush of humiliation that heats my skin turns me on, too, my pussy tightening around my fingers and drenching my hand in my arousal as I buck upwards, grinding against my hand as I climax. The thought of Viktor straining over me, his cock throbbing inside of me as he fills me with his cum, only intensifies it until my entire body is shaking, my thighs clamped around my hands as I squirm and writhe through the orgasm.

"Fuck, oh god, *fuck—*" I whimper, pushing my face into the pillow as I roll onto my side, my fingers still pressed against my pulsing clit. The wave of pleasure satisfied me for a moment. Still, it only leaves a cold emptiness in its wake, a reminder that Viktor isn't here, and he never will be again. I'll never even experience what he's done to me in the past, much less what I just imagined.

The only sex we have in the future will be cold and calculated, meant to create a child and nothing more. And when I've given Viktor what he needs—

I squeeze my eyes shut, jerking my hands free of my clenched thighs, and try to breathe, forcing myself not to cry. I don't want to shed another tear over him, but the hollow emptiness in my chest feels like almost too much to bear.

I'm still aching when I fall asleep, craving something that I can't even put a name to. But even in my sleep, I can't escape it.

I dream about him, forbidding and gentle by turns, my hands bound to the bed, my body stretched out and on display for him as he strikes me over and over again, sending flushes of pleasure through me along with the stinging pain. I dream about his hands smoothing over the marks, his lips tracing them until I'm begging for him to touch me in the places where I need it the most, begging him to let me come. I dream of his smile, gloriously cruel in his handsome face, his breath hovering over my drenched folds as he teases me, making me beg for every caress of his tongue, every press of his lips. I twist and writhe under his touch, so close to a climax, until he pulls away, denying it to me as he starts to stroke himself, watching my twisting, squirming body as he strokes his cock and makes me watch.

The dream is nothing like what I'd imagined as I touched myself. It's Viktor at his cruelest, leaving me punished and wet, aching and needy, forced to watch him pleasure himself until he comes with a groan into his palm, denying me even the feeling of his hot cum on my skin, marking me as his.

I'm not his anymore. I'm nothing. Just something he bought and paid for, another purchased girl meant to serve a purpose.

Those words fill my ears, echoing as he finally reaches for me.

You don't deserve my cock. You don't deserve anything other than this.

His fingers push inside of me, shoving his cum into my clenching, aching pussy, as deeply as he can. I buck upwards, the shame of what he's doing forgotten in my desperation to come, but it lasts only a moment. He pumps his fingers into me twice, three times, rubbing his palm over my heated skin until he's pushed as much of his release into me as he can. And then he stands up, looking at me coldly as he reaches for his clothes.

I hope that gets you pregnant, so I don't have to fucking touch you ever again. You disgust me.

And then his face shifts into Franco's, cruel and mocking, looking down at me.

You disgust me.

Disgust me.

I jerk awake, gasping, my body pulsing with need at the same time that tears are dripping down my face, making me feel almost crazed with the tangle of emotions surging inside of me. I'm painfully aroused and twisted with hurt all at the same time, my heart pounding with fear at the sight of my first husband at the end of the dream. Viktor isn't Franco, he could never be as terrible as Franco was, but the dream lingers all the same, cold chills running over my skin.

I want this to be over. It's all I can think, over and over again, as I curl into a tight ball, trying to push the dream away. I want to forget it, but it lingers, keeping me awake as I shiver despite the warmth of the room.

Will it ever stop hurting? Will I ever stop feeling this way, as if my heart is being torn to shreds? As if I want something so terrible that I hate myself for it?

I don't get any sleep for the rest of the night. I'm too afraid of the dream returning, of making me imagine things worse than anything Viktor has actually done, of making me see him shift into Franco again. I lie awake in the dark instead, waiting for the sunlight to creep through the curtains and push away the worst of it.

The days ahead of me feel endless and nearly unbearable.

Is this what he does? Makes a woman love him and then breaks her?

It would be enough to make me hate him. But the truth is that I don't think he meant to do it. I don't think he meant to break Vera, to turn her life into something so unbearable that she could only see one way out. And I don't think he meant to hurt me.

He certainly didn't mean for either of us to have feelings for the other. *A marriage of convenience.*

That's all I was ever meant to be to him. *Convenient.* It all went too far, and now we're paying the price.

I have to stop thinking of how different it could have been. There's no future in that.

But as the sunlight starts to filter into the room, driving away the worst of the nightmares, I admit something to myself finally, in the silence, somewhere deep in my mind.

I love Viktor. When, I don't know. Maybe in the cabin, when he tended to me, bathing me and feeding me and doing all he could to keep me alive. I can't pinpoint the moment between all the fights and violence and hurt. But somewhere in there, my heart betrayed me as surely as my body ever has with him.

I love him.

If only there were even a single fucking thing I could do about it.

VIKTOR

I haven't slept since the night I left Caterina in the guest bedroom.

A week passes, and then another. The stalemate between us is clear—I won't back down, and neither will she. *If I'd known how stubborn she was*, I tell myself late at night, when I miss her warmth beside me in bed, *I would never have married her.*

Deep down, though, I know that's not true. I wanted Caterina from the moment I laid eyes on her. No amount of fights, defiance, or even her underhanded threats can change that. I viscerally long for her, in a way that I thought I was incapable of feeling any longer.

She's awakened things in me that I thought were dead only to snatch them away again, which makes me crave and hate her in equal measure—or at least I tell myself that too, that I hate her.

The truth is something much worse, which makes men like me weak. Something that can be used against us. And my second greatest fear, right after something happening to my children because of this situation that we've found ourselves in, is Alexei using Caterina against me.

Every day, I do all I can to avoid Caterina. I visit the children when she's not in their rooms, eat my meals alone in my office, throw myself into the work that I can do so far from home and in the meetings I have with Levin, Luca, and Liam, dissecting what information we can find about Alexei's possible whereabouts and the moves he's making on my clients and connections. He's contacted everyone from somewhere remote, but we're able to find out enough about the transactions to discover that he's completed every sale I had lined up before my trip to Moscow and taken the money for himself, as well as brokering sales for the rest of the girls who hadn't been spoken for and taking those profits as well.

"He's positioning himself to take over, once he tells your former clients that you're no longer in the business and that he's the new head," Levin says darkly. "He's building trust so that they'll be more willing to break with you when the time comes, whatever the reason he gives them for your disappearance."

I grit my teeth at that, black fury filling me. "There must be something we can do."

"We need to leave and go back to Moscow. Talk to some of your connections there, and do what we can to flush Alexei out." Levin looks at me. "You know that's what needs to be done, Viktor—"

"I'm not leaving until Anika is well." I shake my head. "I can't do it."

"She's well protected here." It's not often that Levin pushes a point with me, and I know he must be concerned to do so now, especially on this topic. "We'll bring either Luca or Liam with us, and the other stays here to help oversee the security guarding the women. A few days, no more. It would be worth it to eliminate the threat—"

"Anika will be well enough for me to feel comfortable leaving her soon," I insist. "But until then—"

Levin lets out a frustrated sigh, something else unusual for him. Normally he would never let me know if he was displeased with a decision I'd made, even if he was. I can tell that he's as concerned as I am for what this means for our future.

"How trusted is Levin in Moscow?" Luca interjects. "If we send him with enough security to keep him safe, could he seek out that same information while you stay here?"

Inwardly I can't help but grit my teeth at Luca's use of *we*. There was a time when he wouldn't have been party to any of this. I haven't yet entirely gotten accustomed to sharing decision-making with a man whose blood I once wanted to splatter across the Manhattan streets. But a truce is a truce, and part of that is recognizing that a hitch in my business dealings also affects Luca's—and by extension, Liam's as well.

"Do you have any input?" I shoot across the desk to the redheaded Irishman, who has been notably silent throughout the discussion.

Liam shrugs. "I trust both of you to make the appropriate decisions. You know your business, your connections, and most importantly, you know Alexei better than I do, Viktor. I'm not sure my input would be useful."

Well, at least one of them knows when to be silent. I don't say it aloud as I might once have, though, aware that my irritation stems from my worry about my children and my frustrations with Caterina as much as my desire to keep my business dealings close to my own chest.

"Perhaps—" I start to say, but my sentence is abruptly cut off by what sounds like nothing so much as a rattle of gunfire from outside.

"*Bladya!*" I leap up from the desk, moving towards the door. "Levin, where the fuck is security? Get a camera feed for me, now!"

Levin is on his feet as well, moving towards the monitor that has a security feed on it, which is right now set to the children's rooms. He presses a button, flipping through the feeds of the rooms in the mansion before it switches abruptly to the front gates, where the scene I've been dreading is playing out in real-time.

A horde of men dressed in black, with flak vests and automatic weapons and their faces covered, are pouring through the broken gates, a tactical vehicle parked in the gateway where it slammed through. Several members of my security are already on the ground, and I curse aloud as I come around the desk, snatching my own gun out of the top drawer.

"Get Luca and Liam armed," I snap at Levin. "And any other man here who isn't already carrying a gun. Make sure the women are safe in the house somewhere—"

The slamming of the front door and another rattle of gunfire interrupts me, and I rush for the office door, throwing it open as I stride out with Levin on my heels. I can hear the click of loading pistols behind me, but I don't bother to look. I see Max coming out of a doorway further down, his forehead creased, and I grab a pistol from Levin, holding it out to him.

"Take this," I say sharply, but he shakes his head.

"My vows—"

I glare at him, a piercing stare that could freeze ice. "Son, I don't give a fuck about your vows. You've killed one man already, and you're under my protection for it. If you want that to continue, you'll take this gun and defend my family." I narrow my eyes at him. "You wouldn't want anything to happen to Sasha, would you?"

Max's cheeks flush, but he takes the pistol. "I won't use this unless necessary," he says stiffly, but I'm already turning away from him.

I start to turn to Levin to say something, but a piercing scream from upstairs stops me.

"Viktor!" Caterina's voice cuts through the house, followed by a soft shriek that sounds very much like Sofia. A masculine grunt follows it, with loud cursing in Russian, and I dash for the stairs, the sound of more gunshots and the acrid scent of smoke and gunpowder filling the hall from the foyer and living room.

"This is fucking insane," Luca growls. "Liam, come with me. We'll handle what's happening out there. Max, Levin, stick with Viktor—"

"I give orders in this house," I snap, and Luca narrows his eyes at me.

"Then give orders," he says curtly. "But I just fucking heard my wife scream, and—"

We're both interrupted by the sound of crashing from the top of the stairs. I turn to see three men, two of them struggling to hold Caterina while the other has Anika slung over his shoulder and Yelena gripped by the wrist. "I'll throw you down the stairs, you bitch!" he shouts as Caterina tries to claw his face.

"I don't care what you do to me," she spits, wrenching in his grasp, but the man just laughs.

"I'll throw one of the brats down then," he says, picking Yelena up by one wrist as she squirms, starting to cry.

"Put her down!" My voice roars through the air as I stride towards the staircase, but the man just laughs.

"Back off, *Ussuri* or I start taking pieces off of this one." He reaches up, and I catch sight of a hunting knife in one hand, headed for Caterina's ear. "She's pretty, but there's men that will buy a slut even with bits cut off, so long as they're permitted to keep cutting more."

Caterina shrinks back, naked terror in her face, and I can see every bit of blood draining out of it. Her eyes go wide at the sight of the knife, and I can see her reliving every cut that Andrei and Stepan ever gave her in that cabin.

A hot, furious rage wells up in me, and I aim my gun squarely at the man's face. "Put the knife down, and step away from my wife."

He just laughs, pressing the point of the knife into Caterina's jaw. "Go ahead, shoot me. I'll cut this one on my way down, and one of your daughters will wind up tossed down the stairs at your feet. Alexei told us to make sure we kept one alive for bargaining purposes. But two little girls is one too many, as far as I'm concerned."

"Papa!" Yelena shrieks tears streaming down her reddened face. "Papa, help!"

Anika is limp, which tells me she's passed out. I grit my teeth, incandescent with rage. "Levin, where the fuck is security?" I growl, speaking in a low tone, but the man holding Caterina hears it anyway.

"Your security is all but wiped out. Alexei had twice the men you do." He grins, showing a mouth half-empty of teeth. "He made quite a profit from that warehouse full of girls. Turns out, what men he lacked from turning half yours traitor, he bought with the earnings. There are plenty of mercenaries happy to go up even against the *Ussuri* for the right price. And there were some fine fillies in your stable." He laughs then, shaking his head. "Big, bad bear. We snuck up on your fortress and slipped in, disabled your guards long enough to drive that truck through your gates, and let the rest in. So much for your safe house." He grins down at Caterina. "This one is fucking gorgeous. Your wife?"

"Let me fucking go, ah!" Caterina screams as he twists a hand in her hair, wrenching her neck back.

"I'll cut out your tongue if you scream again," the man threatens. "Throw it down at your husband's feet." He jerks his head in the direction of the living room. "We're rounding up the rest. Get going, *Ussuri*. The quicker you meet Alexei and hear his terms, the sooner we can all be done with this messy business."

I've never wanted to kill anyone as badly as I want to murder the three men at the top of the stairs holding my wife and daughters. I've rarely felt this kind of burning urge not just to kill, but to make it last, to take them apart piece by piece and show them exactly where the reputation that they've chosen to ignore came from. But Yelena's tears and the fact that I don't doubt that they won't hesitate to follow through on their promises keep me from charging up the stairs, or taking the shot that I know I wouldn't miss.

I'd take at least one of them down, but there would be casualties, and at least one of them would be one of my daughters and quite possibly Caterina.

The helpless feeling that washes over me only adds to my fury. Caterina looks at me, her dark eyes miserable and terrified, and at that moment, I know that somewhere along the way, I've made a terrible mistake.

For all my wealth, all the men I've hired to protect myself and my family, all the efforts I've made, it's come down to this. I can't protect those I love most, even after everything. And when a door opens, and I see another two men come out with Sofia held between them and another with Ana slung over his shoulder, I feel a despondent pit open up inside of me.

I failed to protect Vera and the child I hadn't known she was carrying, and now I've failed again. For all that I've followed the path that my father and grandfather set me on, for all that I've tried to lead fairly, follow a code, and be a man that other men could follow and respect, this is where it's ended.

"Let her fucking go!" Luca snaps, seeing Sofia. "Both of them! They've got nothing to do with this—"

"You made a bargain with the *Ussuri*."

A voice comes from behind us, clear and sharp, and I know it. Slowly, I turn, along with Luca, Levin, and Liam, but I already know who I'll see.

Alexei is standing there, flanked by a dozen men with automatic weapons. He smiles coldly at me, his white-blond hair combed back and blue eyes glittering icily. "Mr. Romano, you made a bargain," he repeats, glancing over at Luca. "Which means that the *Ussuri*'s business affects you and yours, as well. And you too, by extension, Irishman. Although if you wish to change sides, flesh isn't the only business I have an interest in. Your arms-dealing is a market I wouldn't hesitate to tap into. I hear your father was excellent at changing sides when the wind blew according to his favor." He looks at Liam, his face impassive. "So I'll give you, at least, a chance to choose the winning side today."

Liam, to his credit, doesn't so much as flinch. "I'm not my father, ya wee shite," he says, his accent thickening as he speaks, almost drawling in a heavy Gaelic affectation. He looks at Alexei almost carelessly, as if he isn't the slightest bit intimidated by the man or his backup, and it's almost enough to impress me.

I haven't thought much of Conor's youngest son, but it's clear that he has bigger balls than I gave him credit for.

"Shame." Alexei shrugs. "I imagine if your brother had inherited, he might have chosen the side that would make him a wealthy man and protect the families he's meant to lead. I'm coming for Boston next, Irishman, once I've finished making over Viktor's businesses."

"Isn't Manhattan enough?" Luca glares at him. "If you're targeting me and mine, then I assume you're looking at my territories, too. So you'll try to take Boston after that? Ambitious, for one man."

"I've got my eye on the entire Northeast," Alexei says with a cold smile, glancing at Luca. "From Newport to Baltimore. So yes, Mr. Romano, I intend to take Boston when I'm finished putting my mark on Manhattan."

"Ambitious, indeed." I look at him coolly. "It's a shame you didn't put all that focus into being a better brigadier. You might have been more pleased with your rewards—"

"Shut up, old man." Alexei sneers at me. "And get moving. We'll finish this discussion in a more comfortable place." He gestures towards the living room as the men above us come down the stairs, Caterina, Sofia, Yelena, Anika, and Ana in tow.

He jerks his head towards me, Luca, Levin, and Liam, glancing at the men next to him. "Disarm them."

VIKTOR

I grit my teeth as the men stride forwards, only their eyes visible under the balaclavas and tactical gear they're wearing. They grab all of us roughly, and everything in me screams to fight back. I can see Levin's face go hard, his muscles tensing as he looks at me with an expression that says clearly, *what do you want me to do, boss?*

I want him to fight back. *I* want to fight back. I don't want these sons of bitches touching me or any man or woman in my house. I want to rip Alexei to shreds, peel his skin from his bones while he watches for daring to step foot in my home or allow his men to touch my wife and children. But fighting will mean injury or death for the women and children I'm responsible for. And that thought hits me like a ton of bricks, Caterina's voice echoing through my head.

You were responsible for them the moment you brought them here. It's your fault—

My fault. My fault. A high-pitched scream whips my head around, and I see another of Alexei's men manhandling Sasha down the stairs.

"I'm sorry!" she gasps out as she sees me, her face paling as she catches sight of the man holding Yelena. "I tried to stop him, I'm so sorry, he took her, and I couldn't—"

I'm not entirely sure why it's that, of everything, that makes it click for me at last—everything that Caterina has said to me. But the sight of Sasha, beaten for trying to save my daughter, slides some final piece into place. I feel a wave of cold, sick guilt that I've only ever felt hints of before as if some barrier in my mind and in my soul has been broken down at last.

This girl that I had abducted, held in a warehouse to be sold, this girl who had her virginity stolen by one of my own men, this girl who was then given a place in my home or being turned out on her own as options, risked herself to save my daughter. And all it brought her was more pain.

In Alexei's hands, she won't fare any better, either.

I look at Caterina, and I can see the same thoughts on her face. Her eyes meet mine, and there's a sad resignation there. She's not fighting any longer, just standing there, the man's arm wrapped around her throat as she watches Sasha being dragged down the stairs.

I'm sorry, I want to say. *I understand.* But it's too late.

"Sasha—" Max calls out, his face pale as he twists in the hands of the man holding him, but all it gets him is a fist to the jaw, his head snapping around and a deep groan coming from his lips as he sags forwards. Alexei's men are hustling us towards the living room, the women and children behind us. There's more of his men in there already, Olga and the other staff in a huddle surrounded by soldiers.

"Get them over there." Alexei motions to one side of the room. "All the women and the kids. I want their men to see this. Get the men lined up." He jerks his head, and his soldiers start to manhandle us into place, putting us in a line in front of one of the couches. Levin next to me, Luca, Liam, and Max, who is wobbling slightly, his mouth bleeding.

Caterina starts to fight again as one of the men drops Ana like a sack of potatoes to the floor, leaving her there in a heap as she groans. "The fuck is wrong with that one?" Alexei asks, narrowing his eyes.

"She's injured, you piece of shit!" Sofia snaps, lunging forwards. "Her feet—"

One of the men holding her slaps her in the face, hard. "Shut your mouth and speak with respect, bitch," he snarls. Luca nearly comes undone, twisting so viciously against the grip of the men holding him that he gets one arm free, swinging at the nearest one.

It takes two men to restrain him, one delivering a punch to the gut that makes him double over before Luca stops struggling. He glares at me, spitting mad as he curses in Italian at the man who punched him.

"Are you just going to stand there and take this?" Luca is breathing heavily, turning his head to look at Sofia, who has gone pale as death. When she starts to step forward, and one of the men twists her arm, Luca makes a noise that's almost animalistic.

"She's pregnant, you piece of *merda*!" he snaps, and I groan, shaking my head as Alexei looks at him with interest.

"For fuck's sake, Luca, shut up," I hiss. "You're going to make it worse."

"At least I'll fucking fight!" Luca is looking at Alexei with the kind of hatred I've rarely seen in a man's face.

"They have my children," I growl under my breath. "Fighting won't get us out of this. Keep your cool, Luca."

"He's right," Liam says tightly, his gaze fixed on Ana. "I hate it as much as you do, lad, but he's fucking right." He turns his gaze to Alexei, calm despite the flashing in his green eyes. "What do you want, ya wee shite? You've already taken half of Viktor's business. And I know, I know, you've got designs on all of the Northeast, but think with your head, man. Not one man can hold all that. Even my father knew enough to try to make alliances."

Alexei smirks. "Your father was as stupid as you are, then. One man can rule anything if he's feared enough."

"Fear will only get you so far." My voice stays steady, despite the anger shuddering through me. Yelena has fallen to the floor, curled into a ball, the man watching her looming over her. As I look squarely at Alexei, I see the man drop Anika none too gently next to her sister. It's all I can do not to fly into the same rage that Luca did, seeing Anika jerk with pain and her sister gasp, reaching out for her. Caterina twists in the grasp of the man holding her again, trying desperately to get to the girls, but he's holding her too tightly.

"Fear will get me far enough." Alexei's mouth curls upwards in that cruel smile again. "You see, Viktor, your problem was that pesky moral code of yours. You traffic in sex, sell women, profit off modern slavery. Still, you think you're above others because you kill discriminately, refuse to rape, rarely torture. You think that you rule because you have respect, but in truth, you are nothing but a bear with no claws. An old grizzly whose teeth have fallen out. And I'm here to tell you that fear will get you farther than respect, farther than a moral code. You see, Viktor—" he balances his pistol in one hand, his gaze sliding over the gathered group, and my heart stutters in my chest.

"The difference is that your men knew exactly how far you could be pushed," Alexei continues. "One of them dared to *rape* a woman in your warehouse, steal her virginity because he believed that you would deal with him mercifully."

"I killed him, if you recall," I reply through gritted teeth. "I wouldn't call that merciful."

"Indeed." Alexei considers. "A bullet to the head. A kinder death than I would give a man who stole from me. But you see, my men fear me to the point that it would never happen in the first place. Do you know what I did to the men back home who failed to join my side?"

A sick feeling curdles in my stomach at the look on his face. "No," I say quietly. "I don't."

"I carved them into pieces while the others watched and thanked God that they chose the right side." Alexei slides his pistol back into his hand, wrapping his fingers around the butt of it. "You can take a lot of pieces off of a man before he dies. Some pass out sooner than others, but it's all a part of the fun. Some of your men who switched sides were placing bets, by the end of it, on who would last the longest."

He frowns then, considering. "Of course, I lost Mikhail. It was a disappointment; I think he would have lasted the longest. He was very loyal to you. Loyal enough to try to get all of your staff out, although he failed."

"What did you do to them?" My teeth ache with how tightly I have them clenched in an effort not to lose control. Not to twist loose and attack him, an action that would have disastrous results for my family.

Alexei shrugs. "The prettiest, youngest women I took to sell. The men I shot, the older and uglier women I gave to my men, to dispose of when they were finished. Some men will fuck anything if they can get it to lay down for them." He smirks. "Mikhail got away with a few. But not to worry, I have men looking for him as we speak. I would say that I'll give you the privilege of watching while I see how many pieces I can remove before he loses consciousness. But you'll be dead."

"No!"

A cry comes from the left side of the room, and my heart sinks as I see Olga step forward, her wrinkled face creased as she looks pleadingly at Alexei. "Viktor is a good man," she says calmly, holding out her hands. "I know you, son," she says quietly. "I've cooked you dinner, served you at Viktor's table. This isn't you."

"Shut up, hag," Alexei snaps. "If you know what's good for you, you'll step back and shut your wrinkled mouth. I can fetch a price for you, with your skills at keeping house. But if you don't leave me to my business–"

"Olga, please–" I start to say, but she's still talking, her chin held high as her watery blue eyes fix on Alexei.

"It's a shame you don't have respect for your elders," Olga murmurs. "But whatever you have planned for me, spare Viktor and his family. He's been good to me and to the others in his household."

"I'll warn you once more–" Alexei's eyes narrow, his mouth thinning. "I don't like to lose money. But you're pissing me off, you old bitch. You should know your place."

But to my horror, Olga doesn't back down. Instead, she sinks to her knees, hands still outstretched. I hear a gasp from my right, likely Caterina, but I don't look away. I can't because I know what comes next. And it's my fault.

All of it, my fault.

" I'm begging you," Olga says as she settles onto her knees clumsily with the weight of age, more clearly now, though her old voice wavers with a hint of fear. "If there is any mercy in you, don't—"

M JAMES

The crack of the gunshot is deafening. Yelena starts to shriek as Olga tumbles to the floor, blood dripping from the wound in her forehead, clearly visible. Her piercing screams fill the room, loud enough to be heard even over the temporary deafness from the gunshot, and Alexei turns on his heel, annoyance plain on his face. "Shut that fucking brat up," he snaps. "I only need one child alive, if she won't shut the fuck up—"

"No!" It's Caterina's turn to scream it. She wrenches herself loose from the man holding her with a ferocity that I've never seen, her delicate body jackknifing as she drives an elbow backward into his ribs, stomping on his foot as she gets free, flinging herself onto the floor next to Yelena and Anika. "Shh," she whispers, gathering Yelena into her arms, physically blocking her from Alexei's line of fire and anyone else's. "You've got to be quiet, baby, please. I know you're frightened, I am too, but you've got to be quiet now, for your father and I. Shh, shh—"

She keeps crooning to Yelena, stroking her hair, all of her attention focused on the little girl despite how terrified I can see that she is. I know that she's not past the trauma of her own kidnapping, and I know that this must be bringing it all up again. But I can see in her face that nothing can keep her from protecting my daughters, and my heart swells with a feeling for her that I wish more than anything I'd put into words before this moment.

"The mama bear." Alexei laughs. "Is this one pregnant, too?" He looks at me, and I know he's expecting me to answer.

I don't know which answer is better. Sofia hasn't been hurt since Luca shouted it, but I have a decent idea of what Alexei is hoping to do with the women here. A pregnant woman is a novelty, but not many men looking to buy want the result. It would lower her price.

It makes me sick to think of Caterina like that, but I have to think of how best to protect her while Alexei has the upper hand. And I realize, with the fresh eyes with which I saw Sasha, that I've thought about hundreds of women in exactly that way. It just hadn't mattered to me because they weren't my wife or my daughters.

Still, I was responsible. Just as I'm accountable for everything that's happened to Sasha, Caterina, and Olga. I look at the old woman, her body very still on the carpet, blood leaking from her forehead as Alexei motions for her to be taken away. Her life ended in an instant, because she spoke up for me.

I didn't deserve it. She was loyal to me, and I didn't deserve it. I'd treated her well over the years that she'd worked in my household, but what had she turned a blind eye to all that time? How had she justified it, continued to care for my family and me so faithfully?

Only Caterina has stood up to me. Only Caterina has refused to give me her love and devotion unless I saw myself for what I truly was. Even Vera couldn't put her feelings into words. Only Caterina was strong enough.

And now it's too late.

"She's not," I say quietly.

"Good." Alexei smiles with satisfaction. "Divide up the rest of the staff," he tells the men flanking them, glancing in that direction. "Women under the age of twenty-five with decent enough looks separate out for sale. The others keep separate, we may find some buyers for them still. The Italian woman, the blonde one, Viktor's wife, and that little spitfire—" he nods towards Sasha, "they come along with me, back to the main house. Along with the children." He smiles at me; his expression is as cruel as anything I've ever seen. "Those two girls are very pretty. Imagine the price—"

The noise that comes from my mouth is like nothing I've ever heard, an animal sound as I lunge towards him, my control finally broken. Alexei steps back, making a *tsking* sound. "Now, now, Viktor, remember that your behavior matters. The harder you make this on me, the more I'll take it out on them."

"Before we go," he continues. "It's clear that I can't leave you alive, Viktor. You're not willing to retire with grace. And I can't have any of your compatriots trying to avenge you. So the lot of you will have to die. Since we don't have time for fun, I'll make it quick. Shoot them." He steps back, nodding to his men, and they raise their weapons in unison.

A fucking firing squad in my living room. And I'm on the wrong end of it.

I'm not afraid of dying, exactly. A man in my position doesn't remain there this long without a healthy realization of the fact that he lives on the knife's edge of death all of the time, if the wrong people get the wrong ideas. A man of my age, looking forty squarely in the eye, also knows that he's lucky to have made it this far with everything intact and his life still his own. In our world, making it to a ripe old age is a success in and of itself, as impressive as any financial success. It means you're intelligent, savvy, wise, and respected or feared enough to have escaped the plots, hits, and general ill-will that men who hold power in our world attract.

It's caught up to me at last. And for myself, I don't care. I'm not afraid of death itself. It's a shame to lose out on the trappings of life so soon, of course—the luxuries I've worked hard for, the pleasures of sex, the enjoyment of a good meal or a good cigar or glass of top-shelf vodka. I know that Luca feels the same. He's younger than I am, in his thirties—he knows the accomplishment of having ascended to his place while still remaining alive and whole. And he's had closer calls than I have.

Liam—well, he's young enough to regret a life mostly unlived. I feel for him. And Max fears his God and the vows he's broken. Death won't come comfortably to him.

But mostly, it's everyone else that fills me with regret. Sofia, who will bear her child alone, a widow. Ana, left alone in a world that has beaten her down enough already. Sasha, once again a prisoner. My children, in the hands of a man who will do things that sicken me. *Caterina.*

I should have told her that I love her. I should have understood what she was trying to say to me so much sooner. If only—

But there's no point. I might have a few seconds to speak before the men fire, but I can't use those seconds to tell Caterina what I want to say, no matter how desperately the words rise to my lips. It's a selfish desire, and with death only seconds away, I don't have time for that.

The thought of leaving Caterina at their mercy, never knowing how I feel, makes my heart feel as if it's being ripped out of my chest. But it's not her who needs me the most.

"Not my children, Alexei, please." I hold my hands out, aware of how similar it is to how Olga begged only minutes ago, but I'm far from caring about my pride in this moment. "My business has never been trafficking children. The women have always been of age, and my clientele reflects that. If there is an ounce of goodness in you, an ounce of respect for the years we worked together, not my daughters. Kill me, do what you wish, but not—"

"Shut up, old man." Alexei laughs. "I care about profit, not morality. Those girls are perfection. The one is wounded, of course, but I can work around that. The littlest one, though—"

"Alexei."

Caterina's voice cuts through the air, and everyone goes very still, mostly because of the way she says his name. It's not a shriek or a plea. It's cold and clear, the voice I would have expected from one of my men, and even the soldiers holding guns on us waver, wanting to turn to look at her. They don't dare to incur Alexei's wrath, though, and they hold their position, the muzzles of the automatic weapons pointed squarely at the five of us. At any moment, they could shred us, killing us before we hardly have a chance to hear the shots. *It'll be quick, at least.*

It's not death or pain that I fear. But the thought of leaving my daughters and Caterina behind is an unbearable grief, an agony like nothing I've ever felt.

Alexei turns slowly, a smirk spreading across his face. "The mama bear speaks. What do you have to say, *Mrs. Andreyva?*" He inclines his head sarcastically. "What would the *tsarina* like to say to me?"

Caterina takes a breath, her chin tilted up. "If you let the men live —all five of them," she specifies. "My husband, Luca, Liam, Levin, and Max, all of them live and go free. If you do that, I and the other women and the children will go with you."

Alexei stares at her for a moment, dumbfounded, and then he starts to laugh. "Did you not hear what I just said, you stupid bitch?"

He snorts. "I said you're all coming with me once I dispose of your husbands. Are you an idiot? What kind of fucking bargain is that?"

Any other woman might have wavered or crumpled. Even Sofia is trembling, her face so pale and bloodless that I can't believe she hasn't passed out already. Her gaze is fixed on Luca, tears streaming down her face, her lips making wordless sounds. *I love you, I love you.*

The things I want to say so badly to Caterina. My fierce, beloved bride. My heart swells as I watch her face down Alexei fearlessly, even though I know it's useless.

She smiles at him, and it's enough to make him falter. "Are you stupid?" he asks again. "What the fuck are you smiling about, cunt?" He takes two steps towards her, sneering. "I'm going to sell you to someone who will cut that smile right off of your pretty face. I'll find the most vicious man in Russia, someone who likes hurting women, and I'll sell you for a price that will justify everything he'll do to you. Someone willing to pay for his specific predilections. Can you imagine—"

"I can," Caterina says evenly, though I can see the fear flickering in her eyes. "And you can do what you like with me, Alexei, if you let Viktor and the other men here go and promise to be gentle with the other women and my daughters. You can do anything you like, now or later, and I won't struggle. None of us will fight you when you take us away. But if you kill our men—" she takes a breath, never breaking eye contact with him. "You'll still take us, that's true. But we'll make it hell for you. We'll do what we can to hurt your soldiers, we'll try to escape, we'll bite and claw and scratch no matter what you do to us for it. We'll act out when you try to sell us, and drive down the price. We'll make every moment you have us in your possession a living hell if you do this. You'll sell us for far less than we're worth, just to be rid of us."

Christ. The bravery in her words, the steel in her spine, takes my breath away. She looks at him unfalteringly, offering herself up most of all. It rips my heart out of my chest even as I know without a doubt that no woman in the world could have been a better match for me.

I wish I hadn't realized it so late.

BELOVED BRIDE

Alexei snorts. "You'll do what I want and come quietly anyway. Or I'll hurt those two girls—"

"No, you won't." Caterina looks at him evenly. "You want a good price for them. And besides, what will you do? Will you hurt them? If you do, you won't get more than pennies for them. Kill them?" She smiles coldly at him. "Death is better than what you have planned for them. If I thought there was no other way, I'd do it myself before I let you sell them."

I don't know of another woman who could have discussed something so terrible so calmly. Sofia looks as if she's going to be sick, Sasha staring at Caterina with horror. But Caterina knows as well as I do a simple truth—begging and pleading with Alexei will change nothing. The only way to win against a man like him is to appeal to the only thing he cares about—greed and results. The practicality of the situation is what will change his mind, not moralizing.

He doesn't care about right or wrong. He cares about efficiency and profit. And by removing her emotions from the situation, Caterina has appealed to both.

She might have just saved us all.

Alexei presses his lips together, scowling. "Fucking bitch," he snarls between clenched teeth. "What if I tell you that I'll hurt your men anyway, even if you go quietly?"

"You can do what you like," Caterina says, her voice trembling slightly. "As long as you let them go. We'll do what we have to in order to keep them alive."

He takes a step forward, his left hand darting out and grabbing her breast roughly. I see the pain in Caterina's face, but she doesn't flinch. "You're no virgin," he says, laughing. "So there's no difference who fucks you before you sell. I think I'll take you for myself, for a while. Enjoy what Viktor's been enjoying. I've already taken everything else of his. What do you think of that? Will you fuck me in exchange for your husband's life?" His lip curls. "For all of their lives? You'll have to do it willingly."

Caterina is trembling all over now, a fine tremor running through her body from forehead to toes, but she nods. "Yes," she says quietly. "If that's what your price is."

"What if I tell you to get on your knees now and suck me off in front of your husband?" Alexei laughs aloud, an almost crazed sound. "God, wouldn't that be fun?"

Caterina swallows hard, her eyes darting to me. She's shaking now, but she starts to sink to her knees.

"Caterina, no!" I start to call out, but one of the men drives the butt of his gun into my stomach, making me double over coughing. "Cat—"

She sinks down, and Alexei cackles again, his hand wrapping tightly in her hair. "God, you must fucking love him. Or else he knows how to give you his cock, to inspire such devotion. But don't worry, mama bear." He tips her chin up, grinning down at her. "I'll fuck you until you can't remember any cock but mine."

Alexei tightens his grasp in her hair then, hauling her up to her feet. "Alright, stand down," he says, almost carelessly, waving at the men. "Keep an eye on them, though, and keep them restrained until the women are loaded up. When we're on our way, you can release them. Or—" he amends, "leave them bound, so they can't follow. Make sure every other member of security is dead. Do a sweep." He waves a hand, and some of the men break off obediently. "They can figure out their own way loose. Gives us time to get away."

Then, he looks at me, his blue eyes piercing as his gaze fixes squarely on mine. "Be careful, Viktor Andreyev. If you come after me, the price your family pays will be dear. Don't make your wife's sacrifice for nothing. And don't even think about going back to Manhattan and picking up where you left off. You have no home now, no business. Beg your Italian or Irish friends for help, if you can. But you are finished."

He grabs Caterina then, shoving her towards me. "Say your goodbyes while we load up your friends."

"Let them say goodbye too—" she starts to say, and Alexei's hand comes up in a flash, striking her hard across the cheek.

"No more," he grinds out. "You've bargained all you can, *tsarina*.

You get goodbyes. No one else. See how much your friends care for you after that, since you already bargained with their lives too."

"Max—" Sasha's mouth is swollen, but she manages his name, looking over at him with eyes filling with tears. "Max, I'm sorry—"

He strains against the men holding him, his face going from crumpled to fierce in a matter of moments. "Stay strong, Sasha!" he calls out. "You've survived this long. You can survive until we can come for you."

It's difficult for Alexei's men to keep ahold of any of us now. Liam is trying to see Ana, twisting past the men who have blocked him in. "Ana!" he calls out, but there's no answer. She's passed out cold, from pain or fear or both, and one of Alexei's soldiers hoists her unceremoniously over his shoulder, carrying her out towards Sasha.

"You despicable fucks." Luca is trying to get free, too, his gaze desperately searching out his wife's. "She's pregnant, I swear to god if she loses the baby—"

"What does it matter to you?" Alexei laughs. "You'll never see her again, Romano. Who knows what will happen to the child if it's born. Perhaps I'll keep her until she gives birth and find a use for the baby once it's old enough to turn a profit."

Luca's face is red with rage, and he jerks hard against the hands holding him. Alexei lets out a long-suffering sigh.

"Get them under control," he snaps. Luca lets out a grunt of pain as one of the men holding him punches him hard, another delivering a shot to the kidney that has him nearly falling to the floor in pain. I want to do something, to stop what's happening to him and what will certainly happen to the other men soon, but Caterina is being pushed towards me, and I know I only have moments with her.

"Viktor—"

"You shouldn't have done this," I tell her, shaking my head. "Alexei will hurt you. He'll do terrible things to you simply because you're my wife, and the others—"

"It's okay," she breathes, her eyes fixed on mine, her voice low to keep him and the other soldiers from hearing. She reaches out, gripping the front of my shirt, bringing me closer. "You'll save us. I know you will. I have faith in you, and in Luca, and Liam too, even. Whatever I have to endure until then, it's worth it to keep you alive."

Her words stop any that I might have been on the verge of saying. I look at her, my gaze searching her face. "You mean that." It feels unbelievable, having left things as we did. Without her knowing that I've had a change of heart, or how I feel—

"We don't have time, Viktor," Caterina whispers, her voice low and desperate. "We don't have enough time to say anything, really. But yes, I mean it. Whatever we've done, whatever we've said to each other, I couldn't watch you die in front of me. You saved me once. You'll do it again. I know you will." She breathes in sharply, her hands tightening in my shirt, and then my Caterina, my wife, lurches towards me with a wild look in her eyes that I've never seen before.

She drags me to her, her mouth crashing down on mine. She kisses me as fiercely as I could ever have imagined she might, her tongue plunging into my mouth as she kisses me like it's the last time, like she's memorizing my lips. And I know that she is because it very well could be.

I want to touch her, to hold her, to gather her in my arms and never let her go. I want to feel her body in my hands, her hair, her face, but my hands are bound behind my back, and during this last kiss with my wife, I can't touch her at all.

"Caterina, I l—"

"Shh." She pulls away, shaking her head. "Tell me when we're free of this, Viktor. Not here, not with them."

"What if—"

"No." Her voice is firm, and she reaches up, clasping my face in her hands. "You'll save us. I know you will. We'll be waiting for you."

"Hurry up, bitch." Alexei's voice cuts through the air. "Enough of this shit. You have ten seconds."

"I'll take care of them," Caterina whispers hurriedly. "The girls. I won't let him hurt them, whatever I have to do. I promise. I—"

His men stride forwards, grabbing her, pulling her off of me. I try to lunge forwards to go to her, but there are hands on me too, dragging me back towards Luca and the others. Luca is slumped on the carpet, bleeding from his nose and mouth. Alexei grins cruelly at me as he grabs Caterina by the chin, forcing her to look at all of us as Yelena and Anika are carried out to the waiting vehicles.

"Remember this when I'm fucking you," he says, his lips near her ear but his voice loud enough to carry. "This is the last thing I want you to see."

He nods to his men, and they surge forwards, all of them descending on us at once. Luca is already beaten to the point of passing out, but the rest of us—Max, Liam, Levin, and myself, are instantly their focus as if Alexei has flipped a switch. I hear Max's grunts, Liam's groan of pain, and then I catch one more glimpse of Caterina's pale, tearful face before a fist drives my face sideways, and I lose sight of her.

When I manage to dodge the blows long enough to look again, she's gone, and so is Alexei. The door is hanging open, but I can't see her or any of them.

They're gone.

I might never see them again.

The next blow knocks me to the floor, and I know the one after it will knock me unconscious. But at this point, I don't care.

When it comes, I welcome the darkness.

CATERINA

The ride to our destination is a long one.

We're crammed into a van, all of us pushed to one side of it while Alexei's soldiers, all of them armed, sit and crouch on the other side, watching us with predatory gazes. "It's a shame he's got plans for all of them," one man mutters. "I'd like a taste. Especially the blonde."

"I like the redhead, myself," another says, motioning towards Sasha, who squirms backward with frightened eyes.

"The *Ussuri's* wife has claws," the man on the far left says with a smirk. "I'd like to get my cock up her. I like them feisty. Plus, what a fuck you to the boss, eh? Fucking his wife. We should all pass her around if Alexei wouldn't lop our balls off for it."

"What about the Italian slut?"

"I don't like pregnant bitches. Creeps me the fuck out."

I ignore them. They can't touch us, Alexei would do worse than kill them, and they know it. This is one moment where Alexei's cruelty will work in our favor. Instead of gratifying them with a reaction, I focus on calming the others. Sofia is pale but remarkably calm —or maybe just in shock—so I turn towards where Sasha is huddled next to Anika and Yelena; Ana still passed out next to her.

"I'm scared," Yelena whimpers, her face swollen from crying and her nose red. "They killed Olga, Cat, they killed her—"

"I know, baby. I know." My chest tightens with grief as I reach for Yelena, gathering her into my arms along with Anika. Anika is starting to come back to her senses, but she doesn't fight me. Instead, she curls into my embrace along with Yelena. Under other circumstances, my heart would have swelled with happiness to have Anika be so sweet and trusting with me.

But all I can feel is barely controlled terror. Alexei is worse than I thought, tipped over the edge from merely being a traitor to having become a power-hungry madman. What he has planned for us —for each of us—is terrible, but what he has planned for Anika and Yelena is worse than that. And I won't let it happen.

I don't know how I'm going to stop it, though. I can pacify him for a little while, keep him occupied so that he doesn't have time to hurt anyone else. But unless Viktor and the others find us quickly, it might not be enough time to make a difference. Alexei isn't going to bide his time for long. He can't possibly believe that Viktor will slink off into the distance with his tail between his legs when Alexei has just kidnapped his wife and children, along with two women under his protection and his ally's wife and unborn child.

I meant it when I told Viktor that I believed he would come for us. I just don't know how long we have.

"I'm scared," Yelena cries again, dissolving into sobs, and I clutch her to my chest, muffling them as best as I can so as not to piss off our guards. Even beyond the fear, I'm seething with anger and hatred like nothing I've ever felt before for Alexei and everyone who's helped him. It's one thing to kidnap and brutalize adult women. Still, I know that Anika and Yelena will bear the emotional and mental scars from this for the rest of their lives. The trauma they've endured just in the past hour is unthinkable.

If they make it that long. The thought creeps in, but I shake it away just as quickly. I won't let myself think that for even a moment. I won't allow myself to consider a possibility where, at the very least, Viktor's daughters aren't rescued.

I'll do anything it takes to save them. No matter what it costs me.

I glance towards Sasha, still holding Yelena and alternating between stroking her hair comfortingly and Anika's. "Are you alright?" I ask quietly, and she swallows hard, her chin trembling as she fights not to cry. Her mouth is swollen, her face bruised, and her arms are wrapped over her chest, trying to hold her shirt in place so that the guards can't see her breasts.

"No," she whispers. "But what the hell am I supposed to do about it?"

Her honesty is startling. My heart aches for her because she's been through so much already. "We're going to be okay," I whisper back, and Sasha smiles sadly at me.

"I don't know about that, Mrs. Andreyva. But we'll hang in there as long as we can. They're the most important thing." She nods at Anika and Yelena. "As long as they're safe, it doesn't matter what else happens."

"I don't know what they're going to do to me," Sofia murmurs through her pressed-together, pale lips. "My baby—"

"I'm going to keep you all safe," I whisper fiercely. "I promise. I'll distract Alexei as long as I can—"

"It won't be enough." Sasha is pale, too, her hands trembling where she's clutching her shirt. "You don't know men like him, Mrs. Andreyva. Your husband is one of them, but even he's not so evil."

I'm taken aback briefly at that. *Your husband is one of them.* I know that, of course. It's why the rift between Viktor and I is so deep, still not healed even after those last few minutes between us. I didn't want to leave him with so much hurt, didn't want our last conversation to be the stilted, angry ones we've had over the past weeks. But it's not magically better. And even if he rescues us, nothing will change if he doesn't.

There will still be an impassable, impossible gulf between us. But in this moment, I'd give anything just to be back home, even if it means living alongside my sometimes cruel, distant husband without the love or pleasure that I'd so briefly hoped for.

The last night we spent together seems so far away now that I could almost think I dreamed it. It feels like nothing but a fantasy now, like I can't even be quite sure that it happened. Here in the cramped, cold van, jostling between Sofia and Sasha with my stepdaughters in my arms, armed men watching us like hawks, that warm, firelit night feels like something out of a movie. Something I made up.

He'll come for us. I tell myself over and over as I glance towards Sofia. Viktor won't let Alexei win, for his pride if nothing else, but I know that it's more than that. I don't know what there is between us, exactly. He'd wanted to say something to me before Alexei dragged me away, but I hadn't let him, for more reasons than one.

If he'd been going to say what I think he was, that wasn't how I wanted to hear it. Not there, not like that, not in front of Alexei as my friends were being hauled off to be sold as sex slaves, with me headed directly after them. Not with only seconds left before we might never see each other again.

More than that—I want him to be sure. *I* want to be sure. And if either of us are ever going to say those words to each other, I want it to be when I don't have to tell him, *I love you, but—*

I love you, but I can't act on it when you do the things you do.

I love you, but only if you change.

I love you, but not like this.

It would be better not to say it at all. *If he rescues us,* when *he rescues us,* I tell myself, *we can talk about it then.*

Sofia stirs next to me, pressing her hand to her stomach, and I glance over at her. "Are you alright?" I ask softly, and she shakes her head, wincing.

"I'm in a little pain," she says quietly. "They weren't exactly gentle. But it's not me that I'm worried about."

The baby. I look at her protective hand pressed against her belly and feel the same fear that I have for Anika and Yelena stirring again. "They didn't do anything rough enough to hurt the baby, did they?"

"Not yet." Sofia swallows hard; her face and lips are bloodlessly pale. "But that doesn't mean that they won't."

It takes me a second to realize what she means. "No," I whisper. "No, they wouldn't. Not even Alexei—"

"He wants a good price for me," Sofia speaks with some difficulty as if it's hard for her to get the words out. "Being pregnant will only hinder that. I'm not that far along. It wouldn't be hard to…to —" her voice breaks and her hand flattens tightly against her stomach, her eyes brimming with tears. "I fought so hard for this baby. I put us both in danger to keep it from Luca when I thought that he wouldn't want it, that it would break our contract." She sniffs, obviously trying not to break down in front of our guards. "And then he was happy, and everything was good, and, and—"

"Oh, Sofia." I wish I had more arms to hold her and the girls, but instead, I lean my forehead against her shoulder, still cradling Anika and Yelena. I can feel the weight on my shoulders, the responsibility of trying to ensure everyone's safety. No one has explicitly told me that's my job, but I'm Viktor's wife, the wife of the *pakhan*. The wife of the man whose rival is causing this. I've lectured Viktor about responsibility, and now I've got to take my own words to heart.

"I don't think they'd do anything that would damage me," she manages in a choked voice. "Alexei is interested in profit off of this, not just in hurting Viktor and Luca. But if he can get a doctor to—"

"Shh." I reach out and grab her hand, shaking my head. "Don't say it out loud. Don't even *think* it, Sofia."

"But what if—"

"If that's what he's got in mind, then we'll cross that bridge when we come to it. But you can't work yourself up being afraid of something that hasn't even happened yet. It'll only be worse for you and for the baby."

Sofia nods, taking as deep of a breath as she can. "I saw what they were doing to Luca, as they took us out—and the others—"

"Luca is strong." I squeeze her hand. "I know it's horrible. They were starting in on Viktor when Alexei dragged me out. But they've been through beatings before. We married men who know how to survive in this world, Sofia. They're all strong. They'll survive it, and they'll come after us. As soon as they can make a plan."

"Do you think Max will?" Sasha's voice comes from the other side, smaller and softer than usual. "Do you think he'll come with them?"

I pause, considering. "I don't know," I say carefully, glancing over at her. "I don't know Max very well. But I don't think he's the same kind of man that Viktor and Luca—and even Liam—are. He's a priest, Sasha, you know that, right?"

"He used to be." There's a hint of stubbornness in her tone that sets off a pinging alarm in my head. I remember how Max's face looked when he caught sight of her in the hall, how they'd spoken to each other earlier, before Alexei's men took us away. "He was defrocked."

I lick my dry lips, considering what to say. On the one hand, I don't want to deny Sasha anything that might give her some comfort or hope. She's been through so much, and it's far from over. But just as I'm unsure that Liam's interest in Ana is wise, I feel the same about Max. Even if he had stepped fully away from the priesthood, he clearly comes with a good deal of baggage.

"I'm under the impression that he still tries to keep to his vows, though," I tell her gently. "I don't know his story. But he broke at least one of them, I know that much, and he's under Viktor's protection now. I don't think he's open to romantic connections. And beyond that, he's complicated, Sasha."

She looks away, her arms tight over her torn shirt. "So am I," she says quietly. And then she goes very quiet, refusing to look at any of us.

I start to say something else to comfort her, but Ana starts to stir on the other side of Sofia, and Sofia turns immediately towards her.

"Hey. It's okay," Sofia says softly, reaching for Ana as her eyes go wide and she starts to push herself up, scrambling backward.

She can't go far because we're already on one side of the van, and I can see panic rising in her eyes.

"What's happening?" Ana breathes, starting to shake as she sees the men guarding us. "What the fuck is going on? What the fuck—"

"Alexei attacked the safe house," Sofia says, keeping her voice low and soothing even if her words are anything but. "He forced Viktor and Luca and the others to let him take us. The men are still alive, though, if a little worse for wear. And I know they'll come after us—"

"Liam." Ana looks up at Sofia and then at me, her eyes wide and terrified. "Is he okay? Is he—"

"He's fine, as far as I know," I tell her quickly. "Maybe a little roughed up, but he's alive. I bargained with Alexei to make sure that he wouldn't kill them."

"What did you say?" Ana's expression is suddenly guarded. "What did you promise them, Cat?"

I bite my lower lip, seeing her putting the pieces together before I can even say it aloud. "He was going to force us to go with him anyway. I told him we'd go quietly and not fight back if he didn't kill Viktor, Luca, Liam, and the others. That we'd do what he wants. He would have killed them if I didn't."

"And what does he want?" Ana's voice is trembling. "He's taken over Viktor's business, right? So what? He's going to sell us?"

"He's going to try," I clarify. "I have faith that they'll rescue us before that can happen. He's not going to be able to arrange for that right away. We just have to think of how to protect ourselves until then—"

"What do you think he's going to do to *me*?" Ana asks, her voice wavering. "I'm not going to be worth anything, you know that. My feet—"

"You don't know that," Sofia says firmly. "None of us know anything about how this works. Except maybe Cat—"

"I don't." I shake my head. "I hated that Viktor had anything to do with this business. It's been a point of contention in our marriage for a while now. I don't know anything about it. Sasha might—"

Sasha makes a small noise from where she's curled away from us. "I don't want to talk about it," she mumbles. "Anyway, I don't know anything about the business side of it. I was a product—no one really discusses sales tactics with the merchandise."

Her voice is bitter when she says the last bit, and I can't blame her. She's here because of Viktor—maybe her life in Russia on her own would have been brutal and unforgiving, as he's often insisted, him taking her to sell set the wheels in motion that had led her here, in the state she's in now.

I feel a cold twist of guilt in my stomach, even though I know it's not my fault, any more than what Franco did to Ana was my fault. But she's hurt, nonetheless, by someone close to me. Someone that I love, more than I ever came close to loving Franco, and the dissonance that causes inside of me is miserable.

"It's not your fault, Mrs. Andreyva," Sasha says quietly as if she can read my thoughts. "Viktor was the man he is long before you married him. And as you can see, he's far from the worst."

"But you still wound up here." The words slip out before I can stop them. "I'm sorry."

"I did." She shrugs, her tone defeated. "Maybe this is just my fate."

"I don't believe in any of that."

"Good for you." It's the most combative she's ever been with me, and I can see her careful politeness starting to slip away. "You were born in better circumstances, Mrs. Andreyva, with more control over your fate. And yet, you still were married off without your consent. You're in this van too." Sasha turns her head, glancing back at me. "So, what does that make you think?"

"It's bad luck," I say firmly. "Bad luck and a complex world that we're born into, one made for men. But it's not over, Sasha. We've got time. And they'll—"

"Save us. You keep saying that." Sasha rubs a hand over her

mouth. "You, maybe. Mrs. Romano. Miss Ivanova. But me? Why would they save me?"

Because I'll have Viktor's head if he doesn't.

"Because Viktor knows he bears responsibility for you, too," I tell her firmly. "Just like anyone else in here. You're not going to be left behind."

"We'll see." Sasha's expression is one of someone who has seen a decent bit of the world and found very little in it to make her hopeful. Still, she pushes herself up, wiping at her cheeks. "I'll help with the little ones." She reaches for Yelena. "To give you a break."

I don't entirely want to give them up, but my arms are tired, and Sofia is trying to calm Ana down, who is on the verge of a panic attack. I'm sure she could use help, so I disentangle Yelena's now sleeping, small form from me, handing her to Sasha as I squeeze Anika's hand.

"Let Sasha watch over you, okay?" I ask. "I'll still be right here."

"It's not like you can go anywhere," Anika mutters sarcastically, wincing as the van hits a rough spot in the road and jolts all of us. "We're kind of stuck."

If anything, her attitude lifts my spirits. Anika's smart mouth returning means that she's healing, at least, and maybe not quite as traumatized as her younger sister, although her pale face and the flickering fear in her eyes tell me that it's mostly bravado.

Which makes me angry all over again because no nine-year-old should have to learn to shield her emotions like that. She should be home in Manhattan, playing or fighting with her younger sister, doing homework, complaining about school, refusing to listen to me. She shouldn't be crammed into a dirty van with guns a few inches away, listening to us worry about what happens next. She shouldn't have seen the woman who was like a grandmother to her murdered in cold blood.

None of this is okay.

And all I can do is hope that somehow, Alexei will pay for it.

Once Sasha has distracted Anika, I move closer to Ana,

taking her hand that Sofia isn't holding. "I'm going to do everything I can to keep you safe," I tell her gently. "All of us. Whatever Alexei wants as payback, I'll try to get him to focus it on me if I can. We just have to hang in there, okay?"

Ana nods wordlessly, her eyes glimmering with tears. "I want to go home," she whispers softly. "Luca said I'd be safe if I came to Russia with him and Sofia. That Viktor wanted me to come with them to keep me away from Alexei. But it didn't help at all in the end."

"I know." I look at her helplessly, at a loss for anything to say. "I'm so sorry, Ana, for everything. I've said it before, and I'll say it a million times again. I'm sorry for what's happened to you. I wish more than anything I could have stopped it."

"It's not your fault," Ana says dully. "Franco hurt you too. And now—Alexei certainly isn't your fault."

"He's after my husband. You being close to me is why—"

"And me," Sofia interjects. "You can't take it all on yourself, Cat. Luca made a bargain with Viktor, and I'm his wife. Ana is my best friend. All of this is just as much because of my husband's business dealings as yours." She looks at me sympathetically. "Cat, I wasn't born into this life, and even I know that now. You know it too. You grew up around all of this, even if you were sheltered from it. You're just so caught up in your guilt that you're ignoring that. We've all been pushed into decisions we didn't want to make." She rubs her free hand across her eyes, wiping away the remainder of the tears she'd been blinking back earlier. "The Bratva hurt me once, but I don't hold it against Viktor. I've learned there's a lot of things in this life that aren't the way we want them to be. We can't hold onto it all."

Sofia gives me a soft, sad smile. "You helped me so much, Cat, when I was struggling. And what I learned is that this world that I was dragged into, that you were born into, is very cruel. But there's love to be found anyway if we look for it. For me—it's Luca and my baby. The friendship I have with you. You have to find what that is for you."

"You, of course." I squeeze her hand. "And Ana, and my stepdaughters." *And Viktor,* I want to say, but I can't because I don't know how to reconcile that with myself yet. I'd resented being married to a Bratva man so deeply, felt as if I were being sold off to the enemy, to someone far beneath me. That Luca had handed me over to a brutish, savage man.

But that's not Viktor at all. And try as I might, I can't make myself wish to go back before all of this. If I could undo what's happening now, I would. But the things I've experienced with Viktor, the things he's made me feel?

I can't regret it, even if I know I should.

CATERINA

When the van finally comes to a stop, it's several minutes before we have any idea where we are. We haven't stopped once since leaving Viktor's safe house, and all of us are in desperate need of water and a chance to use some kind of bathroom and starving on top of it. I don't know how much time has passed. It feels like hours, but it was hard to tell in the darkness of the van. Both Anika and Yelena have soiled themselves, much to the disgust of the guards, who made a point of mocking them to tears over it. Sasha and I both tried to comfort them, but all of our nerves are at the breaking point, and I'm seething with anger like I've never felt before.

I've never wanted to *hurt* someone as violently as I want to hurt Alexei. Not even for myself, but for my friends, and most of all for my stepdaughters. The fact that I've promised to willingly do anything he asks makes me sick to my stomach, but I know I can't go back on it. I have no doubt that he'll make me rue the day I broke that particular bargain, even if he can't outright kill our men any longer.

He'd find some way to make up for it, I'm sure of that. Which means that I have to stick to my word and hope that I can be a barrier between him and the others. I have to hope that I'm strong enough.

After what happened to me when I was abducted in Moscow, I'm not so sure. Every moment since Alexei and his men stormed the safe house has made me feel as if I'm reliving it all again, the trauma that I haven't even really had time to process rearing its ugly head and making me want to dissolve into a panic.

I've held it together, somehow. And I have to keep doing so, just for a little while longer. Alexei is more sophisticated than the men who tortured me in that cabin, even if he's also clearly a sadist. He has a use for me, so he won't hurt me the way they did. I just have to be strong.

I can do it. All my life, I was raised to be a mafia wife, to stand at my husband's side and turn a blind eye, to raise children and kiss him when he came home and warm his bed and never, ever judge anything that he did. By the standards of a good woman that I was raised with, I've failed.

But no one ever told me about this darker side of it. No one ever told me I might face things like this, that I might have to face men like Andrei and Stepan and Alexei down and hold my ground. That I might have to save my husband instead of the other way around.

No one ever told me that it might not be all babies and dinner parties and ignoring the lipstick on my husband's collar and pretending that I don't know about the blood on his hands.

No one said there might be blood on my hands, too.

And now, I want it. I want Alexei's blood. I want to pay him back for everything he's done. It's more visceral even than what I felt when I held that gun to Stepan's head. I wonder if instead of being the good mafia wife that I was raised to be, I'm becoming one of them instead.

Strong. Fierce. Ruthless when it comes to the ones I love.

I'd rather be that than a woman like my mother, no matter how much I loved her. She never stood up to my father even once, never talked back to him, never suggested that anything he did might be wrong, even when I knew she thought it.

I refuse to be spineless or cowed in the face of anything that Alexei might throw at me.

When the van doors open, I make sure I'm at the front. Sasha is just behind me with Anika and Yelena, and Sofia sticks close to Ana, so that when I hear Alexei shout orders for the men to hustle us out, we leave the van roughly in that arrangement.

It's dark out. I can barely see anything, other than the vague outlines of where we are, illuminated by the moon overhead. We're still in the mountains—further in, quite possibly, from what I can see—and there are no lights on in or around the house in front of us. I can see the shapes of high walls and a gate further down the drive and gravel crunches under my bare feet as the guards jostle us forwards, my skin prickling from the cold.

It's much colder here, the kind that crawls along your skin and sinks into your bones. None of us are dressed for it, and we're all shivering as we're marched towards the front door of the house. As we get closer, I can see that it's large and made of dark stone, rising up three or four stories and sprawling out over the cleared land in the middle of the forest around us. It's not as large as Viktor's fortress that we just left, but it's still sizeable, and I glance towards Alexei, narrowing my eyes.

"This isn't yours." I nod towards the house. "You were my husband's brigadier. You couldn't have something like this."

"That's none of your business, bitch," one of the guards snarls, jabbing me hard in the ribs with the butt of his gun.

"Now, now." Alexei smiles, his teeth white even in the darkness. "There's no reason to be rude to Mrs. Andreyva, even if she's making assumptions. But of course, you're right. It's not mine." His smile broadens, not quite meeting his eyes, but wide nonetheless, almost mocking. "It used to be your husband's. He gave it to one of his business associates as a gift for their long history of working together. It doesn't seem that history prevented them from working with me. However, when I offered them something that Viktor wouldn't. And now I have use of this house while I work on completing my takeover of everything that should have been mine all along."

Something curdles in my stomach at the expression on his face. "What did you offer him?" I'm not sure I want to know, but I can't stop myself from asking.

Alexei shrugs. "It's not appropriate for your ears or some of the more delicate ones here. Let's just say he wanted a rare pleasure that your husband's moral code, such as it is, wouldn't permit him to provide."

A shudder ripples through me, and I press my lips tightly together. I don't want to know. Viktor has done things that I think are truly despicable, but I'm glad to hear he has limits. I just don't want to know what could be so horrible that Viktor would refuse to sell it or what kind of depravity exists in the world that I'm not yet aware of.

I've become aware of far too much in the past weeks. I'm not sure how much more I can take, if I'm being honest.

"The girls are cold," I tell him, glancing at Anika and Yelena, shivering hard enough to make their teeth chatter as they cling to Sasha. "They need to be inside, warmed up, and given a bath. No one stopped to let us use the restroom."

Alexei smirks. "My apologies. I'm unused to children and their needs, as they differ from adults." He pushes the heavy wooden front door, swinging it open with a groaning creak, and gestures. "Go on in, and we'll discuss what happens next."

The last thing I want to do is walk inside that house. To bring my stepdaughters, Viktor's children, into that house. But I know I don't have a choice. And I need to be brave for everyone else.

So I tear my gaze away from Alexei's face and stride forward into the dark house, my heart pounding in my throat as my bare feet strike the cold wooden floor.

"There's no staff here yet," Alexei says in his cool, accented voice as the rest of the group files inside. "It will be somewhat different from what you're used to, *tsarina*. You'll have to take care of yourselves here, for now at least." He hits a light switch, and the room is suddenly full of yellow light, illuminating a large foyer with slightly dusty hardwood, opening out into an open-plan living room with covered furniture arranged in front of a massive stone fireplace.

"Don't bother lighting a fire," Alexei tells the men standing behind him. "We won't be down here long. Besides, I enjoy watching them squirm." He motions for two men to come forward and points at Sasha, who is still holding onto Anika and Yelena. "Take the children upstairs. They don't need to be here for this."

My blood runs cold at that, my stomach twisting. I don't know what Alexei has in mind, but if he's actually having the girls removed, it can't be good. My mind runs to all sorts of horrible places, but I force myself to do what I told Ana to and not think too far ahead.

"They stink," one of the men complains, and Alexei narrows his eyes at him.

"Just get them upstairs," he snaps. "You don't have to clean them up. Just lock them in one of the bedrooms until I'm finished with the women. Then they can deal with the brats."

"Yes, sir." The two men stride forwards, and Sasha shrinks back instantly, her hands tightening on Anika and Yelena's shoulders. Yelena is already beginning to cry again, and I can see the irritation plainly on the guards' faces.

"Can't they stay here?" Sasha asks, her eyes wide and frightened, and Alexei's eyes narrow.

"Unless you want them to see things that children shouldn't, no," he growls. *As if they haven't already, today.* "Get them upstairs, now!" he barks at his men. "If she fights back, give her a good slap. Nothing hard enough to bruise, just enough to sting."

"Alexei—" I step forward, and he wheels, pinning me with that icy glare. I was already freezing, but even so, it feels as if the temperature in the room drops by a couple of degrees. "Let me go with them. They need to be bathed, and a change of clothes—"

"Fuck." Alexei grimaces. "I swear to Christ, this is why I don't bother with children. Look in the upstairs rooms," he directs one of the men, the one currently reaching for Anika, who looks as if she might try to bite his fingers off. "See if there are any clean clothes for the brats. As for you—" he turns back to me, his mouth twitching in an evil smile. "You're not going anywhere. In fact, since you decided to speak out of turn, *tsarina*, you can go first."

Go first? My heart skips a beat in my chest, anxiety twisting in my gut. I have no idea what he's talking about, but it can't be good. The sound of him saying *tsarina* makes my skin crawl, reminding me of Viktor growling *printsessa* at me, but so much worse. This isn't even sarcastic; it's mocking, a reminder of my position and just how low Alexei plans to bring me.

"What are you talking about?" I manage, my mouth feeling as if it's gone dry and stuffed with cotton. My hands are starting to shake from cold and nerves, but I do my best to stay still and unmoving, looking at him squarely as if I don't fear him at all.

"Undress." Alexei waves a hand at me. "Each of you, in turn, strip. So that I can see what I'm working with."

Oh god. I hear Sasha make a small noise, see Ana shrink back as if she can hide behind Sofia. The men behind Alexei shift with anticipation, some of them starting to grin with almost predatory expressions. *In front of everyone.* I feel like I'm going to be sick.

Stripping naked in front of strangers would always have been something that made me feel sick to my stomach with anxiety. But now, when I've been so badly scarred, the thought is even worse. And I know it will affect Alexei's plans for me.

"At least send your men out." I swallow hard, forcing myself to keep speaking even though I know I'm probably only making him angrier. "They don't need to appraise us, do they?"

Alexei frowns. "There you go again, telling me what to do, *tsarina*. What do I need to do to teach you just how bad of an idea that is?"

"Not telling you," I say hurriedly, shaking my head. "Suggesting. We're valuable assets, aren't we? Do you think your buyers would like to know that mercenaries and low-level soldiers got to see the same flesh that they're paying a premium for?"

I feel sick just saying it. But it makes Alexei pause. "Clear the room," he says finally. "This isn't a public show."

"Boss, should we leave you unguarded—"

"Stay just outside the door," Alexei snaps. "And don't think I don't know what you're trying to do, sticking around to get a glimpse of these women. Keep the door shut, and I'll call if I need you."

The men nod, filing out, and I can see the looks of disappointment on their faces. I feel a small flare of triumph. I might be losing the overall war, but I've won this battle at least. I know how to reason with Alexei, how he thinks. I can't help but think it will come in handy again.

The triumph is short-lived, however. I might have avoided having to strip in front of his entire security team and band of mercenaries. However, I'm still going to have to do it in front of Alexei. And there's no getting out of it.

"Don't make me wait." Alexei's voice drops an octave, full of a warning that I know better than to ignore.

I swallow hard, reaching for the hem of my t-shirt. I hadn't been wearing anything special today—a t-shirt and jeans, barefoot in the house. I definitely hadn't been prepared for this. I'm freezing, and the idea of taking *off* more clothing sounds awful.

"Hurry the fuck up," Alexei growls. "We don't have all night."

I take a deep breath and strip off my shirt.

"All of it," Alexei snaps. "Quickly. Let's go, *tsarina*. Every bit."

Just get it over with, I tell myself. I undo my jeans, pushing them over my hips and ignoring the gooseflesh that springs up over every inch of me as the cold attacks my skin. I reach for the clasp of my bra, quickly undoing it and letting it fall to the floor.

My panties are last. I don't look at Sofia, Sasha, or Ana, feeling my cheeks flush at being naked, not just in front of Alexei but in front of them. I can feel them looking at me, wondering what Alexei will do to them, worrying anxiously about when it will be their turn.

I shove the black bikini panties over my hips and down my thighs, stepping out of them. I haven't shaved since Viktor did it for me, and I see Alexei's displeased look when his gaze flicks between my thighs.

"That bush will have to go." His eyes rake over me, and I can see the disappointment that I'd expected written across his face. "Fuck, you're cut to shreds. Or healing from it, at least." He steps forward, forcing the other women to move out of his way as he circles me. "That's a fucking shame. You're perfect in every other way. A bit thin, but that can be helped. Perfect breasts, good hips, long legs. Gorgeous face, thick, healthy hair." He tips my chin up, talking about me as if I'm livestock, and it's all I can do not to bite his fingers. "Good teeth. Lovely dark eyes." His gaze rakes down the front of me again, taking in the scars on my breasts and belly and thighs, the still-healing wounds that are scabbed and nearly turned to scars themselves.

Alexei steps back, frowning. "I might get a decent price for you still. You're young. Not a virgin and marked up, but there are men who won't care. Some will even get off on it, although I doubt you'd enjoy being sold to one of them." He chuckles. "Not that I care what you enjoy, either way. I might take some pleasure in selling Viktor Andreyev's wife to a dungeon or maybe a hunting grounds." He glances over me again, tapping his fingers against his thigh. "In the meantime, I'll enjoy you. Like I said earlier, it won't matter who fucks you before I sell you, so keep that in mind. Anger me, and I just may let a few of my men take their turn, so long as they don't leave marks."

This time, I can't hide the shudder that ripples through me. The last thing I want is to go anywhere near Alexei, but if the alternative is being tossed to one of the brutes who just looked at me as if I were meat ready to be served up, I will take Alexei. At least for him, I have some idea of how to manipulate.

"You." Alexei jerks his head towards Sofia. "You next. Ah, ah," he adds, glancing at me as I reach for my clothes. "Stay just like that until I tell you otherwise."

It's clear that he's enjoying this, and it makes me hate him all the more. I don't bother trying to cover myself; I know he'll just put a stop to that as well, and I risk making him angry. I'm flushed with embarrassment despite the cold, my nipples stiffening in the frigid air, and I can't look at Sofia as she starts to strip down next to me.

"Much better," Alexei says with satisfaction. "No marks on

this one. Except—" He taps her belly, only faintly starting to round, shaking his head. "I can charge a premium for a pregnant woman, but once the child is born and weaned, the novelty is gone. Usually, the child is discarded, and her owner gets her pregnant again." He smirks. "How many orphans in Russia are from just such a thing?"

Sasha makes a small sound of desperation, and I glance at her. She's as pale as Sofia, her hands shaking, and she's kneeling on the floor next to Ana, who is unable to stand. She's squeezing Ana's hand, and I've never felt more helpless in my life than I do at this moment.

"Please," Sofia whispers, her words coming out numbly. "Please, just don't hurt my baby—"

"Do you know the sex?" Alexei asks abruptly, and Sofia stares at him, shocked.

"No," she manages finally. "I'm not far enough along."

I can see the effort it takes for her to say that, the fear in her eyes. She's terrified that Alexei will do something to hurt the baby, and rightfully so. It's not a difficult leap to imagine him doing exactly that.

"Good," Alexei says, to both of our surprise. "I might have a buyer, in that case." He lifts a lock of Sofia's hair, letting it trail through his fingers before it falls back onto her bare shoulder. "Very beautiful. A shame that perfect body is going to be ruined by a child."

Sofia stiffens at that, her lips pressing together, but she doesn't say anything. When he fails to get a reaction from her, Alexei turns away, glancing towards Sasha and Ana.

"The fuck is wrong with the blonde one?" he asks, reaching down to push Ana's hair out of her face. "Russian?"

Ana doesn't say a word, only flinches away from him.

His hand moves too fast to see, grabbing her chin and tilting her head up. "Answer me, bitch," he growls. "What's your name?"

"Anastasia Ivanova," Ana manages, her eyes wide and terrified, the words coming out stilted through Alexei's grip on her chin. "Please, you're hurting me."

"Then get the fuck up."

"I can't, my feet—"

"The fuck is wrong with you?" Alexei shakes his head, hauling her up by his grip on her chin. Ana cries out in pain, her toes curling as he tries to set her on her feet, and she immediately crumples again.

"Her feet were injured," I cut in, feeling my stomach twist again at the look on Ana's face. "She can't walk very well or stand for long periods."

"Christ, this one is worthless." Alexei's mouth turns down, a look of disgust crossing his face. "Pretty enough, but fucking worthless if she can't even stand up. And she cowers away like a whipped dog. I ought to have my men come back in here and put her out of her misery."

"No!" Sofia cries out before she can stop herself, her hand going to her mouth. "No, please don't hurt her. Please—"

"Oh, shut up." Alexei spins on his heel, his hand cracking across Sofia's cheek. "I'm not going to kill her. I'll find some use for her. In the meantime—" he looks pointedly at Sasha. "Get up, girl, and prove to me that this hasn't been a complete waste of my time."

Sasha looks as if she's about to burst into tears, but she pushes herself up to her feet slowly.

"Good, very nice…" he says creepily, as tears roll down Sasha's face. In an instant she shrieks, and I turn away seeing his hand come from between Sasha's thighs.

"Fuck! If only you were a virgin." He scoffs, angrily.

"So. What do I have outside of used goods? One scarred, one pregnant, and one crippled. Fuck if I shouldn't have just killed the lot of you. But at least I ought to be able to get something for each of you, except for the crippled one." Alexei shakes his head. "Get out of my sight."

All of us scramble at once, reaching for our clothes, only for him to kick them out of the way.

"I said, get out of my sight." His upper lip curls. "Find something else to wear upstairs."

Sofia and Sasha go to Ana at the same time, helping her up

as I walk behind them, agonizingly aware of my nudity. I feel embarrassed and exposed, helpless and vulnerable, and I know that's the point. Alexei is enjoying this, sending us naked and scrambling for the stairs, hurrying to obey before he changes his mind and comes up with something worse.

None of us want to walk in on the children like this, so we find the first guest bedroom upstairs that's still dark, pushing open the door and making a beeline for the closet and dresser. There's no telling what we'll find or if any of it will fit, but it's clear that at least one woman stayed here in the past. I manage to find a cotton long-sleeved shirt and a pair of jeans that fit loosely, and Sofia finds a black sweater dress from somewhere in the depths of the closet. She quickly hands Sasha another, and the three of us get dressed as soon as we can, painfully aware of the lack of underwear or anything beyond these borrowed, ill-fitting clothes.

"Let's go find the girls," Sofia says, and I nod.

"They will have left them in one of these rooms." I glance over at Sasha. "Sasha, find a bed for Ana, and then find the bathroom on this floor, if there is one. Heat up the water so we can get the girls clean."

Sasha nods, looking almost relieved to have been given something to do. She wraps an arm around Ana's waist as Sofia goes to the other side, helping her hobble down the hall until we see a room with light coming from under the door. When we open it, there's a large bedroom on the other side with two beds, one on either wall, the same sort of dresser, and a chair and desk by the window. Anika is huddled beside one bed, picking at her lips as Yelena lies next to her on the rug, curled into the smallest possible ball.

"I'll go figure out the hot water," Sasha says quickly. "Girls, we're going to get you baths, okay? You'll be nice and warm when we're done."

I'd give anything for a hot bath. Hell, even a five-minute hot shower would be acceptable at this point. But the last thing I want is to take off my clothes in this house again, even for a moment.

Anika narrows her eyes at me as Sasha leaves, and Sofia sinks down onto one of the beds. "Is the mean man letting us take a bath?"

"He is," I tell her tiredly. "Both of you. And then we're going to stay in this room, and neither you nor Yelena are going to leave for anything, do you understand me?"

Anika nods, but I don't break eye contact with her. "I'm serious, Anika. You know how you came out of your room even though your father told you to stay because you were curious? And that's how you got hurt?"

The little girl purses her lips as if she wants to argue, but she finally nods. "Yes," she mumbles. "I remember." She presses her small hand to her stomach, where I know there are still bandages ensuring the wound heals. It needs to be cleaned as badly as the rest of Anika does.

"You have to obey this time, okay?" I let out a breath, wondering how much to say. "Anika, the man who took us, is bad. He's a very bad, very dangerous man. He's responsible for you getting hurt in the first place, okay? Do you understand?"

Anika nods wordlessly, her eyes starting to blink rapidly as if she wants to cry, but refuses to.

"I need you to stay in here, unless I'm with you, so that I can protect you. Okay?"

"Okay." Her voice is smaller than I've ever heard it, as small and fragile as Yelena's, and I hate it. I hate that Alexei has managed to take even Anika's spark to frighten her to the point of being timid.

I'm going to make sure he pays for this if it's the last thing I do. I think as I gather Yelena up in my arms; Sofia gets up to help me with Anika.

And if I'm being honest with myself, it very well might be.

CATERINA

We manage to get the girls bathed without too much hassle. To my surprise, there's plenty of hot water and towels in the bathroom cupboard, and Sofia even discovers a children's room further down the hall with clothes that look like they'll fit Yelena. All she can find for Anika is an oversized t-shirt that looks like it was worn by a very petite woman at some point. I can't help but notice the array of sizes in the women's clothing. Alexei had said the man who owned the place was a client, so I can only imagine why there's a variety of women who have stayed here.

A client was given this place by Viktor. The reminder is sharp and painful. It's easy to forget, especially when faced with a horror like Alexei, that my husband isn't without fault. He isn't the sadistic sociopath that Alexei is, but neither is he blameless. He's sold women to the man who owns this house, the house that his family and associates' family are being held prisoner in.

It will be a long time before I forget the burning humiliation of Alexei forcing me to strip in front of him and my friends. I'd thought that Viktor had made me feel humiliated in the past, in the bedroom, but now I know the difference. Nothing about what Alexei had made me do had felt arousing in the slightest. It just made me feel sick.

With Viktor, it's different. His dominance, orders, and demands all make me feel things that I've never felt before, that I'd never imagined I could feel. I realize now, still shuddering from Alexei's ordeal, that while Viktor's humiliations of me might be very real, they come from an entirely different place.

Viktor doesn't want to *hurt* me. He wants to possess me. Own me. Dominate me. But he doesn't truly want to harm me, and he doesn't take pleasure in my real, true pain, only the pleasurable pain that he sometimes inflicts on me.

When I step out of the bathroom with Anika in tow, Yelena in Sasha's arms, Alexei is waiting for us. I feel my stomach drop the moment I see his hard expression and icy blue eyes. Still, I force myself to keep an even expression, meeting his gaze as if I'm a guest in his home and not a prisoner waiting to be sold to a new master.

"You'll stay in that room where my men left the girls," Alexei says coldly. "All of you. Divide up the beds how you like. Your door will be guarded, and there will be men all down this hall and at every door throughout the house, so don't bother thinking of escape. You won't make it, and I'll ensure that you regret it." He pauses, his gaze raking over us. "If you remain on your best behavior, you'll continue to sleep freely in that room without being restrained."

I feel my mouth go dry at that thought. Viktor tying me to the bedpost is one thing, the idea of anyone tying me up with the intent to keep me prisoner after what happened in that cabin is enough to make a sick panic flood through me.

Keep it together. I force my hands not to shake, gripping Anika's in mine. "Thank you," I manage, the words burning like acid on my tongue. The last thing in the world that I want is to thank Alexei for *anything*, but I know it will help us.

Whatever will help us, I have to do.

He eyes me as if it's some kind of trick. "I'll have buyers lined up soon," he continues casually, as if we were discussing the price of meat at the butcher shop. "Until then, behave like good girls, and things will go easier on you," Alexei smirks. "Viktor's clientele has jumped ship all too easily. But then again, Viktor never was good at changing with the markets. It's a new day, and I'm ready to greet it."

"Viktor had a moral compass," I grind out through my teeth, my anger rising up again, sharp and hot. I can feel Anika shrinking back behind me, and the thought of Alexei finding a *buyer* for her, separating her from us, makes me see red. "One in need of a good cleaning and polish, that's for sure, but a moral compass nonetheless. You—"

"I am a man who can see where the future will take us—myself and the Bratva who stand with me." Alexei shrugs. "I wouldn't expect you to understand. You are nothing but a woman. After all, a Bratva wife meant to suck, fuck, and bear children. But I do feel sorry for you, in a way."

I blink at him, startled. "Sorry? For me?"

"Certainly." Alexei's mouth twitches. "You thought you married a powerful man, but you married a bear with no claws. And now you're here, at my mercy. Such a tragedy for a pretty *tsarina* like you. He even let the men I hired kidnap you from Moscow and rough you up. Let them take you and scar you so that you're worth almost nothing. An old, tired bear indeed."

"My worth has nothing to do with my body," I snap at him. I know I should keep quiet, but I can't. I'm exhausted, cold, frightened, and trying desperately to keep up hope that's slipping away quickly. "And my husband is a man who is respected among other men. Just because you don't respect or fear him as you should mean nothing. And you'll regret your words when you find his claws in your back."

I half expect Alexei to hit me, but he starts to laugh instead. "I see you've developed feelings for your Bratva husband," he says with a smirk, still chuckling. "How embarrassing for you. I wonder what your father would think to know his daughter is taking Bratva cock nightly. You were meant for better than one of us, I know that. And yet Luca Romano sold you for a promise of peace that is worthless now. Viktor couldn't even keep the promise that bought him your body in his bed." His eyes rake down the front of me lasciviously, and I repress a shudder.

"What a sight you must have been in your wedding bed before you were scarred." Alexei licks his lips, and to my horror, I see him reach down to adjust himself. "A mafia princess, a Rossi girl, sold to the Bratva because the Rossi heir was so desperate for peace. I wonder if Viktor knew what a prize he had."

Of course, he did, I want to say. *That's why he demanded Luca give me to him. Why he threatened war and bloodshed if Luca didn't concede, or I didn't agree.* But I don't. I've said too much already.

"And now I can see from your face that you've fallen for him." Alexei laughs again, shaking his head. "What a problem that must be for you! I know how much you detest his business. I was there that day in his office, remember? When you knocked over those files and found out what your husband does to give you that mansion to live in and the fine food on your plate and the unlimited credit cards in your wallet? But you've fallen in love with him anyway. Which makes this all the sweeter, if I'm being honest."

"What?" I croak the word, my senses pinging with alarm, picking up where Alexei is headed before he even says it.

"You've only had one Bratva cock since Luca bartered you away," Alexei says with a smirk. "I think it's high time you had something to compare it to."

My stomach drops. I'd known this was coming, of course. With how I'd bargained for Viktor and the others' lives, there was no way that Alexei wouldn't capitalize on it in this way. But I hadn't expected it to happen so soon.

"I need a shower—"

"You can bathe later." Alexei reaches out, stepping forward so he can tip my chin up with one finger. "I like it, I think. The princess in borrowed rags, dirty and on her knees. Give the girl to her," he orders, jerking his head at Sasha. "And come with me."

I don't have a choice. I'd promised him my willing compliance, and if I go back on it now, I know he'll make someone other than me pay. One of the girls, maybe, or Sasha. Maybe Sofia or her baby. There's no way to know, and anyway, I can't let someone else be hurt because of me.

Not again.

I have to do what I'd said I would.

"The entrance to this floor will be locked," Alexei says, looking at Sasha and Sofia. "Guards posted all along it and at every exit, as I said. So I advise you to go back to your room and get comfortable. You'll be there for the foreseeable future, unless I say otherwise. And trying to escape will, as I also said, come with penalties. Punishments, you might say."

Sasha and Sofia say nothing, pale and white-lipped, clinging to Anika and Yelena. Alexei's hand is on my elbow, gripping it tightly as he leads me down the hall, out of the door that leads to our rooms, and towards the main hall by the staircase, which spirals up to another floor.

"This way," he says firmly, and I have no choice but to follow him.

Alexei has, of course, chosen the most elaborate suite of rooms for himself. It's still nothing like the rooms I shared with Viktor back at his fortress of a safe house. The bed in the center of the room is bigger than any others I've seen. This bedroom has a fireplace and a door to another room filled with covered furniture and an attached bathroom.

I don't have long to take in my surroundings, though. Alexei locks the door behind us and strides towards the fireplace, which has been lit by someone. It casts odd, frightening shadows around the room as Alexei beckons to me with one finger, and I walk towards him, knowing that I have to do as he asks.

Whatever he asks.

That was the bargain I struck for Vincent's life. For Luca's, Liam's, Levin's, and Max's. And now the time has come to pay the piper.

Alexei grins as if he can read my thoughts. He's already erect, I can tell, pushing against his fly with an urgency that makes me feel nauseous.

"On your knees, *tsarina*," he says, one hand going to his belt. The other goes to my hair as I sink down obediently, my heart hammering in my chest as I do all I can not be sick. When I see him, eager and ready as he slides his zipper down, it takes more than a little effort.

He's not as large as Viktor, not even close. I could almost laugh if the situation weren't so awful. *He wants so badly to be Viktor, and yet his cock can't even measure up.*

The thought makes me feel a little better. It's a ridiculous thought, but I cling to it because I have nothing else. Nothing except gallows humor and the knowledge that by being on my knees right now, I'm protecting everyone who came here with me.

My responsibility. My duty.

"Suck, *tsarina*," Alexei orders, his voice thick with lust. "And swallow it all when it's time. Every drop. Don't worry, we won't be finished then. We have all night."

That's what I was afraid of. But I don't say it aloud.

I simply bend my head and obey.

VIKTOR

Alexei's men didn't beat us hard enough to leave serious injuries, but we're out cold for a decent amount of time. When I come to, it's starting to get dark outside, and my stomach drops as I realize that Alexei has had enough time to put a good bit of distance between him and us. I have no idea where he's headed, no clue where he might be taking them.

I hear a groan from the far end of the sofa and see Max sitting up slowly, his hand pressed to his nose. "I think they broke my fucking nose," he growls.

Liam is sitting up too, and he laughs, looking sideways at Max as he touches his mouth gingerly. "Watch your language, priest. You'll end up in the confessional. Or do you just confess to yourself? How does that work, exactly?"

Max glares at him irritably. "If you ever found yourself on the right side of the door for Mass, you'd know."

"How do you know I don't?" Liam gives him a cheeky grin, then winces. "Ah, shite. Bastard split my lip open."

"Call it a hunch." Max grimaces, reaching up to grasp his nose and move it back into place. "Fuck!" he yells, and I can hear the crunching sound as he does it.

Liam makes a face. "Do that somewhere else next time, aye? Enough to make a man lose his breakfast."

"Luca is still out cold." Max ignores Liam's ribbing, moving around the other man to crawl alongside Luca, reaching for his shoulder. "Luca. Wake up, man."

"He got the worst of it, I think," Liam says. "Him and Viktor." He glances up at me, his face creased with concern. "You alright, lad?"

"I'm fifteen years your senior if I'm a day," I tell him darkly, getting to my feet and crossing to where Luca is still lying on the floor. "So "sir" would be more appropriate than "lad," I think."

"Viktor it is."

"You're in a remarkably good mood, considering the beating you just took, and the fact that the woman you've been flirting with for the better part of three weeks is in Alexei's custody, along with our wives and my children." I look at him darkly. "Or maybe you missed that?"

"I didn't." Liam frowns. "I saw it all, Viktor. I apologize." He shrugs, watching as Luca starts to come to, Max helping him to sit up halfway. "The best way to keep a bad situation from getting to you is humor, I've found."

"Not my experience." I glance at Luca. "How is he?"

"I'll live," Luca speaks before Max can, with some difficulty, although it doesn't look as if there's any permanent damage done. "I think they might have cracked a rib or two. It feels like a knife in my side every time I breathe. But I'm not dead."

"Well, that's something." I frown, looking at the three of them. "Alexei has already put too much distance between him and us. It's going to be difficult to find out where he's taken them. It sounds strange to say it, but the one thing that we have in our favor is that we don't have to be concerned about him hurting them. He'll want to get a good price, which means keeping them in good condition. That will buy us a little time."

Luca narrows his eyes. "That doesn't protect *my* child. And there are other ways to inflict hurt that don't leave marks. You know that very well, Viktor."

"I do." I let out a breath. "But we have to think about our options. Alexei has the upper hand now, no matter how much we might hate it. We're playing his game, and we need to do it carefully. He's calculating—more so than I ever realized," I admit.

"You didn't see signs of this?" Liam narrows his eyes. "Not a single hint that one of your closest men was on the verge of betraying you?"

"No." I glare at him. "If I had, I would have taken steps to prevent it."

"Given what happened to Sasha, I think it's safe to say there was dissent in your ranks well before Alexei decided to—"

Something snaps inside of me. I'd held back my rage the entire time that Alexei was here, knowing that losing control of my emotions meant harm or death to my family and those depending on me. But now that the immediate danger has passed, I'm on the knife's edge of losing it. And being on the other end of questioning from a cocky Irishman fifteen years my junior is the last straw.

I swing at him, intent on landing a blow square on his jaw. I've punched a man or three in my lifetime, though I don't usually rely on my fists. But Liam dodges the blow neatly, smirking as he sidesteps me.

"Got to be faster, old man," he says with a grin. "Or maybe you are losing your edge."

"That's not an improvement on *lad*," I growl and swing again.

I miss. It's not all that strange, considering I was out cold a few minutes ago. And Liam moves like a boxer, lithely going up on his toes and getting out of range like it's second nature to him.

"Viktor!" Luca's voice, thick with pain but still commanding, rings out through the room. "Enough!"

I grit my teeth, swinging to face him. "You're going to give me orders in my own home, Romano?"

"I'm going to tell you to pull it together." Luca pushes

himself upright, his face going slightly grey with pain as he gets to his feet, but he manages it anyway. "Every minute that we stand here fighting instead of tracking Alexei down is another one that he's using to put more distance between him and us, another chance for him to make sure we don't find him until it's too late." He glares at Liam. "That goes for you too, son. Keep that smart mouth of yours to yourself."

Liam's green eyes glitter at that, and I catch a glimpse of the man under the careless, cocky exterior, someone who doesn't appreciate being told what to do any more than Luca or I would. He has a backbone and balls of steel; I know that much from how he stood up to Alexei. But I'm not about to be questioned by a boy still wet behind the ears, leader of the Kings or not.

"We can get some men together," Levin says from where he's sitting on the edge of the couch, his dark hair matted with dried blood at one temple. "We'll call into Moscow, get reinforcements. Hell, we'll take a page out of Alexei's book if we need to. I still have some contacts through the syndicate, I might be able to find some mercenaries who would be willing to back us up for a decent payday—"

"I'll leave you in charge of that," I tell him firmly. "Liam, you have connections with hackers in DC, right?"

Liam smirks. "A hacker," he says casually. "She's come in handy a time or two."

"She?" Levin glances up, and Liam grins.

"Yeah, *she*. Women know how to use computers, Petrov. She's not hard on the eyes, either."

"Focus," Luca snaps. "Liam, you should see if this hacker friend of yours can dig into any transactions Alexei might make in the next few days, see if we can pinpoint a location. We'll have you and Max stay here while Viktor, Levin, and I take some men and go as soon as we have—"

"Absolutely fucking not." Liam narrows his eyes. "You think I'm staying here behind these walls while Ana is out there suffering, being kept captive by that monster? Fuck no. I'll be coming along as well."

Luca frowns, and his face suddenly goes very serious, almost fatherly. "You've got feelings for her, son?"

Max rolls his eyes. "I think anyone with decent vision could tell that."

I let out a heavy sigh. "I think it's been quite clear that Liam here has an attraction to Miss Ivanova. But this is hardly the time—"

"No, I think it is before this goes any further." Luca doesn't look pleased. "How much do you know about her, Liam?"

Liam has gone very still, his expression suddenly guarded. "Enough," he says curtly, the cocky boyishness gone in an instant. "As Viktor said, I think this is hardly the time—"

"Ana has been through a lot." Luca crosses his arms, his eyes narrowing. "She's my wife's best friend, and I've come to care for her as well, like a sister. Since—"

"What happened?" Liam interrupts, his brow creasing. "Did someone hurt her?"

"That's not my place to discuss," Luca says firmly. "But she has been badly abused. It's taken a toll on her, physically but also mentally. Whatever your feelings for her are, she's not in a place to return them or even to consent to them. She's barely able to take care of herself." Luca lets out a breath, frowning. "Anyway, I'd heard there was talk of you marrying the O'Sullivan girl."

"For an Italian mob boss, you sure do know a lot about the inner workings of the Kings," Liam growls. "I can't see how it's any of your business."

"Ana's wellbeing affects my wife, and therefore the peace and stability of my household. And beyond that, there is an alliance between our families. If the Kings are destabilized, it also affects me and mine." Luca shakes his head. "Come with us if you must, but put Ana out of your head. Marry the O'Sullivan girl. It will strengthen your position and set you up well, increasing your favor with the other Kings. Ana can do nothing for you when it comes to your position in the families."

Liam's jaw tightens, but he says nothing more about Ana. "I'm coming with you," he says instead, his voice ringing with finality.

"I'll talk to Beth and see what she can dig up. But when it's time to go, I won't be staying here."

"I'm not either." Max swallows hard, uncertainty in his face, but his jaw is set too, his shoulders squared. "Sasha has trusted me in the past. I want to be there to bring her home." He catches the look on my face and shrugs. "As a friend," he says, emphasizing the last word. "Someone in need of spiritual guidance."

Liam's mouth twitches, but he holds back whatever remark is on the tip of his tongue, to my relief and Luca's too, from the look on Luca's face.

"Come on," Levin says, standing up with a groan. "Let's patch ourselves up and piece ourselves back together. A few cuts and bruises won't stop us, eh?" He looks at me with the gruff resilience of a man who has seen much worse than even what happened here today.

He hangs back as Max, Liam, and Luca start to make their way out of the living room, stepping around bodies and shattered glass. "I'll call for a cleanup crew," Levin says grimly, looking around at the carnage. "It's a fucking shame. Good men, all of them."

"Alexei needs to pay for this." I follow Levin's gaze, taking in the gruesome scene. "He's slaughtered my men and taken my family from me. This cannot stand."

"It won't, *Ussuri*," Levin says firmly. "He'll pay ten times over. But first, we have to find him."

"It's not going to be easy."

"Liam has his ways, and I have mine." Levin smiles coldly, and I see a hint of the man he was before he came to work for my father, the mercenary who was once feared across four continents. "I'll contact the syndicate. What Alexei has done cannot stand. And he will pay for it, I promise you that."

That, I believe beyond a shadow of a doubt.

I just hope we can accomplish it in time to save the woman I love.

CATERINA

To my relief, Alexei doesn't demand that I stay the night in his bed. When he's finished with me, he leans down and scoops my clothes from the floor, tossing them at me as he disposes of the used condom in the trash, barely looking at me as I dress and retreat for the door.

That, in and of itself, is another relief. Alexei seems to have no interest in taking a chance that he might get me pregnant, which I'd feared even more than him forcing me into his bed. I still have no idea if it's even possible for me, but I know that there's one thing I couldn't bear, and that's to carry a child that wasn't Viktor's. I can't imagine what Viktor would do in that scenario, what he would demand, how he would handle it—but I don't ever want to have to know.

It's an odd thing to feel relief in the bed of the man forcing you to sleep with him, but that's exactly what I'd felt when Alexei had pulled out the foil packet. I'd almost felt grateful to him.

Is this what Stockholm Syndrome feels like? The thought flits through my head grimly, gallows humor making the corners of my mouth twitch as I move as quickly as I can towards the door before he changes his mind and decides that the night is still young.

It's not—it's nearly two o'clock in the morning, and I feel broken in both body and mind. I'd done my best to shut my mind off as soon as Alexei had ordered me to my knees, telling myself to simply not exist for as long as it took. It wouldn't be *me* that he was taking, just my body. Just the shell that I inhabit. *It means nothing*, I'd told myself over and over as I looked up at the raftered ceiling, following the knots and whorls in the wood as Alexei thrust into me. I tried not to think about the reality of what was happening, that he was taking what belonged to Viktor, leaving a mark on me that neither of us can ever wash away. I'd thought Viktor was the last man who would ever be inside of me, but that wasn't the case any longer, and it wasn't my choice.

How many times has going to bed with a man not been my choice? More than I can count, if I'm being honest with myself, between the majority of my marriage to Franco and the beginning of my marriage to Viktor. The last night I spent with Viktor stands out in my head as the one true time when I chose, all on my own, to seduce and sleep with a man.

I couldn't let myself think about it then, though. Not with Alexei inside of me, doing his best to fuck every trace of Viktor away. He'd grunted things to the effect of that throughout the entire thing, reminding me with every second that passed the reality of the situation that I was trying to escape.

Take that Bratva cock. I know you like it. Once you get one, you get a craving for them, eh? Behave, little tsarina, *and I won't throw you to my men. You'd like that, wouldn't you,* tsarina? *Italian whore. You'd like to see how many Russian cocks you could take at once.*

I'd ignored him, my eyes glued to the ceiling, while he grunted out insults, spewing them faster as he got closer to his climax. He'd made a sound like an animal when he'd come, rolling onto his back instantly, his muscled abdomen gleaming with sweat as he'd pushed his white-blond hair out of his face with one hand and peeled off the condom with the other.

"I'll make you come next time, *tsarina*," he'd promised with a cruel smirk. "You'll see."

Not a chance in hell, I'd wanted to say, but I'd just given him a small, forced smile, feeling something crack inside of me as I'd done so. It seemed to have satisfied him because he'd turned away from me, tossing the condom into the trash and getting up with a groan, striding past me towards the bathroom. He'd finished with me.

Please hurry, I think silently to Viktor as I step outside into the hall, immediately greeted by a large guard who takes my elbow, hustling me towards the stairs and down to the floor where we're being kept. *I don't know how long I can bear this.*

I will, for as long as I have to. If it keeps Alexei mollified and pleasant, prevents him from using my friends or my stepdaughters as punching bags, I'll go willingly to his bed. But I can feel that I'm going to lose a small piece of myself every time.

I hope that there's something left by the time we're rescued.

The room is quiet when I slip back in. I can barely see, but as my eyes adjust, I manage to make out the makeshift sleeping arrangements that the others came up with while I was gone. Anika and Yelena are sleeping soundly in one bed, and Sofia and Ana are squeezed together in the other, with Ana on the outside. Two piles of blankets are next to the bed, with Sasha curled up on one and the other empty—meant for me, I imagine.

Sasha stirs as I kneel down on the pile of blankets. I want desperately to shower, but I have a feeling that we're not allowed to do that without express permission, and I don't want to risk incurring Alexei's wrath.

"Mrs. Andreyva?" she whispers sleepily, and I reach out, patting her hand as I lie down. "Are you okay?"

I let out a sigh. "Just call me Caterina, please? Or Cat? Especially after all of this, I think we're past formalities."

Sasha hesitates. "Okay," she whispers finally in the darkness. "Caterina. Are you okay?"

"No," I answer honestly. "But I'm alive, and I'm not hurt. So all in all, I'm as good as I can be, I think."

"He didn't hurt you?"

"Not—" I swallow hard. "Not physically, no." Alexei had been a surprisingly boring lay, all things considered, especially after the things that Viktor had opened my eyes to. He hadn't tried to hurt me during sex or really been violent in any way, which, again, I'm weirdly grateful for. It's strange, the things that seem to matter when everything else is so terrible. He'd gotten off on the fact that he was fucking his former boss's wife, apparently, and not much else.

"That's good," Sasha whispers. "We weren't sure where to put you to sleep, if—" she hesitates, and I hear the sound of her swallowing hard in the darkness. "With Sofia being pregnant and considering Ana's condition, I thought they should have the bed. I don't mind the floor. But I wasn't sure—"

"I could probably fit in the bed with the girls if need be," I murmur tiredly. "But this is fine." At least down here, I can stretch out, which wouldn't be possible sharing a bed with a nine and seven-year-old. "Did they go to sleep alright?"

"Almost immediately," Sasha says ruefully. "Children are resilient."

She says it in a way that makes me think there's more to it. I remember what she and Viktor had both said about her being in foster care, aging out of it before Viktor took her. I want to ask her to tell me more about herself, to get to know her better. But I don't, because lying there in the darkness in this monstrous house, it feels as if going to a place that dark is more than either of us can take.

"He'll want you again," Sasha says softly. "Men like him always do."

I want to ask how she knows that, too. But I don't. "I know," is all I say, simply, and then I lay back on the makeshift pillow that was left for me, staring up at the ceiling.

More than anything, I want to forget the feeling of Alexei's hands on me, his fingers traversing my body, his pathetic cock inside of me. I want to pretend that it never happened, but I can't. I can't even get rid of his smell, still clinging stickily to me, leftover from his sweaty skin sliding over mine.

I'm afraid to sleep because I don't want to dream. But eventually, my exhausted body gives in, and I slip into a deep, thankfully dreamless sleep.

* * *

I'M awoken sometime early in the morning by the sound of someone crying, small shrieks, and stuttering sobs drifting through the air towards me from Anika and Yelena's bed. I'm up in an instant, pushing my sore body up from the floor, aching in every bone and muscle as I make a beeline for their bed.

"Shh," I whisper, reaching for Anika, who is twisting in the covers, her small fists beating against them as if she's trying to fight someone off. "It's okay, sweetheart. It's just a bad dream. Wake up, baby. You're alright."

"Are we home?" she whispers, her eyes still tightly shut. "Are we back home, mama?"

I suck in a breath, my chest tightening as I feel tears spring to my eyes. I don't know if Anika is awake enough to see that it's me holding her and not her late mother. Though, right now, when I'm desperately craving anything to make me feel something good, I can't bring myself to care.

"Not yet," I whisper, pulling her into my arms. Blessedly, Yelena is still asleep, somehow not woken up by her sister crying. "We will be soon, I promise. Just as soon as your father comes to get us, he's going to take us home."

"Is he coming?" Anika's eyes pry open a fraction then, peering at me through the tears still streaming down her reddened face. "Is daddy really coming for us?"

"He's going to do his best." I press a kiss to the top of her head, desperately wanting to promise her that he is and also not wanting to lie to her at the same time. "I know he's looking for us right now. He's going to do everything he can because he loves us so much." *I'm not sure about myself,* I think grimly, rocking Anika as her sobs slow. *He loves* them *so much. His children.* But I don't say that out loud. There's no need for Anika to hear it, and it's not something she can understand. Better that she thinks that her father loves all three of us deeply, that we're a solid, unshakeable family unit.

I wish so much that could be true.

I hear the soft sounds of crying from the other side of the room, and I realize that Ana's woken up, probably from the noise that Anika was making. "It's alright," I hear Sasha murmur. "It's going to be alright."

I look up to see Ana curled into a ball, her hands pressed against her face. "No," she mumbles from between her fingers, her shoulders shaking. "It's not okay. It's never going to be okay again—"

"It will," Sasha insists, with surprising vehemence considering the fact that I know she has similar concerns. "Ana, they're going to find us—"

"And until then?" Ana's voice is starting to rise, the sign of a panic attack coming on, and Sasha grabs her hand to try to soothe her, but it's already too late. "You heard what he said," she gasps. "I'm not worth anything. I'm too damaged. So what is he going to do with me? What happens to a woman in this world who isn't worth anything to a man?"

She's crying in earnest now, hiccupping and shaking with sobs, nearly hyperventilating. However, all of us have gone very still at her last words, the weight of them hanging in the air and sinking in slowly.

What happens to a woman in this world who isn't worth anything to a man?

None of us have a good answer for that. Not here. Not now.

"They'll find us," Sasha whispers desperately, looking over at me for help, but I'm preoccupied with the children. Anika is starting to cry again, the collective sadness in the room spurring her emotions on again, and Yelena is beginning to wake up, whimpering and looking confused and upset as she hears the rest of the crying.

"Please, girls," I whisper, looking anxiously towards the door as I try to soothe them. "We've got to be quiet, okay? I know this is scary, but we can't be loud."

But it's already too late. I can hear footsteps in the hall, and I hope it's just one of the guards coming to scold us and tell us to quiet down. But when the door opens, I see polished shoes, and my stomach sinks as Alexei steps into the room.

CATERINA

He's dressed already despite the early hour, and from the irritated look on his face, I can tell that we disturbed him. He grimaces as he looks at the bed where I'm sitting with the girls, and it's all I can do to not shrink backward.

"What's going on?" Alexei demands, annoyance coloring his every word. "Why won't those brats shut up? And the crippled one, is she always like this?"

"She's scared," Sasha hisses, some of her backbone returning as she turns to glare at him. "She can't help it. You're not the first man to—"

"To what?" Alexei's eyes gleam, his gaze fixing on Sasha. "No, go on," he says, as she flinches, paling as she realizes she's said too much. "Tell me what I'm doing. I'd *love* to know."

"You're keeping us prisoner!" Anika blurts out from the circle of my arms, leaning around me to glare straight at Alexei in the way that only a nine-year-old with no concept of just how much danger we're in can do. "You're a bad man! And she's scared because you're a bad man!"

A slow smile curves Alexei's lips. "Oh, so it can speak, as well as cry." He smirks, taking a few steps closer to the bed as my arms tighten around Anika, my pulse speeding up warningly. "You shouldn't be scared, little one. I'm not going to hurt you. I'm going to find you a new daddy, someone who will take *very* good care of you, as long as you're a good girl. You can be a good girl, can't you?"

Anika doesn't understand the double meaning behind his words, but I certainly do. I can feel myself starting to tremble, anger surging inside of me as I look at Alexei's cruel, smirking face and feel a deep, visceral desire to claw the expression off of it.

You can't. You'll make things worse. I repeat it over and over in my head, trying not to think about what he did to me last night, about what he's taken from me, what he's going to take from all of us. I cling to the thought that I have to stay calm, that I have to protect the others, and for a moment, I think he's going to retreat, maybe threaten us, and leave.

But instead, he reaches out to stroke Anika's hair, smiling as he does so. "You'll be a good girl for your new daddy?"

Anika's mouth drops open. "I don't *want—*" she starts to say plaintively. She doesn't get a chance to finish her sentence because I pull her sharply away from Alexei, depositing her on the pillows as I lurch towards him, every bit of self-control that I have fleeing at that moment.

"Get away from her, you fucking *monster!*" I screech, shoving at his chest, my hands clawing as I try to rake him across the face with my nails, only for him to grab my wrist in a quick reflexive motion, his fingers wrapping around it so tightly that I cry out in pain.

Stupid, stupid, stupid. The word echoes in my head, because I know this was the wrong thing to do, that I should never have lost control, that in doing it, I've failed Anika and Yelena and Ana and everyone else depending on me. I've made it all so much worse. Still, my rage feels like a living, breathing thing, twisting in my gut until I feel like I'm going to be sick, until I feel as if I'd sacrifice everyone just to see Alexei's face turn to bleeding ribbons.

"You're not going to touch my children," I hiss, my chest heaving. I can see Sasha moving quickly across the room out of the corner of my eye, grabbing Anika and Yelena and moving them to where she and Sofia and Ana are, out of reach of Alexei. Sofia moves in front of all of them, her face pale and tense, but Alexei isn't paying attention to any of them. His attention is focused entirely on me, his grip tightening until it feels as if he might crush my wrist with his long-fingered hand, and I'm on the verge of tears from the pain.

He looms over me, that cold, calculating smile that I'm beginning to know better than I'd like creeping across his face. "Oh, but they're not your children, are they?" Alexei smiles coldly. "They're Viktor's. Viktor's and *Vera's*, to be exact. Not a drop of your blood in them. Oh, I knew Vera, in case you were wondering. We all envied Viktor. She was perfection—blonde, blue-eyed, porcelain skin, and a figure a man dreams about at night. We all jerked off thinking about her."

He grins, licking his lips. "Come to find out, though, we were all lucky not to have her. You know about that, don't you? How she turned out to be an insane cunt, spoiled and fat, desperate and needy, how she slit her own wrists because she was so weak?"

I hear a soft gasp from the other side of the room and catch a glimpse of Sasha and Sofia moving at the same time, covering the girls' ears so they won't hear. Sofia's mouth has dropped open in shock, but I can't do anything about that right now. Alexei is still leering at me, that malicious smile growing ever wider.

"Viktor picked you next. A beautiful Italian bride. So out of place, among us brutish Bratva. Or that's what you're told, right? We have no sophistication, no manners. Just animals, foraging out in the cold, killing indiscriminately." He laughs, his tongue running over his lower lip wetly. "Life is so much better, really, once you stop trying to be better than everyone else thinks you are. Once you give in to your baser nature."

"Let me go." I try to twist away from him, but his grip only tightens, until I can feel the small bones of my wrist rubbing together. "Please, you're hurting me—"

"I can imagine that Viktor taught you about *your* baser nature, didn't he?" Alexei smirks. "I've been to Moscow on business trips with him before. I've seen the women he seeks out at clubs and brothels. Women who can take pain, but even more to the point, women who *like* it." He raises my hand to his mouth, sucking two of my fingers into his mouth. "Salty. I do enjoy the taste of your tears."

"Alexei, please—" I don't want to beg him, hate that I'm reducing myself to this after attacking him only seconds ago. He's dangerously close to breaking my wrist. The pain brings tears to my eyes, my body trembling with agony and fear, and I'm growing more panicked by the moment.

"Ah yes. I do enjoy hearing Viktor's *tsarina* beg. I'm going to fuck you every night, I think, until you beg me like that between the sheets. Until you give in to your baser nature with me, just like you did with him." He leans forward, his breath tickling the shell of my ear. "Until I've taken everything he has from you away from him."

"Why?" I nearly sob it, gasping. "Why me?"

Alexei smirks. "Why? Because I want everything Viktor has. And you—you're very nearly the most important thing to him. The only thing dearer to him than you are his children."

"That's not true," I whisper desperately. "It's not. I'm not even close to being that important to him—"

Alexei snorts. "If you really think that, *tsarina*, you're stupider than I thought. And I actually thought you were quite intelligent." His eyes rake across me, lingering on my breasts. "So, what should your punishment be, do you think?"

"Punishment?" I croak the word, suddenly very aware of the eyes on me, Ana's soft, frightened gasp at Alexei's words.

"You can't think that I would simply allow you to attack me without consequence. What should it be? Should you blow me in front of your friends? Bend over for me so I can fuck you here? Lashed with my belt?"

I stare at him, dumbfounded, until he *tsks* with irritation, his cruel smile faltering.

"Choose, *tsarina*, or I'll choose for you."

I can't. I simply can't. Not here, not in front of Sofia and Sasha and Ana, not in front of my stepdaughters. "Somewhere else," I beg. "We'll go to your room—"

"Here," he says firmly. "Choose, *tsarina*."

"No." I swallow hard, shaking my head. "No, let go of me. Let *go*!" I try to jerk free, twisting in his grasp, doing my best to ignore the pain as I swipe at him with my other hand, trying desperately to throw him off guard enough to get free. I know it's fruitless, that there's nowhere for us to go, nowhere to run, and what's more, that I've only made things worse. That I've broken my promise to be willing, to not fight back, and I know he's going to make me pay.

The panic takes over, and I writhe in his grasp, forgetting that Anika and Yelena are watching, that I need to worry about them, to protect them, to keep them from being frightened, that they shouldn't see this. I hear Alexei's grunt of frustration, but I don't heed it for the warning that it is.

I don't see the blow coming. When his fist strikes my jaw, it takes me completely off guard. So much so that I don't even realize he's knocked me out until I'm already sinking bonelessly into the bed, the room spinning around me as my vision throbs at the edges and then goes black.

* * *

When I wake up, it feels as if my head is splitting open. A jolt of pure panic washes through me because I remember this feeling from the cabin, how my head can feel as if it's fracturing from the inside out. I start to try to sit up, grasp my head in my hands, push my fingers against my temples to relieve the pressure a little, but I can't move my hands.

Oh god. Oh god. Fuck, fuck, fuck!

I can't move my feet either. For one terrifying moment, I think that he's paralyzed me somehow. I realize a second later that I'm tied to the bed, my wrists and ankles bound to the four corners of the poster bed.

We're not in Alexei's room. I don't know what room we're in. It's not well furnished, just the bed in the center with nothing on my left side but a wall, and then when I slowly turn my head to look at the other side while trying to ignore the shooting pains in my skull, a scene straight out of my nightmares on my right.

There's no furniture on the other side, either. Just a door that's almost certainly locked, four blank walls, and a hook hanging from the ceiling, for all the world like a slaughterhouse.

And Sasha is hanging from that hook, her wrists bound and looped over it, her toes barely touching the hardwood floor as she whimpers, twisting her head as if she's trying to see what's happening even though her eyes are covered with a thick blindfold.

"Sasha!" I gasp out her name, and she lets out a small cry, twisting again on the hook.

"Caterina! Where are you—"

"I'm on the bed." I try to keep my voice steady and calm, as if I'm not panicking. "What's going on? Alexei knocked me out, and then—"

"He had his men take you out of the room." Sasha's voice is trembling, every inch of her shaking as she tries to keep some kind of purchase on the floor with her toes. "We didn't know where you went, and then he grabbed me and dragged me in here—" I can hear the tears threatening in her voice, her breath coming in short quick gasps. "He blindfolded me, and—"

"Did he leave?"

Sasha nods, swallowing hard. "He said he'd be back, he said—"

The door opens, and her words die on a small, mouse-like squeak as she twists towards it, looking sightlessly in the direction of the footsteps walking towards her. It's Alexei, striding into the room in slacks with his shirtsleeves rolled up and his collar open, a hunting knife in his hand. Two men follow him in, closing and locking the door as they take up a position on either side of it. Neither of them looks directly at us, as if they'd been ordered to keep their eyes forward—and knowing Alexei, they probably had.

My pulse leaps into my throat as he strides towards Sasha, not even bothering to look at me. I open my mouth to say something, to beg for her, but the words die on my lips as I realize with a sinking,

BELOVED BRIDE

acid feeling in my stomach that anything I say will only make it worse. And a moment later, Alexei confirms that.

His gaze rakes over Sasha, an anticipatory smile curving his lips as he takes in every inch of her, and then finally, he turns his head to look at me.

"Ah, *tsarina*. You're awake." He reaches up, pressing the tip of the hunting knife into Sasha's chest, just above the neckline of the t-shirt she'd worn to bed last night. "You know," he says conversationally, dragging the knife down so that it begins to cut through the fabric of her shirt, "Sasha is here because of you."

I don't say anything. I can't. I feel my body trembling, every muscle rigid, poised for a flight that I can't take and a fight that I can't participate in because I'm tied down. All the trauma from the cabin comes rushing back, the feeling of being bound and helpless, the memory of Andrei and Stepan's knives biting into my skin bright and vivid, seeing Alexei pushing the hunting knife against Sasha's skin. The blade must have been impossibly sharp because it's slowly slicing through her shirt like tissue paper, with hardly any resistance.

"I thought of how I should punish you," Alexei continues, dragging the knife down as he cuts her shirt open, the tip scoring her flesh just slightly, so that a raised pink line appears, small droplets of blood springing out like a leak. "I thought of *so* many creative ways, but then I realized something fundamental about *you*, Caterina."

His use of my name is startling, piercing me in a way that his mocking *tsarina* never does. It feels familiar, intimate, and my stomach twists because it reminds me that he *has* been intimate with me, that he knows the innermost parts of me now, and I can never change that. He's indelibly sunk into my skin, whether I somehow managed to destroy him in this instant or not.

"What's that?" I manage to ask it with some difficulty, my lips feeling numb and thick, my entire body shifting into a panic mode that threatens to overtake me.

"You're brave when it comes to your own pain. I could threaten you all day long, punish you in the worst ways, and it would take a long time for you to break. I think you could endure more than some of my men." He looks at me appreciatively. "In a way, I admire you, Caterina. Not many women have your strength or your bravery. But you see, I don't really have time for all that. I need you obedient, pliant, because I have a business to run and deals to make. I can't afford to spend time breaking you, as enjoyable as it would be to see how much you could bear before you started to beg me for mercy. And don't mistake me, you *would* eventually. I can be very talented at torture when I put my mind to it."

He slices through the rest of Sasha's shirt, cutting it away from her so that it floats in white cotton ribbons to the floor. Almost absentmindedly, he shoves the knife into his belt then, reaching for the waist of the too-big sweatpants that she found. He jerks them down with one motion, baring her entirely as he pulls them off and tosses them aside, leaving her dangling naked from the hook.

"Your weakness, Caterina, is others. Those you care about, those you feel responsible for. You would let me torture you, but if I hurt someone dear to you, it will cut you more deeply than any knife, sear you to the very soul more than any brand. So I brought dear Sasha in here to punish instead, because by watching this, you will understand the severity of what you've done and how very serious I am."

He reaches up, running his finger around her nipple, and Sasha squeals, twisting away from him with a gasping sob. "I can't leave marks on her, of course. Not lasting ones. This one is the only one of you that's unblemished, except for her lack of virginity. But she'll fetch the highest price." He sets the knife aside then, undoing his belt. "But I can still teach you a lesson in this way."

Alexei circles around her, folding the belt over in his hands. And then, as Sasha sobs aloud, twisting on the hook, he brings the belt down on her ass with all the force in his arm.

Sasha's scream is like nothing I've ever heard. She screams again when he does it a second time, and Alexei laughs, a sound that's almost a cackle. "When you defy me, *tsarina*, when you refuse to bend to me the way you've bent to your husband, when you argue with me or try to harm me, when you try to thwart me, it won't be you who receives the lash. It won't be you that I push to the very edges of your limits to bear the pain. It won't be you that I torment and violate." He smiles cruelly, his eyes lighting up with pleasure as he strikes Sasha again, hard enough to send her body swinging on the hook.

"It will be her, or the crippled one, or Romano's wife. And if you haven't learned your lesson by then, after I've grown tired of taking out my anger on them, I'll turn to something more—convincing." His eyes gleam, and I know with a bone-chilling fear exactly what he means.

"After all," Alexei says pleasantly as if we were discussing the weather. "Don't most children need a good spanking from time to time?"

"Fuck you!" I twist against the ropes tying me to the bed, baring my teeth at him in a near snarl. "You won't lay a fucking hand on them—"

"Oh?" Alexei raises an eyebrow, and then he brings the belt down on Sasha's thighs. Not once, not twice, but over and over, swinging in a relentless rhythm that peppers her butt and thighs and hips with the crack of the leather until she's nearly glowing red and sobbing, dangling helplessly.

"Please," Sasha whimpers, and I wait for Alexei to beam with pleasure that she's begging him. But then she turns her head in my direction, and I feel something in my chest crack open with a specific, excruciating agony. "Caterina, please—"

"What?" I gasp the word, feeling as if I can't breathe. "Sasha, I—"

"Stop fighting him. Please." She's crying harder now, gulping for air, her body shaking as if she's nearly seizing from the pain. "Please don't make him mad. I can't take anymore, please, it hurts, it hurts so bad, Caterina, please don't—"

I feel myself go limp, every bit of fight that I ever possessed draining out of me. It's as if Alexei reached inside of me and tore out a piece of my soul in that instant, as if he crushed my heart in his fist. I'd thought that I'd felt broken before, leaving his room, but I'd been wrong.

I hadn't known just how broken I could be.

"I'm sorry," I whisper. "I won't—I promise I won't. I won't fight. I swear, Alexei, please don't hurt her anymore—"

"Louder." He moves as if to swing the belt again, and I nearly scream it, jerking at the ropes.

"I won't fight back! I swear, Alexei, I promise, just don't hit her again! Please! I'll do anything you say, I swear—"

He steps back, a satisfied smile curving his lips. "Very good, Caterina." He motions to one of the men at the door, and the guard strides forwards, stretching up to pull Sasha off the hook. She crumples into his arms, unable to stand and seemingly uncaring who is holding her, as long as it keeps her from falling to the floor.

"Take her back to the room," Alexei orders. "And bring in the other one."

"What?" I gasp aloud, my eyes going wide. "But I said—"

"You aren't arguing with me, are you, *tsarina*?" He looks at me calmly, his mouth twitching with obvious pleasure at the corner that he's backed me into. "You said you would go along with whatever pleased me, yes? That you wouldn't fight or thwart me if I let your friend down? Because I can bring her back if you didn't mean it—"

"No!" I shake my head fiercely. "I'm not—I meant it. I promise. I'm not arguing with you, I just thought—"

"Women." Alexei clicks his tongue. "You all think too much. It's not necessary. All that we need from you is a hot mouth and tight pussy on our cocks, a pair of hands to keep the house, and a fertile womb to give us an heir. None of that involves *thinking*. So less of that, please." He motions to the other guard, who opens the door, and a moment later, I gasp as I see Ana being dragged in, her ruined feet barely touching the floor.

"You see," Alexei begins, as the guard drags her wrists over her head to hook them like Sasha's had been. "I can't trust you, *tsarina*. You promised me once before, after all, to behave, and obey me willingly if I spared the lives of Viktor and the other men. But you broke that promise. Now I'm going to give you another chance to keep the one that you just made." He moves towards Ana, who looks at him with terrified eyes. She hasn't been blindfolded, and she whimpers as he comes closer, trying to move away. But of course, she can't. The rope holding her wrists is over the hook, and her feet barely touch the floor.

"I'm going to punish this one now," Alexei says calmly, "to drive home the point that I've made. I need you to understand, Caterina, that your husband is not coming for you. None of them are. They are not coming to save any of you. Your only hope of survival, and your only hope for your friends and for those two precious children, is for you to submit to the situation that you've found yourself in—for you to submit to *me*. This—" he gestures at Ana, shivering in fear on the hook, "is *your* fault. You attacked me, and now these poor girls are paying for it." He shakes his head as if deeply disappointed. "Your obstinacy is the reason why they're in pain."

I wanted to be strong. I wanted to be brave. More than anything, I wanted to protect them. And as Alexei starts to methodically cut away Ana's clothing, ignoring her sobs and pleas, I can feel every ounce of strength I had draining out of me, leaving me feeling empty and hollow, more hopeless than I've ever felt in my life.

I'd thought that I'd hit rock bottom before. But clearly, there was further down to fall.

I don't bother begging. I know it won't help. What Alexei wants isn't me pleading and crying. He wants me silent, compliant, obedient. He wants me to submit, to accept his decisions without argument, and this is one of those. If I beg, if I argue, if I fight back, I'll only make it worse.

Ana doesn't meet my eyes. She doesn't plead like Sasha did either or say anything to me. She hangs there, head down so that her chin is almost brushing her chest, tears dripping onto the hardwood as she cries, waiting for the blows.

When Alexei starts in, he doesn't stop. I want to look away, but I force myself to watch all of it. Because he's right—this is my fault. All of it. I let my emotions get the better of me, lost control, gave into the gratification of fighting back instead of keeping my word and protecting the ones I have responsibility for. And now I'm responsible for something so much worse.

He brings the belt down, hard and relentless, again and again until Ana is so limp that I'm afraid she's passed out. Alexei doesn't stop, doesn't take a break, just beats her until her skin is welted and burning red, visibly bruised and decorated with broken veins. Finally, breathing hard, he steps back, admiring his work.

"I could go harder on her," he says, his voice pleased. "She's worth nothing at sale anyway. Not like the other one. Beautiful, isn't it? Such a lovely red." He reaches out to touch her, and Ana shudders away from him like a fly-bitten horse, a cry escaping her lips.

"I'm done with her," he says, glancing over at the guard. "Get her out of here."

I nearly gasp with relief as the guard pulls her down, practically dragging her out of the room as she slumps against him. Alexei doesn't even glance after them, striding towards the bed instead as he throws his belt to one side, the leather skidding across the floor.

"In two nights," he says casually, "I'll be throwing a party for potential buyers. They'll be coming here to see what I have on offer. Do you understand what I'm saying?" He reaches out, grabbing my chin so that I'm forced to look at him. "Tell me you understand, Caterina, or it'll be Romano's wife I drag in here next. And after that—"

Not Sofia. The thought of her on that hook, the belt coming down on her relentlessly, threatening her unborn child, is too much. And Anika or Yelena—it's unthinkable.

I'd do anything to prevent that. And Alexei knows it.

"I understand," I whisper.

"If you act out, or defy me, or try to escape or fight back, the consequences will be your fault." He looks down at me sternly. "And remember, it won't be you who bears them."

"I know." I swallow hard, nodding. "I understand, I promise. I won't—I'll behave."

"Good." Alexei beams as if we've settled something between us. "That's the *tsarina* I know." He reaches for the button of his slacks then, and I see that he's rock-hard, bulging against his fly. It makes me sick because I know he's aroused from the beatings, from whipping Ana and Sasha.

I've seen Viktor turned on from my punishments, of course. But it's not the same. Viktor knows that deep down, I want it, that I get unimaginable pleasure from riding that line of pain and ecstasy, from taking his punishment and submitting to him. What he does to me is a back and forth, a game that I'm a part of that ends in pleasure. Even when it hasn't, even in our worst moments, he's still always drawn something out of me, some deep and depraved need that only he can satisfy, and he knows it.

This was nothing like that. There was no pleasure, no symbiosis, no game. It was just torture, just pain, and that's what Alexei is getting off on. He's a sadist in the purest sense, and it's nothing like what I've experienced with Viktor.

"Open your mouth, *tsarina*," he says, reaching into his slacks. "I'm so hard I could burst, and I need a place to put my cum."

My stomach turns over, but I don't argue. I know better now. So I turn my head and open my mouth.

When he stuffs himself into it, groaning as he grabs the back of my head and begins fucking my face, I feel the last shred of hope that I had drifting away.

Two days until the party. I don't know if he'll be brokering deals that night, but if not, it won't be long after.

I'd lied.

No one is coming to save us.

And all of our lives as we knew them are over.

VIKTOR

*C*aterina leans over me, her lips brushing my chest. She's naked, entirely so, and her nipples brush my skin too, hard and pointed, evidence of her desire. But that's not what I'm most interested in.

My cock, heavy and swollen, throbs between us, the tip brushing against the soft skin of her belly and leaving a trail of my arousal there. I want to grip it, stroke it, angle myself so that I can slip into her, into that wet heat that I crave like air itself.

But that's not what I seek out either. Instead, my hand finds its way between her spread thighs, up the soft inner flesh, feeling the heat radiating from her before I even touch her. Hot, for me. Wet, for me. Smooth and yielding, slick and inviting.

My fingers slide between her folds, trailing in her arousal, soaking myself in her as I find her clit, circling it so that she gasps against my skin, her ass arching upwards as she presses against my hand, seeking more of that delicious friction as her lips make their way downwards.

My cock throbs in anticipation, knowing that her soft lips will be wrapped around my tip any moment now, her tongue circling the sensitive spot beneath, slipping down, taking me into the tight confines of her throat. No one gives head like Caterina. She can suck a cock better than any woman

I've ever known, and it's just one of many reasons why I'm glad that I married her.

I could list off so many more, and I will, later when she's lying breathless and sated in my arms. But for now, I settle for groaning in pleasure, my other hand making a fist in her hair as she slides another inch downwards, guiding her mouth towards my throbbing length. She's taken her sweet time, but now it's time that I remind her who's in charge, that I decide when my cock gets sucked.

Her eyes roll up to meet mine, heated and glazed with lust. Her mouth opens, that soft pink tongue darting out to run along the length of my shaft, teasing the prominent, pulsing vein along the top. My head tilts back as I groan again, tightening my grip on her hair as her mouth moves upwards, her lips parting to wrap tightly around my cockhead, sucking me into her mouth with wet, hot friction that threatens to send me over the edge far too soon.

Some nights, that's all I want—just to pour myself into her mouth and down her throat, a hot rush of my cum spurting over her tongue, hearing her moan as she drinks me down, licking every last drop away. But tonight, this is just foreplay. I want my wife's pussy, and she knows I get what I want.

And she's happy to give it.

She's not trying to make me come, so Caterina licks me almost lazily, with long slow strokes as she sucks at my head and shaft with her full lips, until my cock is so swollen and hard that I'm not sure it's possible for me to get any more erect, my thick shaft stretching her lips as she struggles to take it all.

"Down your throat once, yes, ah, fuck!" I curse aloud as her throat muscles tighten around me, my cock choking her as she slides down to the base, engulfing all of me. When she comes up, her eyes are watering, her lips puffy and shiny with her spit, and my cock is glistening, aching to be inside of her.

My hand relaxes in her hair, and Caterina pulls back, tossing her head and sending all of those cascading dark locks tumbling over her shoulders. She gives me a wicked grin as she straddles me, her hand wrapping firmly around my throbbing shaft as she guides it between her legs, her thumb stroking that vein as her hips rock downwards onto me, her folds *parting and wrapping themselves around my head as I penetrate her with a sensation that outstrips any other pleasure I've ever felt.*

She fucks me slowly, tantalizingly, drawing out every moment, making me ache for more even as I'm inside of her. When I finally take charge again, grabbing her hips and thrusting up into her hard and fast, the grin on her face tells me that she was waiting for it. Waiting for me to take her, to show her that even with her on top of me, I'm in charge.

I'm the one who possesses her, claims her, owns her. Mine, forever and always.

My beloved bride.

I hold back until she's grinding down onto me with fast, helpless motions that tell me she's close, the muscles of her inner thighs trembling as she pushes herself towards her orgasm. My own muscles are rigid with the force of holding back my cum, my body tense and ready for it. The moment that I feel her clench around me, her nails digging into my chest, I throw my head back with a roar of pleasure as I thrust up into her hard, seating my cock as deep inside of her as I can as I start to come.

I pour into her, her pussy gripping me, milking me as I throb and spurt inside of her, the pleasure almost unbearable. Nothing has ever felt as good as Caterina; no woman could ever compare. Nothing could ever make up for the loss of her, if that day ever came.

She's my obsession. My drug. The only woman who could ever match me.

Mine. Mine. Mine.

I grab her hips, rolling her onto her back as I stay buried inside of her, keeping my cum there, letting it take root. My hands sweep over her body, caressing her as she sighs softly with pleasure, and I kiss her lips gently, knowing that she'll fall asleep in my arms tonight. Whatever problems there once were between us, they're gone now, drifted away until I can't even entirely remember what they were or how we overcame them. There was some gulf between us, but now—now I can't even recall why, or how there could have ever been a single night when I didn't hold my wife close to my chest, cherishing her. Adoring her. Claiming her for my own.

Caterina tilts her chin up, arching up to kiss me. I meet her halfway, kissing her again fiercely, feeling her warm, full, soft lips—

--go cold under mine.

I jerk backward, feeling her skin turn waxy, her body go limp, and when I slip out of her, sliding back on the bed, my hands trail in something warm and sticky.

Blood. There's blood on the bed, on my hands, everywhere. I hold my hands up, watching it drip down my palms, and when I finally look out from behind them, I feel my own blood run cold.

It's not Caterina on the bed, naked and beautiful. It's Vera, her face twisted with sorrow even in death, her wrists laid open and streaming blood.

* * *

THE DREAM JERKS ME AWAKE, leaving me in a cold sweat as I lie there, the dawn light greying just outside my window. I hold my hands up in front of my face, half expecting to see them streaked with blood, but they're clean and bare. *It was a dream*, I tell myself, and I try to think back to the first part of it, Caterina atop me, her lips wrapped hungrily around my cock, Caterina straddling me, riding me to a climax.

But try as I might, the sickening final act keeps creeping back into my thoughts, driving away anything else. And if I'm being honest, even remembering the first, best part of the dream does little to make me feel better.

Caterina isn't here. She's gone, captured by Alexei, his prisoner, along with Sofia, Ana, Sasha, and my daughters. She's in some other bed right now, if she's lucky. I can't help but wonder if she's thinking of me at all, if I've crept into her dreams, if any part of her misses me with the deep and intolerable ache that I've felt every second since Alexei dragged her away.

There's no way to know.

The truth is that we might never know.

Liam's hacker dug deeply enough to uncover traces of Alexei's whereabouts. We managed to pinpoint an area where he might be. That in and of itself gave us a clue—I had once owned a house in that region, a mountain chalet that I'd gifted to a particularly lucrative client.

If Alexei has poached that client from me, it's possible that he has use of the house. And if so—if he's there—we have an advantage that I hadn't dared hope for.

The house had once been mine. I know it fairly well, even though I hadn't spent much time there while it had been. Of all the places Alexei could be, it's the one that offers us the greatest chance of circumventing his guards and sneaking in.

Through my remaining connections in Moscow, we managed to find out that several well-known men who had purchased from me in the past had plans to attend a "retreat," which I know is code for a party where deals will be brokered for illegal merchandise that requires discretion. It could be drugs, it could be big game or live bodies for the hunting parties that some of the Moscow elites hold at their estates, it could be weapons or deals for arms trading.

It could be women.

I'm betting on that—and that it's not only women, but the women that Alexei stole from us. Caterina. Sofia. Sasha. Ana. My *children.*

When dusk falls tonight, we're going to begin the trek to the mountains and Alexei's possible hideout. And once we arrive, nothing short of a nuclear blast could stop me from finding my way inside.

And what then?

That's a question that remains to be answered. When Caterina is rescued and back home with me—I refuse to couch it in terms of *if*—what happens then? I can tell her that I love her, but I have no idea if those feelings will be returned, not vocally, at least. I would bet a great deal that Caterina loves me in return, but my wife is a stubborn and willful woman. If she doesn't feel that our marriage can exist on even ground, she won't say something that means so much. And in order for her to feel secure in that—

I have to change. My *life* has to change.

Something had shifted in me when I saw Sasha being dragged down the stairs, abused, and violated yet again because she'd tried to save Yelena. I'd seen what Caterina had been trying to tell me all along—that no matter how much I might have believed that I was giving these women a better life, in the end, I'd only opened up more opportunities for them to be hurt, brutalized, and enslaved. I hadn't given them anything, and I'd taken away every chance they had to make lives of their own, created by their own choices.

I don't know how it took me so long to see it, except that for nearly forty years, it's all that I've known. My grandfather built this business, passed it down to my father, who did the same with me. I'd never had reason to think differently about the world I'd been raised in.

At the end of the day, it's no different than any other one of us. Not a single one among us—not Luca or Levin or Max or Liam—has clean hands. We've all done immoral things, pushed at the edges of the code we claim to hold dear, grown rich on the addictions, vices, and pain of others. I had meant it when I'd once told Luca that his business was no better than mine, simply because it was a more sophisticated way of accumulating wealth. But now, I see that wasn't entirely true, either.

The Rossis, and then Luca, have been in the drug trade for years. At some point, of course, the addiction takes hold in those that have access to their supply, and there's no longer any choice in whether or not they'll continue to buy from those that deal those drugs. But at least in the beginning, it's their own choice. Their own choice to get high, to lose themselves in a chemically-induced ecstasy, to shut out whatever part of the world has become unbearable to them, or even just boring.

The only choice that has ever existed in my business is my own.

I'll do something differently. What, I don't know exactly. Stepping away from the sex trade will mean leaning on my connections outside of it, relying on men like Luca to point me in the direction of a fresh start, a new horizon.

But it could also mean another kind of fresh start, one no less daunting, but potentially equally rewarding. A marriage on equal terms with my wife, a partnership built on love, trust, and mutual desire.

A marriage where the games we play with each other are only in the bedroom, and outside of it—

I don't know how to describe it, exactly. I don't know what it looks like or how to be that kind of husband.

But for Caterina, I want to try.

Outside, the sun is beginning to rise. In twelve hours, we'll leave for the mountains, and what happens after that remains to be seen.

But silently, I whisper a promise that I hope is the last one I'll ever have to wonder whether or not I can keep.

I'm coming for you, Caterina. I'm going to save you.

I'm going to bring you home.

CATERINA

The party, both is and isn't what I had expected.

I feel numb with grief as Alexei's men bring us downstairs, into another part of the house that seems made for big gatherings. It's well lit, huge wrought-iron chandeliers with Edison bulbs hanging from the ceilings, and a roaring fire built in a stone fireplace at one end of the room. Several feet in front of the fireplace, there's a series of round stages, and it's there that Alexei's men lead us, pushing us forward so that we don't hesitate or try to run.

To my horror, on the center one, I catch a glimpse of Ana.

The last few hours have felt like a fever dream. Alexei had "clothing" brought to us and told us to make sure we all bathed until we were spotlessly clean. The minute we were all scrubbed and "dressed," the guard marched us downstairs into a room where a tall, elegantly pretty blonde woman that none of us had ever seen before was waiting, her face blank as she led each one of us in turn to a chair and started to make us up and do our hair—including Anika and Yelena.

That made me shudder with anger, seeing her making up the girls like they were in some Southern beauty pageant. For Yelena, at least, it was a distraction that left her giggling and happy for the first time in days, touching her face curiously as the woman expertly and quickly curled her long, silky blonde hair. Anika viewed it with the same suspicious irritation that she viewed most things, but she sat very still, intuiting that this wasn't the time to cry or fight back.

If only I'd figured that out, too.

Sasha and Ana have barely spoken to me since the episode with Alexei. I apologized to both of them, and both of them had said, of course, that it wasn't my fault. That anyone would have lost control, hearing Alexei talk about and seeing him trying to touch Anika like that. That we're all pushed to our breaking point. *He's the sadist,* Sasha had said quietly. *He found your weak point and exploited it, but that's not your fault. It could have been any one of us.*

It's not your fault, Ana had echoed, just as she had to me in the past. But somehow, this time, it held less weight.

The fact remained that it *hadn't* been any one of us. It had been me, and the guilt feels as suffocating as Alexei forcing himself into my mouth. Every time I see Sasha or Ana limping or unable to sleep comfortably as they heal from the lashing he gave them, I feel a fresh wave of cold, sickening responsibility that weighs me down until I feel as if I could crumble under it.

I don't know what happens tonight. I don't know if deals are brokered, our prospective new buyers come for us later, or if we're handed over when the festivities end. I don't know how much time there is between now and the moment when I'm separated from my friends, my stepdaughters, and the possibility of ever being saved by my husband forever. But I can feel it coming, rushing towards us with a sickening speed, and I'm helpless to stop it.

I'm helpless to do *anything* now except be silent and keep Alexei from using me as an excuse to hurt anyone further.

Ana wasn't with us when we took turns showering and scrubbing ourselves clean or when we were hustled downstairs to be primped and curled and made up. I didn't know where she was taken, and the ever-present pit of anxiety in my stomach yawned wide and all-encompassing, making it impossible for me to think about anything else.

Alexei had clearly chosen what we were each wearing. Sofia, Sasha, and I had each been given a short silk slip dress with nothing underneath that barely grazed below the tops of our thighs, with a draped neckline that swooped down to a few inches below our breasts. Mine was a deep cranberry color that set off my deep olive skin and dark hair and eyes beautifully, Sofia's a jewel blue that accentuated the paleness that she'd inherited from her Russian mother and the dark hair she'd gotten from her Italian father, and Sasha's a deep emerald green that made her strawberry blonde hair look redder than ever and set off her sea-colored eyes, drawing the green out more than the blue. The woman who put on the finishing touches left our hair loose in heavy, cascading curls and applied makeup with a light touch, adding false eyelashes and expert contour and eye makeup to make each of us look more like a runway model than everyday women.

Which was the point, of course. We were meant to look as if we were worth an astronomical amount of money. And since Sofia and I both had irreparable flaws—my scars and her pregnancy—looking extraordinarily beautiful was even more important.

All of us jumped when the door opened, and Alexei strode in, stopping in the middle of the room and ordering us to turn around so that he could see the woman's handiwork. He looked pleased enough when he saw Sofia, Sasha, and myself, but the minute that his eyes landed on Anika and Yelena, his expression turned dark and irritable.

"Why the fuck are they wearing so much makeup?" he'd demanded, glaring at the woman. "My buyers want them to look like *children*, not like miniature whores. Get that shit off of their faces."

Something dark and terrible had surged up in me at the word *buyers*, fueled by the sudden, terrified look that Anika shot me, understanding beginning to dawn on her too-young face. She went slightly pale, stiffening as the woman reached for her to start cleaning the makeup off of her face with shaking hands, stuttering apologies to Alexei. But she hadn't struggled, as if she'd come to understand that he posed a danger. And I held myself back, shoving the feeling down until my throat felt tight and choked with emotion, my stomach roiling until I was certain that I was going to be sick.

Yelena had started to cry when the woman began to take her makeup off. "No!" she'd cried, stamping her foot in frustration. "I *like* it!"

Alexei had shot me a look of warning, and I'd stepped out of my spot in line immediately, reaching for Yelena.

"Shh," I'd told her, taking the makeup wipe out of the woman's hands and starting to use it on Yelena's face myself. "It's okay. This just wasn't the right look for you tonight, okay? When we're home, you can play with my makeup all you want."

"I looked like a princess," Yelena mumbled, trying to pull away as I wiped the tears away from her eyes.

"You can be a princess again later," I promised her, trying to keep the thread of desperation out of my voice. "Okay? You're still dressed like one." Alexei had had them put in frilly pink dresses that suited Yelena very well, and Anika not in the least.

"Okay," she mumbled, wiping at her eyes. "I thought daddy was coming."

"He is," I whispered, hating myself for the lie. "He's just running a little late."

When I looked up, I saw Anika's eyes meet mine, and I knew that she understood far more than she should.

For instance, Viktor almost certainly wasn't coming.

It made my heart sink to my toes.

Yelena started crying again, silently, and I'd looked desperately at Alexei, wiping at her face. "I'm trying," I'd told him, fear licking at my spine, but he'd just shrugged, coolly meeting my gaze.

"It might be for the best," he'd said with a casual, one-shouldered shrug. "Some of the buyers like it when they cry."

It had taken everything in me not to try to murder him on the spot. I'd never wanted to commit violence so deeply, until the hatred seemed to have crept into my bones, my blood, until I would have gladly died if it meant he would too.

The problem, of course, is that it isn't me who would suffer if I lost control again.

Alexei has made that very clear.

"Take the girls to the party ahead of time," he'd told two of the guards, who strode forward immediately. "The others will be along shortly."

One of the other guards pulled me to my feet, away from Yelena, and I forced myself to go limp, standing up and tottering backward on my high heels as the girls were led away. It felt as if my heart were being ripped out of my chest, but I'd forced myself not to speak, not to cry, not to scream.

It felt like dying.

When we're led into that huge room, I catch sight of the round stages, and my heart stutters in my chest as I see Ana on the central one, her eyes glazed over almost as if she's been drugged.

She's been dressed in a ballerina's outfit, complete with a skin-tone leotard cut down nearly to her navel and a frilly white tutu around her hips. But she's motionless, her hands bound above her head to a rigging suspended from the ceiling, and her injured feet stuffed into pointe shoes, one leg bent at the ankle and tied with a looping ribbon to another around her waist, so that she looks like nothing so much as one of the small plastic ballerinas that are in the music boxes every little girl has as a child.

The stage is rotating, so she faces us at one point as we're led forward. But her eyes are unfocused, and it's as if she doesn't see us, as if she's completely out of it.

It might be better for her if she is.

The guards get each one of us up onto our own rotating stage, grabbing our wrists and chaining them in front of us with a thin, bracelet-like chains that almost seem like jewelry. They're still too strong to break, though—I surreptitiously try to test them as Sofia and Sasha are led up onto their own stages, and there's not even the slightest bit of give. Nor is there much room left between our wrists.

There's nothing left to do but stand there and watch.

If you took away the chained women on stages and Ana

bent into a caricature of a music-box ballerina, like some grotesque decoration, it would seem like a normal party for outrageously rich men. At least it's mostly men as the room begins to fill up, of varying ages and ethnicities, all of them dressed in tailored and bespoke suits. There are a few women in evening gowns, mostly on the arms of the men who brought company. Still, a couple of them appear to be on their own, eyeing us with the same appraising expressions that the men wear but less lecherous.

At this point, being purchased by a woman seems like a possible salvation that I hadn't thought of. I have no interest in women sexually, but neither would I have any interest in the kind of man who would purchase a woman. And though I'm well aware that women are capable of equal cruelty, the prospect somehow seems less terrifying.

I still have a faint hope that Viktor will come for us, but it's rapidly fading, minute by minute. When we'd been getting dressed, Sofia had spoken up, saying that she was sure the men were coming. "They're planning something, I know it," she'd said aloud, looking at Sasha and me. "They'll be here. I know Luca will come for me."

I'd nodded, but something in my face must have given away my uncertainty.

"You must think Viktor is coming for you," Sofia had said, a thread of desperation coloring her tone. "He loves you. He wouldn't abandon you like that."

"I don't think he'd abandon me, or any of us," I'd said quietly. "But if he can't find us in time—"

"He will," Sofia had whispered, pressing her hand to the silk draped over her slight bump. "They all will."

But when I catch a glimpse of her face as the stages turn, I can see that she's losing hope, too. We all are.

I catch sight of Anika and Yelena in the crowd, being paraded around, two guards watching them. They both look pale and anxious, occasionally looking around as if searching for someone familiar. Yelena catches sight of me on the stage at last and tries to make a run for it, bolting in my direction, only to be scooped up by the irritated-looking guard who is none too gentle with her. She slaps at him, trying to struggle out of his arms, and I see a pretty, elegant brunette woman move in their direction, cooing at Yelena as if she finds her struggle endearing.

I can feel myself trembling with helpless anger. It takes everything in me not to leap down from the stage and go to her. But I can't stop hearing Alexei's voice in my head, telling me that Sofia would be the next one punished, and then Anika and Yelena after that. It would feel good to rush to them, to momentarily save them from the fear I know they're feeling, the panic and confusion, but it would just be worse in the end.

I'm not sure how much worse it can get. But I have a feeling we're about to find out.

It's clear that Alexei is soaking up his new position, preening like a peacock in his elegantly fitted navy suit as he makes the rounds of the room. I keep an eye on him, watching as he moves from one important-looking guest to another; I can't overhear anything he's saying. I can only see the arrogant expression on his face, the self-satisfied smile that tells me that as far as he's concerned, the night is a success so far.

Which doesn't bode well for us.

He must have given the guests permission to start approaching us at some point because several of the men start to make their way towards the stages. One man goes so far as to reach for my breast, squeezing it so hard that I wince, and the guard standing by my stage steps forward, his face hard and impassive.

"You're not allowed to hurt the merchandise," the guard says in a firm, almost bored tone. "You may touch and examine them, but with care. These are all very valuable."

The man fondling my breast, who is easily forty years older than me if he's a day, looks disappointed. But he withdraws his hand, choosing instead to slide a hand up my thigh and push my skirt up just enough to get a glimpse of me beneath it. According to Alexei's instructions, I'm shaved bare, and I feel my face heat with shame. *Not this one, at least,* I think like a prayer, as if I can bargain my way out of this.

More of the guests are starting to come forward, several men gathering around Sasha's stage to eye her like a zoo animal in captivity, running their hands over her butt and breasts and thighs, one even going so far as to ask her to open her mouth so that he can check her teeth, like she's a prize horse. Alexei joins them a moment later, clearly seeing that most of the interest is in Sasha, and I wince as he lifts up her skirt, slapping the inside of her thigh to make her spread her legs apart so that the men can get a better view. "She's not a virgin," I hear him say, as if he's describing some deep flaw. "But from what I understand, she's only ever been fucked once. Still a tight pussy." Alexei looks up at her, his hand tightening on her thigh. "That's right, isn't it? Only the once?"

I can tell that Sasha is trembling, her voice stuttering as she tries to speak, and Alexei smacks her hard on the outside of her leg, where I know she's still sore from the lashing he gave her. "Answer me! Don't keep my guests waiting."

"Y-yes," she manages. "Just once. Not—not since then."

"See?" Alexei beams. "She's never sucked a cock, never been fucked in the ass. Plenty of new territories to tread." He notices another couple examining Sofia, a man who appears to be in his late forties and his beautiful, much younger wife, and inclines his head to the guests still looking at Sasha. "Please, take your time. I'll be right back."

There's a small crowd gathering around me as well, but I do my best to ignore them, wanting to keep an eye on what's going on. So far, no one has approached Ana, walking past her like she's a statue, and I wonder if Alexei has told them that she's off-limits, not for sale. A few men glance at her with barely concealed interest, though, and my stomach clenches with anxiety. Alexei might have assumed that he wouldn't be able to sell her, but if he thinks he can turn a profit, I don't doubt that he wouldn't change his mind.

The couple looking at Sofia seems to have two very different interests. The man is visibly undressing her with his eyes, but the woman is focused on the slight swell of her belly, going so far as to reach out and touch it. Sofia visibly shrinks back, and Alexei slaps her hard on the ass.

"Be still and let them look at you." He smiles pleasantly at the couple. "I know the price is a bit high on this one, but it's not just her that you're buying. As I'd mentioned, she's pregnant."

What the fuck? Alexei had made that sound like it was a detriment when he'd appraised us, but now he's playing it up, driving up Sofia's price. It doesn't make sense—until it does, and my skin starts to crawl.

"That's precisely why we're interested," the woman says in her smooth, cultured Mediterranean accent. "My husband wants her for pleasure, but it's the baby that I want. We haven't been able to conceive, you see. My issue, not his. We'd raise the baby as our own, and with luck, she might even be able to give us more."

Sofia can't hide the look of utter horror on her face. I feel like I'm going to be sick, and I catch her gaze when she turns her head to look miserably at me, all pretense of hope gone. It's as if whatever she'd been buoying herself up with has drained out of her entirely, and she blinks rapidly, trying to hold back the tears so that she doesn't make Alexei angry.

I hate you. I hate you, you fucking monster. The words echo over and over in my head, my blood boiling as I watch Alexei bargain with the couple, who appear ready to make the sale at this very moment. "A million and a half, at least," he tells them, gesturing to Sofia. "She's very beautiful, the daughter of an elite Italian-American mafia family. She has all the social graces. And as you can see, she's fertile."

"*Excusez-moi d'interrompre.*" A smooth, heavily-accented, masculine voice speaking French comes from behind Alexei, and he stiffens in surprise, turning. There's a flash of irritation on his face, but it seems to disappear the instant he sees who is standing there, and he straightens, inclining his head.

"*Monsieur*! I hadn't thought you would come. I'm pleased you accepted my invitation," Alexei says, stepping aside and giving the couple room to continue looking at Sofia. It gives me a clear view of the man who interrupted, and I blink, startled.

I'd been expecting another garden-variety billionaire, some generic man with nothing particularly interesting about him. Most of the men in this room are like that, as if they'd been designed from a drop-down list—choose ethnicity and age, pour into a tailored black suit. Rinse and repeat.

But the Frenchman is nothing like that. He looks to be in his mid to late thirties, a few lines creasing his forehead, but his skin otherwise smooth, without a hint of stubble, his jaw strong and chiseled, with a long and aquiline nose that could be considered the only flaw in his otherwise startlingly handsome appearance. However, combined with the rest of what could only be described as a *look*, it gives his appearance character. His dark hair is expertly cut and styled, like most of the men here. Instead, he's wearing a *velvet* suit of all things in a shade of royal blue that makes him inescapably stand out in the crowd, with a pink paisley handkerchief square, satin lapels on the jacket, and no tie.

Almost every man in the world would look ridiculous in an outfit like that, but he somehow pulls it off.

"*Monsieur* Egorov." The Frenchman smiles, displaying gleaming white teeth. "I'm sorry to interrupt, but it did not appear that the couple you were conversing with were quite ready to make a sale. And I am."

My stomach is instantly in knots. *Here it is. Who? Who does he want to buy? Please god, not Anika or Yelena.* I feel as if I'm going to throw up, the room tilting dangerously as I wait for him to speak again.

Alexei perks up instantly, looking at the other man with keen interest. "Of course," he says politely, doing an excellent job of shielding his eagerness. "If you are ready to purchase, you are my first and foremost concern. Which of the girls were you interested in? If it's one of the children, I can fetch them for you to inspect more closely—"

The look of utter disgust that crosses the Frenchman's face is some relief, even if it doesn't fix the situation entirely. "*Merde*," he groans, shaking his head. "My God, man, I am not interested in *children*. No, I wish to buy that one." He nods in Ana's direction, and for a moment, I think he must be mistaken, that he must have meant to gesture to Sasha.

"The ballerina," he clarifies, and my stomach drops.

Alexei looks startled. "I'm very sorry, *monsieur*, but she's not for sale. She was brought out as a decoration, nothing more."

"Is she yours?" The answer only seems to pique the Frenchman's interest more. "Your private possession, I mean."

"Er—no. Not precisely." Alexei looks flustered. "She came with the most recent group of girls—the others here tonight. But she's too flawed to sell—damaged goods. I couldn't sell her for any price. It would damage my reputation to let that sort of merchandise change hands under my purview."

"What's wrong with her?" The Frenchman glances towards Ana. "She's quite beautiful, from what I can see. Russian, yes?"

"Ah—yes." An expression of frustration crosses Alexei's face as he tries to divert the other man. "I have others in much better condition—"

The Frenchman is already turning away, walking back towards the stage where Ana is trussed up in her dancer's pose. "What is your name, pretty one?" he asks, his accent so thick that it's almost hard to understand him at first.

"She won't answer you," Alexei says, with barely disguised irritation. I see him glance back towards Sofia and the couple still standing there speaking in low tones. It's not hard to parse out what he's thinking—that he stepped away from an almost certain sale for what seems to be a dead end.

For myself, I don't know whether to be relieved that Sofia's sale has been delayed, or worried for Ana. *He won't buy her once Alexei explains*, I think to myself, desperately trying to believe it. *Surely he won't.*

"Why not?"

"She's been medicated," Alexei explains. "When I say she's damaged goods, I don't just mean physically. She has regular panic attacks, lashes out if anyone tries to touch her. It's like trying to contain a feral cat." He laughs, and in that moment, I want nothing more than to strangle him.

"Then why is she out here?"

Alexei shrugs. "I didn't want her to be a total loss. She makes a lovely ornament—as you said, she's very beautiful. But she's not suitable for sale."

The Frenchman appears to consider, his gaze drifting over Ana appreciatively. He's looking at her differently from the way most of the men and even the women in the room are looking at us—less as if he wants to strip her bare and fuck her, and more the way you might look at a particularly moving piece of art in a museum. He lingers for a long moment, then turns to look at Alexei, squaring his shoulders.

"I disagree," he says simply.

"Excuse me?" Alexei blinks. "I'm sorry, *monsieur*, but I simply cannot—"

"Fifty million. Transferred to an account of your choosing immediately."

Alexei goes very still. Everyone within hearing distance does as well, turning to listen to the conversation with significant interest as Alexei struggles to formulate an answer.

"You must be joking," he says finally. "It's a remarkable jest, but you can't be serious."

"I am." the Frenchman says firmly. "Actually, you're right. She's worth *far* more than that. One Hundred million for the damaged Russian ballerina. I'd like to take possession of her immediately. My plane leaves in two hours, and my driver is unused to these mountain roads."

No. Oh god, Ana, no. I feel as if I can't breathe. Sofia is staring at Alexei and the Frenchman with mute horror, her face so pale that I'm afraid she might pass out.

"She's not worth that—people will think I've cheated you."

"I'll be happy to inform them that you have not. She is worth it to me. Now please, *Monsieur* Egorov, my time is as valuable as yours."

"Why?" Alexei stares at him, seemingly unbelieving.

The Frenchman shrugs. "Some of the finest artwork in the world has flaws, *Monsieur* Egorov. Even Michelangelo's statues have flaws in their design. Did you know that? The Japanese art of *kintsugi* is built on the concept that by embracing broken things, filling their cracks and flaws with gold, something that was damaged can become beautiful again. I find that to be a very interesting concept, do you not?"

It's an impressive argument. If the man weren't currently bartering for a human being and one of my closest friends at that, I could almost have liked him. The dumbfounded expression that he's put on Alexei's face is enough, as it is, for me to feel a flicker of respect.

"A hundred million," he repeats, becoming irritated. "You would be foolish not to take it. You said yourself that you cannot sell her."

"Ah—yes." Alexei seems to recover from his shock, nodding. "Please, come with me to my office, we can complete the sale there—"

"No need." The Frenchman motions to a man in a black suit hovering nearby, who steps forward with a briefcase and opens it, revealing a laptop. With a few quick keystrokes, he accesses an account and holds the computer out to Alexei. "Please enter your information, *monsieur*. A hundred million, transferred immediately."

Alexei looks vaguely as if he's not sure whether or not he's dreaming. He steps forward, quickly typing in the required information, and with a press of a button, a satisfied smile sweeps over the other man's face.

"Very good." The Frenchman beams at Alexei. "Please bring her to me. I wish to leave immediately. She is medicated, you say? So she cannot walk under her own power?"

"Ah, no." Alexei looks faintly pale, as if that information might suddenly change the man's mind.

"Jacques." The Frenchman waves to the black-suited man. "Have the driver bring my car around and have two men help the ballerina outside. What is her name?"

"Anastasia," Alexei says quickly. "Her name is Anastasia Ivanova."

A pleased smile crosses his face. "Ah, how lovely. The name of a princess. Another lost and broken thing, if I recall."

"No!" Sofia screams it, lurching forward and startling the couple still standing nearby. "No, you can't take her! You can't! Please, no, *ah!*"

She screams as the guard standing behind her reaches out, shocking her on the back of her thigh with what I see is a small, compact taser that I hadn't noticed until just then. Sofia nearly crumples, and the woman standing next to her reaches out, grabbing her arm to steady her.

"She's pregnant," the woman snaps at the guard. "Don't you think that's a bad idea?"

"My apologies," Alexei says quickly, striding towards them. "My security is sometimes overeager." He glares at the guard, who pales, realizing that whether he made a mistake or not, he's about to be punished for the guest's displeasure.

"Get out," Alexei snaps. "Tell someone else to come and replace you." He smiles pleasantly at the couple, returning his attention fully to them. "I'm so sorry for the interruption, but as you can see, it was urgent business. If you're still interested—"

I can't stand to listen any longer. Ana is being brought down from her rigging by three guards, two to support her while another undoes it, untying the looped ribbon holding her foot up and unlocking the chains on her wrists. She slumps against the guard like a disjointed doll, her head lolling to one side as the Frenchman waits impatiently for them to follow him.

I want to help her, to save her, to stop this, but I know that there's no way that I can. Sofia is crying silently, tears filling her eyes and sliding down her face. Her mascara doesn't budge, and I realize with a sick feeling in my stomach that the makeup artist must have used waterproof on purpose, knowing that women in a situation like ours likely wouldn't make it through the night without crying.

God forbid we not still be beautiful and perfect, even in our misery.

"Cat—" Sofia whispers, almost pleadingly, but I know that

she knows as well as I do that there's nothing to be done. The room is full of security, ours and now the Frenchman's, and even if one of us could get to her, there's nowhere that we could go after that. We're helpless, and it's one of the worst feelings I've ever experienced.

I've failed. The same words loop over and over in my head, the sight of Ana being carried to the entrance of the room turning my blood to ice. I can see Sasha staring after her, too, her face pale and shocked. It feels like a dream, a *nightmare*, like at any moment we'll wake up and be back in Manhattan. It can't be real. It can't be happening. But it is.

Ana's purchase seems to have awakened a sense of urgency in the guests. They start to move towards the remaining three of us more eagerly, with renewed interest. I try desperately to distance myself from all of it, trying to ignore the hands and eyes on my body, appraising me, determining if I'm worth whatever price Alexei has set for me. I try to pinpoint Anika and Yelena again, terrified that I might miss someone catching interest in them and have them be gone before I know it, but the party is in full swing now, and I can't always catch sight of them. The room is a swirl of mingling guests interspersed with servers circulating with trays of appetizers and champagne, and I feel dizzy as the minutes tick by, Ana's sale and loss becoming more concrete by the moment. We haven't eaten in hours, and my mouth is dry, my stomach twisted with hunger and grief, my body starting to tremble with exhaustion and the effort of holding back my emotions.

I catch sight of Alexei handing the girls off to a guard, and I catch my breath, fear shooting through me. "Take them upstairs to their room," I faintly hear him say over the ambient orchestral music and din of conversation. "I'm finished with them for tonight."

A wave of relief washes over me, enough to make my knees weak. The night clearly isn't over for us, but at least I don't have to be worried for Anika and Yelena, at least for the rest of tonight. They won't be sold, not yet, and I feel almost faint. One loss is all I can bear for the night.

On the other hand, the fact that Alexei had the children removed doesn't bode well for the three—possibly four—of us at all.

He motions to the guards standing by our stages, confirming my fears. My heart sinks as the guard starts to reach for me, grabbing my elbow and tugging me towards the edge of my stage. I do my best to keep my balance in my high heels as exhausted as I am, stumbling towards the edge as he pulls me impatiently off of it onto the main floor.

I glance over, seeing Sasha and Sofia's guards doing the same, pulling them down from the stages and moving them into a line. The couple interested in Sofia stays close, watching her with interest as Alexei turns towards those same guests, who are starting to gather curiously as we're pushed forward. He opens his mouth as if to say something and I stiffen, dreading whatever comes next. I can only imagine what kind of display he's going to put on to drive up our prices and encourage another sale.

Then, there's a sudden cracking sound, the now-familiar sound of gunshots splitting the air. I hear a crash from the main part of the house, the sound of shouting. I turn, my heart hammering in my chest and my pulse lodged in my throat as I look towards the entryway into the room with a sudden, wild hope that I can hardly bear.

I'm hallucinating.

I must be.

The stress, guilt, and shock must have gotten to be too much. It's the only answer, because what I see is Viktor coming through the door, black-garbed men in tactical gear spilling out on either side of him, and Levin, Max, and Luca close on his heels.

It can't be real.
He's here.
He came.

VIKTOR

The sight of Caterina sets me on fire, relief and fury pouring through me in equal measure as we burst into the room, weapons out and advancing on Alexei and his party.

She's alive.

She's here.

I'm going to kill that motherfucker for ever laying a hand on her.

It only takes an instant for the room to devolve into pure chaos. Several of Alexei's security move towards us with the intent to keep us from going any further, but I'd meant it when I'd said there wasn't a goddamn thing in this world that could stop me once we got inside, and especially not now that I know for sure that Caterina is here. The men we'd hired to come with us spill out on either side, firing at or fighting Alexei's men hand to hand, while Levin and Max veer off to either side, followed by Liam and Luca, and finally me.

There's no mercy given, no one who will escape. As we'd discussed, Levin, Max, Luca, Liam, and our backup go for the guards, while I stride through the room purposefully, gun in hand as I go for Alexei.

It's impossible to find him immediately. The room is a madhouse, guests scattering wildly at the sounds of gunshots, pouring towards any of the three exits, a few even going for the windows. I see Caterina duck to one side, grabbing Sofia and Sasha and getting them all down to the floor behind one of the stages, cowering away from any strange gunfire.

Ana is nowhere to be seen, and neither are my children. I take note of that instantly, a fresh rage rising up in me at the thought that Alexei might have dispensed with any of them, but especially Anika or Yelena.

As the room starts to clear, I catch sight of him trying to make it to the entrance on the far side of the room, where several of his security attempts to fight off Levin and Max. He's flanked by a few more of his security team, and I see more than one face that I recognize, men who turned to his side when he'd staged his mutiny in my absence.

I can't entirely blame them, not when Alexei had murdered the ones who stayed loyal so brutally. But the ones who died will be avenged, and in this world, disloyalty carries a steep price. I won't give them any compassion when it comes to rescuing my family and leaving this house safely.

They're all about to find out exactly how well-earned my reputation truly is.

"Stop right there." Levin turns to block Alexei's path, swinging his gun out to one side as he does and shooting the man who tries to lunge at him to disarm him point-blank in the forehead. A foot away, Max sends one of the guards heavily to the floor with a punch to the jaw, joining the growing pile of dead or injured bodies that once made up Alexei's force of men.

Without missing a beat, Max circles behind Alexei, leveling his pistol at the back of Alexei's head as Levin takes out the two remaining guards, one with a gunshot and the other with the heel of his hand driving up into the man's nose, sending him to the floor with a sudden, heavy drop.

"Viktor Andreyev would like to have a word with you," Max says, his voice even as he and Levin hold their pistols trained on Alexei's head. "So kindly don't move."

I see Alexei pale slightly as I stride forwards, snatching a pair of plastic cuffs off of one of the men as I do. Luca and Liam come in from the sides as they finish dispatching the guards they were fighting, the five of us boxing him in as I grab his arms from behind, yanking his wrists behind his back and securing them with the plastic cuffs pulled just a bit too tight.

"Sit him on the edge of one of the stages," I tell Levin, pushing Alexei towards him. "I want to check on Caterina before anything else."

"Right away, *Ussuri*." Levin grabs Alexei's cuffs, shoving him forwards, and Alexei lurches, throwing his head back to strike Levin. Levin neatly sidesteps, swinging around and delivering a punch squarely to Alexei's gut.

The blond man doubles over, coughing as Levin hauls him back upright, twisting the cuffs until Alexei's eyes widen with pain. "If you think that hurts," he growls near Alexei's ear, "just wait until the *pakhan* has had time to attend to you."

Luca, Liam, Max, and I rush immediately towards the stage where Caterina is still crouched with Sasha and Sofia, the latter of whom looks dangerously pale.

"Viktor!" Caterina gasps, leaping to her feet. "I thought—" she chokes on her words, and I can see that she's shaking. I go to her instantly, reaching for her to steady her as Luca kneels down next to us, helping Sofia to her feet.

"Here, let me help you." Max holds out a hand to Sasha, and her eyes widen as she looks up and sees him, her cheeks flushing as she takes the hand he's holding out, letting him help her up to her feet. For a moment, she sways, as if she wants to topple into his arms, but she steadies herself, looking up at him with those startlingly bright blue-green eyes of hers.

"You came too," she murmurs softly, and Max's expression softens, his eyes locking with hers in a way that I've never seen him do with any woman. For as long as he's been under my protection, he's denied all female company and never so much as flirted with a woman that I've seen. The fact that he hasn't let yet go of her hand is, for him, highly unusual.

"Shit." Luca curses as Sofia totters on her high heels, all of the blood suddenly draining out of her face as her knees give out. Caterina reaches for her instinctively, helping to support her as Luca gathers his fainted wife into his arms.

"There are bedrooms upstairs," Caterina says quickly. "Anika and Yelena should be in one of them. Alexei had them removed from the party not long before you got here."

"I'll take her there, then." Luca lifts his wife as if she weighs nothing, cradling her in his arms bridal style. "And stay with her, if you don't require my presence, Viktor." His voice is terse, and I know that the tensions that have existed between us are far from entirely dissolved. We've worked together these past weeks, the bad blood between the mafia and the Bratva thinned with our truce, but there's still mistrust there, the seeds of bitterness.

It will take time to heal those wounds. But just as I hope to make a fresh start in my own life, I hope to continue to keep our new peace from souring. It's one of my highest priorities—right after dealing with Alexei Egorov.

"We can handle it," I tell him firmly. "Stay with your wife." I glance over at Caterina and Sasha. "Do you want to go with him? You don't need to stay and see what I'm about to do. It won't be…pleasant."

Caterina and Sasha both look at Alexei almost in unison, and the expressions on both of their faces would be frightening, if they had been directed at me. I've never seen such vicious hatred on the face of either woman—*any* woman, I think, and a feeling of sick dread knots my stomach.

"No," Caterina says, her voice firm and cold. "I want to stay."

Sasha lifts her chin, her eyes meeting mine without a hint of reticence. "So do I."

"Very well then." I glance towards the door, where Luca carries Sofia out, flanked by a few men we brought as backup for protection. "Where is Ana? You said Anika and Yelena are upstairs, is she there too?"

The look on Caterina's face changes instantly to one of such grief, tears springing up in Sasha's eyes as well, that I know the answer.

"She was sold?" My voice is tight and hard, the fury that I'd momentarily quelled when I'd gone to my wife rising up hot and fierce again. "To whom?"

"I don't know much," Caterina says quietly. "He spoke French, with what sounded like a native accent, and he dressed very outrageously. He was wearing a velvet suit. He seemed to be a collector of some kind—he looked at Ana…differently." She frowns. "I don't know how to explain it, exactly. It wasn't lecherous. It was like he could have been buying a priceless antique or piece of art just as easily as a human being."

"*Shite,*" Liam curses. "You've got to be *fecking* kidding me. How long before we got here?"

The look on Caterina's face is beyond grief-stricken. "A half-hour, maybe," she whispers softly. "No more than that."

"Fuck!" Liam swears again, rubbing a hand over his mouth. "Mary, Jesus, and Joseph, I'm going to find him if it's the last fucking thing I do—" He's pacing, his hands clenched in fists as he swivels abruptly, turning towards Alexei. Before I can say anything or even guess at what he's about to do, he crosses to the stage where Levin has Alexei sitting in two long strides, a grimace of pure rage on his face.

"Fucking piece of *shite*!" Liam snarls, grabbing a fistful of Alexei's hair in his left hand and yanking his head back, delivering a blow directly to the man's nose with his right. "You don't deserve a quick death, you *fucking—*"

"And he won't get one," I say curtly, striding towards them and interrupting Liam before he can get in another blow.

Alexei spits at me, grimacing, and I backhand him across the face, hard enough to split his lip open. He rocks backward, and Levin grabs his shoulder, pushing him forward to take the next blow, my fist smashing into his jaw.

"You're going to pay for what you've done to my family," I tell him coldly through gritted teeth. "You thought, in your arrogance, that you could take what's mine. You were wrong. And now you'll live long enough to regret it."

"I didn't touch them," Alexei snarls, narrowing his eyes at me. "You can punish me for disloyalty all you like, *Ussuri*, but I didn't touch your cunt of a wife or the other girls—"

"He's lying." Caterina steps forward, her face very pale, but her chin lifted defiantly as she glares venomously at Alexei. "He forced me into his bed the first night that we were here, made me go down on my knees for him, and then fucked me. It wasn't the only time either." Her voice shakes slightly, but she doesn't stop, her hands fisted at her sides. "He raped me," she says, clearly and coldly, the words ringing out between us. "He threatened our children, tried to sell them to men who would have done the same. I want him to hurt for that. I want him to bleed."

"He beat me." Sasha steps up next to Caterina, her gaze equally as vicious as she stares Alexei down. "He hung me blindfolded from the ceiling and beat me with a belt until I nearly couldn't walk. Ana too. He did it to punish Caterina because she attacked him when he frightened Anika and tried to touch her."

It's not even the red-hot, fierce rage that I feel now, as I absorb what my wife and Sasha are saying. I see Liam tense next to me, his hands curling into fists as he rocks forwards, every line of his body screaming that he wants to beat Alexei to a bloody pulp. But I have other plans for the man, and Liam knows it.

The rage I feel now is cold, chilling me down to the bones with the dead certainty that I will take this man apart piece by piece, until he's paid ten times over for what he's done. And I won't feel guilt or regret.

He deserves it.

"Levin," I say calmly, glancing towards my right-hand man, who I trust above all else. "You have the tools?"

Levin nods. "Of course, *Ussuri*. As requested." He pushes a black bag towards me with his foot, sliding it across the hardwood floor, a cold smile on his lips as we both see Alexei start to pale with the realization of what's about to happen.

"You can't do this!" Alexei cries, twisting as he tries to stand up. "*I* was your enforcer, Viktor, your left hand. They're lying, the cunts, I—"

I nod to Liam, who pauses long enough to roll up his shirtsleeves before stepping forward and punching Alexei hard enough to send him reeling to one side, blood spurting from his mouth as a tooth comes loose.

"Again?" Liam asks, and I nod, rolling up my own as Levin stands to one side, watching.

"There's a rigging, there," Levin says, nodding to the center stage. "Should we restrain him there?"

"Excellent idea." I grab his wrists, hauling Alexei to his feet as Levin strides in front of me. When we reach the stage and drag him onto it, Levin pulls Alexei's wrists over his head, lashing him to the rigging so that he's standing with his hands bound above him. There are rings on either side of the stage, and Levin takes more rope, running it through the rings and then looping it around Alexei's ankles so that he's standing spread-eagled, unable to move.

"Strip him," I order, and Levin moves forwards with an anticipatory smile on his face, a hunting knife in his hand.

"You can't do this!" Alexei tries to twist away, but there's no moving. "Viktor—"

"*Ussuri* to you," I snarl, pacing as Levin begins to cut away Alexei's clothes.

"Wait!" Sasha steps forward to the edge of the stage and holds out her hand. "Give the knife to me."

Levin pauses, glancing from me to Sasha, hesitating.

"This is what he did to me," Sasha says, her chin trembling, but her eyes flashing with barely contained vehemence. "He cut my clothes off with a knife while I hung from the ceiling, and then he beat me. Let me do it."

Levin looks at me, waiting for my approval, and I nod. "Give the knife to her."

He holds it out, and she takes it without hesitation, stepping up onto the stage. Alexei rears back, spitting at her, but Sasha only smiles at him.

"You thought you could get away with it," she hisses. "Viktor will do the worst to you, but this is mine." Sasha raises the knife, pressing it into his chest as she starts to slice at his clothing. "Are you afraid? You must know what's coming. You tortured men for Viktor, after all. You know what he's going to do. I hope you're afraid." She drags the knife downwards, between his legs, and Alexei flinches as Sasha cuts down the sides of the suit trousers he's wearing, tearing the cloth away as it gives and tossing it to the floor.

When he's stark naked, she hands the knife back to Levin, but she doesn't get off the stage immediately. She reaches between his legs in a flash, her hand gripping his balls tightly and her nails digging in.

"This is what you did to me on that stage," Sasha hisses. "I hope you die slow."

And then she twists.

She barely manages to let go and get out of the way before Alexei pitches forward, vomiting from the pain. I give him a cold smile as I open the black bag, watching as his head sags, bile and spit dripping from his mouth.

"Just think," I tell him, reaching for a pair of pliers. "This is only the beginning."

"You have no right! " Alexei heaves again, sucking in a breath as he turns to look at me, his eyes flashing with anger and defiance. "No right to treat me this way—"

"No right?" I approach the stage, clicking the pliers in my hand. "You killed my men. You poached my clients, stole my merchandise for your own profits, killed my housekeeper and some of my staff, and sold the rest. For that alone, I ought to shoot you where you stand. But you didn't stop there."

I step up onto the stage, grabbing a handful of his hair and yanking his head back. He gasps, and I use that moment to force the pliers into his mouth, grasping one of his molars.

"You killed my people," I growl, and I yank hard, ripping the first tooth out of his mouth.

Alexei's scream echoes around the room, his body jerking as blood starts to flow. But I don't stop there.

"You sold a woman under my protection." I fasten the pliers around another tooth and yank.

"You kidnapped and tried to sell the wife and unborn child of my closest ally." Another tooth, this time one in the front.

Alexei heaves again, more bile and blood spewing as I step aside. I wait for him to finish, and when he's gasping for breath, I grab his jaw, forcing the pliers into his mouth again.

"You stole my children." Another tooth, and then another. "One for Anika and one for Yelena," I tell him coolly, as the blood drips onto the stage. "But you couldn't stop there, could you?"

"*Ussuri—*" The word comes out thickly through missing teeth and swelling lips. I smirk at him, clicking the pliers and enjoying his sudden flinch.

"Ah, you begin to remember how to speak to me with respect. But you didn't stop there, did you? Abducting my children, my wife, and those under my care, abusing them and terrorizing them, that wasn't enough for you. Stealing what's mine, that wasn't enough, either." I drop the pliers and hold out my hand, and Levin passes me the hunting knife, sharp with a serrated point. As he stands there observing, he takes another knife, flicking a lighter on and passing it over the blade, heating it.

"*Ussuri.*" Alexei gasps, shaking his head, his eyes widening. "*Ussuri*, I didn't kill you—"

"You're right. Your mistake," I chuckle. "A long list you made. Particularly when you decided that you needed to possess *everything* that belongs to me."

I lean towards him, reaching between his legs to grab his balls, dragging the blade of the knife up his inner thigh with my other hand. "No, you must have been out of your fucking mind to think that you could rape my wife and have even the mercy of a quick death."

"*Ussuri!*"

Alexei's scream turns into an animal sound, guttural and desperate, as I drag the knife across his scrotum, yanking down on his balls as I slice them away from his body. Before he can even start to bleed out, Levin is there in an instant, the heated knife pressed against the wound so that it's cauterized instantly.

The smell of searing flesh fills the room, and I hear Caterina and Sasha both gasp from behind me. But neither one of them makes any other sound, or goes to leave the room. They watch, and satisfaction floods me at the knowledge that they both are seeing what happens to anyone who dares to lay a finger on that which is mine to protect.

Particularly what belongs to me.

Alexei slumps forward, his eyes glazing over, and I grab his hair again, yanking his head back so that he's forced to look into my eyes.

"You said when you broke into my house that you took bets on how many pieces you could cut off of the men who refused to betray me before they passed out or died." I smile coldly at him. "I think we'll take this opportunity to see how many that is for you."

It doesn't take long. By the time I've divested one hand of its fingernails, Alexei's screams begin to fade, his body sagging downwards. I nod to Levin, who steps forwards with smelling salts, waving them under Alexei's nose until he comes to again.

"That was disappointingly few," I tell him. "Let's try again."

It goes on for a long time. Caterina and Sasha watch through it all, neither of them flinching or getting sick, which is more than I can say for even some men who have had to watch other men being tortured. Every time Alexei passes out, as I divest him of his nails, his teeth, his fingers joint by joint, Levin rouses him again, cauterizing any wounds that bleed too badly.

Finally, when I step back to breathe, wiping sweat from my forehead with a blood-spattered arm, Liam steps forward.

"My turn," he says quietly, and reaches for the knife.

There are two fingers left on Alexei's left hand, brought down from the rigging briefly for this purpose, and Liam pulls one of them back, pressing the knife against the joint. "This is for Ana, you fucking dogshite," he snarls as Alexei groans.

When he's done, he holds out the knife towards Max, who is standing next to Sasha as she watches, her face pale but resolute.

"Want a turn?" Liam asks, as casually as if passing a controller for a game, and Max hesitates.

His hands aren't bloodless. But I know for a fact he's never tortured a man. I can see the quandary in his face, the fight between his desire to hurt the man who hurt Sasha and the vows he once took.

Finally, he steps forward and takes the knife from Liam. "Give me his right hand," he says quietly. "The one he used to beat her."

Liam trusses up Alexei's left again, ignoring his groans of pain as he jerks the right free. Alexei's head lolls towards Max, his bloodshot eyes rolling up towards the other man's face.

"Aren't you afraid of your God?" Alexei slurs, blood dripping from his lips as the words come out thickly.

Max pauses, the knife pressed against Alexei's forefinger, the nailbed raw and red. "I would be," he says simply. "If I thought God was in this room."

When he's finished, I take the knife back and start in again, cutting away piece after piece of Alexei, Levin rousing him each time he comes close to unconsciousness. Finally, I press the knife into his groin, looking at him with cold, cruel eyes.

"You should have known there would be no mercy for you when I caught up to you." My voice is a low growl, and I slice downwards, taking off the very last piece of Alexei that I'd planned to cut away. Levin is there instantly, cauterizing the wound, and Alexei jerks in the ropes, a deep groan of agony coming from his raw throat. "No mercy for you at all, *kozy'ol*."

Alexei's head drops forwards, his eyes fixed on mine. I see everything that I'd hoped for in them—despair, agony, and above all, a deep and engulfing terror of what he knows is coming next, his own end. He fears death more than any man should; I know that now, because for all the pain I inflicted on him tonight, he hasn't begged for it even once.

If it were another man, I'd respect such restraint. I'd even call it courage. But for Alexei, I know it's nothing but cowardice.

"You said I was old and toothless," I remind him. "You didn't fear me, Alexei. *A bear without claws*, you said." I lean very close to his face then, close enough to smell the stink of his fear, sweat, and piss mixed together in a rank odor combined with the iron scent of blood.

"You should have known better," I growl then, pressing the blade of the knife to his throat. "For what you've done, this bear will rip your throat out."

And then I jerk the knife sideways, laying open his throat from ear to ear.

Alexei jackknifes in his ropes as I step back, watching as the blood starts to run down his throat, his eyes going wide with terror as he feels it streaming from him, his life leaving him in a stream of rich red that slides down him, over his chest and down his neutered body, dripping onto the stage as he jerks and twists, as if he could get free.

As if anything could save him now.

I can see the knowledge of his coming death in his eyes, the cold terror as they glaze over, and I watch him until every last drop of his life has drained away.

"Get rid of the body," I tell Levin. "Have Max and Liam help you. I need to get cleaned up before I see my children."

Caterina comes up to stand beside me, reaching for my hand. She looks up at me unflinchingly, and I know at that moment that I love this woman—completely, entirely, more than I've ever loved anyone else in all my days.

She is, without a doubt, the other half of me.

"Let's go get our daughters," she says quietly, and I nod.

Hand in hand, we leave the room.

CATERINA

While Viktor cleans Alexei's blood off of himself in the bathroom, I go to find the girls, along with Sofia and Luca. I step inside to see Sofia sleeping in one bed, Anika and Yelena curled up together in the other, and I glance at Luca.

"It's been a while," he says quietly, his voice low so as not to wake them. "Is it over?"

I nod. "He's dead," I say flatly. And then, because I know Luca will want to know, "It was slow."

"Good." Luca turns to look at Sofia. "She hasn't woken up since she fainted. Is she—did he—hurt her at all?"

I shake my head. "Not really. He wasn't gentle with her, exactly. But he didn't touch her like that or beat her. He didn't want her to accidentally lose the baby, I think. There was a couple that wanted her because they couldn't have children. I think he was keeping that in mind."

Luca's jaw tightens. "They should be glad, for their sake, that they escaped before I could get my hands on them."

"She'll be alright," I reassure him. "Traumatized for a while, probably. She'll have nightmares, if my experience is anything to go by. But it will get better in time."

"And you?" Luca looks at me sympathetically. "You've been through even more."

I'm quiet for a moment, thinking about it. There are things that have happened in the last weeks that make them seem as if they've been months, abuse and violence spanning things I would have never thought I would endure or see. I've killed a man who laid his hands on me, and tonight I watched as Viktor carved another to pieces, taking out his vengeance and mine on him in inches.

"I'm alive," I say simply. "And he isn't."

"Is that enough?" Luca asks very quietly.

I shrug, looking up at him with a grim half-smile. "It's going to have to be."

The door opens, and Viktor walks in, scrubbed as clean of Alexei's blood as he can be. The moment he steps in, shutting the door behind him, Anika starts to stir, as if she knows he's there.

He crosses the room in two strides, sitting down on the side of the bed as Anika sits up slowly, rubbing her eyes as she peers at him in the dim light from the one lamp in the room.

"Daddy?" she says in a small, hesitant voice, blinking up at him.

For the first time since I've known him, I see Viktor break down.

He reaches out, crushing her to his chest as his shoulders start to shake, pressing his lips to her hair as he squeezes his eyes tightly shut. "I'm so sorry, baby," he murmurs in a broken voice, tears clogging his throat. "I'm so sorry."

"Daddy!" Yelena squeals it sleepily as she wakes up, too, throwing herself at him. He reaches out with one broad arm, pulling her into his embrace too, and I feel tears rise sharply to my eyes as I watch Viktor hug his daughters as if he'll never again let them go.

He holds them like that for a long time, both girls clinging to him as they cry together. Finally, Anika looks up at him, her small brow furrowed.

"Are we going home now, papa?"

Viktor nods, wiping his face with the back of one hand.

BELOVED BRIDE

"Yes, *malyshka*," he says, his voice low and thick with emotion. "I'm going to take you home."

He looks up then, over at me, and meets my eyes from across the room.

"*We're* going to take you home," Viktor says.

* * *

WE TAKE Luca's plane back to Moscow, and instead of going to the loft, where my last memory is of being abducted, we go to a hotel instead. Not the one where I tried to run from Viktor, either, but another that's equally as luxurious. Viktor asks for adjoining rooms for the girls and us. Sasha offers to stay with them in their room so that they're not alone, and Viktor accepts gratefully.

Anika and Yelena are beyond exhausted. Even after sleeping on the plane, they're still out the instant we tuck them into bed. "I'll stay up for a little while," Sasha says, once we've kissed the girls goodnight. "In case they wake up and need you. I'm not all that tired."

From her face and the bags under her eyes, I know that's not true, but it's not hard to guess as to why she might not want to sleep yet. We'll all be having nightmares for a while, I'm certain of it.

But it's over now, and they'll fade in time. "Thank you," I tell Sasha, and Viktor and I each kiss the girls once more on the forehead before we retreat through the adjoining door to our own room.

I turn towards him once the door is closed, opening my mouth to say something to him, but he doesn't give me a chance. Before I can even breathe, Viktor's hands are on my waist, pulling me towards him, one hand going up to slide into my hair as his mouth comes crashing down onto mine, hard and hot and fierce.

I should push him away. I should tell him that I can't, that what's happened hasn't changed anything, that the last night we spent together is still the last time I ever planned to go to bed with him for anything other than duty. But he's kissing me as if he needs me more than he needs to breathe, both his hands in my hair now, clutching my head in his hands as his mouth devours mine hungrily.

I've never felt need in him like this before, not even the night that he was afraid he would lose Anika, not even that last night. He pulls me to him, his tongue plunging into my mouth, breathing me in, tasting me, and I can feel how hard he is against me, how every inch of him is so desperate for me that I think he might die if I don't give in.

Why are you fighting this so hard? Don't you want this, too?

Everything isn't fixed between us. It's not solved; it's not all made right, not by a long shot. But I remember him standing in that room in the mountain chalet, a bloodied knife in his hand like some avenging god, splattered in Alexei's blood as he carved the man to pieces for me.

He took everything Alexei did to me, by proxy and with his own hands, and made him pay for it in flesh. He avenged me, and I'd be lying if I said I hadn't enjoyed every fucking second of watching him kill for me.

Torture for me.

Make a man bleed for me.

My bear. My husband.

My Viktor.

I can't tell him no, and I don't want to. I can feel some emotion that I'm terrified to put a name to surging inside of me, heating my blood as I arch against him. When Viktor starts to pull away a fraction, opening his mouth as if to say something, it's my hands that bury themselves in his hair and drag his lips back to mine, my nails that sink into his scalp as I press myself tightly against him and devour his mouth with mine.

Viktor grabs my waist, lifting me up so that my legs go around his waist, carrying me towards the bed as I kiss him fiercely, letting the desire wash over me, the lust, the need to remember that I'm *alive*. Alexei tried to strip me of everything that made me myself, erase the deepest parts of me, sever Viktor and me from each other and make me into a shell of what I once was.

He failed.

Viktor spills me back onto the bed, stretching over me as he

BELOVED BRIDE

follows me down, his chest heaving as he pushes my hair out of my face. "Do you want this?" he asks, his voice deep and rough with need. "After what he did to you—"

I reach up, pressing a finger to his lips. "I need this because of it," I tell him firmly. "I want you, Viktor." I wind my arms around his neck, pulling him down to me. "I want you to erase it all," I whisper against his mouth. "Make me forget. Make me forget everything."

And he does.

Viktor undresses me slowly, hands caressing my body as if he's unwrapping a gift, sliding over my breasts and waist and hips until he grasps my thighs, spreading my legs apart as he moves down my body, his eyes hot and dark with lust as he presses his mouth against me, his tongue sliding out against my hot and eager flesh.

I cry out when he licks me, the pleasure bursting across my skin, electric sparks dancing over me as he swirls his tongue expertly over my clit, licking and sucking in all the places that he knows I like best, driving me towards a climax hard and fast, knowing that it's what I need. I let it come, hands buried in his hair as he sucks my clit into his mouth, thrusting two fingers into my wet and aching pussy as he pushes me over the edge, reminding me what pleasure is, what desire feels like, what it feels like to *need* so badly that I'd do anything to have him above me, around me, inside of me.

"Viktor!" I scream his name as I come, thighs clamped around his face. He keeps sucking as I grind against him, coming hard on his tongue as my back arches, and I writhe on the bed, riding the wave of pleasure for as long as I can.

The moment I start to go limp, he pulls back, his eyes dark and wild as he jerks open the fly of his pants, his thick cock springing free as he reaches in to pull it out. "I need you now, Caterina," he growls. *"Lyubov moya,* I need you."

I nod breathlessly, swallowing hard as I reach for him, and he leans over me, pressing his swollen cockhead against my entrance and thrusting into me with one hard, hot slide that sends me into another spasm of pleasure, my body clenching tightly around him as I arch upwards, pressing every inch of flesh that I can against his as I cling to him, moaning aloud with the ecstasy of it.

It feels so fucking good. So *right*, no matter what I tell myself. And in this moment, thinking of everything that's happened between Viktor bringing me to his first safe house and now, I have one thought that rings through my head clearly as he starts to thrust with long, powerful strokes that possess me entirely with each one.

We were meant for each other, he and I.

It would take a strong woman to stand at the side of the *Ussuri*. A woman who can be fearless, who can be brave, who can look at blood and death and pain and not flinch. A woman who can rule, just like him.

I could be that woman if he'd let me.

Viktor groans above me, his hand cupping my face as he kisses me hard, panting against my mouth. "Caterina," he whispers as he stiffens, his back arching as he thrusts into me deeply and holds himself there. "I can't—*bladya*, I need—"

His voice breaks as I feel him shudder, his cock going iron-hard inside of me, and I feel him start to come, my body tightening around him in response. He kisses me again, hot and fierce, surging inside of me as he shudders with a ripple of pure pleasure, his cum filling me in a hot rush that sends another wave of pleasure over me too, the sensation almost too much.

"*Lyubov moya*," he whispers as he leans against me, still shuddering with the last spasms of his climax. "Caterina. My love."

The words hit me, sending a flood of emotion through me in an almost dizzying rush, and as Viktor rolls to his side, I pull away, my heart pounding.

"Caterina, no." His arms tighten around me, pulling me closer. "Don't do this, please."

I swallow hard, fighting back the tears that rise up hot and fast, threatening to overcome me. "Viktor, I—"

"No. Let me speak." His arms are hard around me, and I want to lean into them, to sink against his chest and let myself luxuriate in the aftermath, in the scent of his skin and mine on the sheets, in the warmth of our bodies intertwined.

I can't. I swore I wouldn't.

Viktor lets go of me, pushing himself up to a sitting position as he tugs the sheet over his legs, letting it pool around his hips. "I've wanted to tell you, Caterina, every second since we left the mountains how brave I thought you were. How strong to protect the others the way you did, to fight for them. How *grateful* I am that you protected Anika and Yelena most of all, no matter what it cost." His eyes meet mine, holding my gaze, and I feel myself flush under the weight of it.

I want to go to him, to let him hold me. But if I do, I don't think I'll ever be able to pull away again.

"Caterina." He reaches for my hand, and I let him. I don't have the strength to stop him. I can barely control the emotions flooding me now. "Cat, I love you."

I flinch, feeling the words strike me squarely in the chest, a knife to my heart. Pain blossoms through me, an ache that I'd thought I might not feel again, not since that last argument that we had. "I wish you hadn't said that," I whisper.

Viktor looks hurt. "Why not? It's the truth."

"I know." I swallow hard, pulling my hand away from his. "And that's why." I look over at him, forcing myself to meet his eyes. "It makes it so much harder, knowing that, when we can't have a real marriage. I've accepted that you can't change, Viktor. But you need to accept that I can't live with what you are and what you do."

Viktor is quiet for a long moment, his eyes dropping to the bed. When he looks up at me again, his face is calm and peaceful.

"That's where you're wrong, Caterina," he says gently. "Because for me, now, everything *has* changed."

CATERINA

I look at him, speechless, my heart pounding in my chest. When I can finally speak, I look up at him, feeling breathless.

"What do you mean?" I ask quietly, and Viktor takes my hand again. This time, I don't pull it away.

"I see things in a different light now, Caterina." Viktor pauses, meeting my eyes, and I can see the sincerity in them, how hard he's trying to make me believe him. "I almost lost you. I almost lost my *children* to the same ordeal that I've put hundreds of other women through, and I see it now. It shouldn't have taken almost losing my own wife and children, and other women I was supposed to protect for me to understand what you've been trying to tell me all along. But I see it now, and I'm so sorry, Cat. I'm sorry I didn't understand sooner."

He takes a breath, his hands tightening around mine as he reaches for my other one. "I've told myself my whole life the things that my grandfather and father said, the things that I came up with in my own head to justify it. I'm not going to repeat them to you; you've heard them all. But I'm not lying when I say that I've been struggling with it for some time, Caterina. I was just stubborn—too stubborn to admit that you might be right, to admit that my entire life has been built on something that could never be justified no matter how hard I tried."

"What are you trying to say?" I ask him, feeling my pulse lodged in my throat, beating wildly. I'm terrified to trust in what he's saying, to believe him only to be disappointed. I need to hear it aloud, in plain words, to know beyond a shadow of a doubt.

"I'm getting out of the sex trade, Caterina," he says bluntly, and I let out the breath that I've been holding in a rush, my shoulders sagging forward.

"Viktor, I—"

He shakes his head, still speaking. "Luca and I are working out deals to see what businesses we can invest in together instead, perhaps even bring Liam in on it. Our three families, working together. We talked about it on the plane, while you and the others were sleeping." Viktor pauses, breathing in slowly. "I'm never going to be legit, Caterina. I need you to understand that. Men like us—Luca and Liam and myself—we're not made for a straight-edged life. We're always going to be what we were born to be to some extent—mob bosses, mafia, men that other men fear, dealing in things that are illegal and in the shadows. But I won't sell women any longer; I can promise you that."

"There might still be some element of sex to my businesses," he continues. "That's what I know, and there are other things I can invest in. Strip clubs, porn—there's always a market for anything involving sex. But whatever I do, the women involved will want to be there. It will be consensual, and I'll make sure that none of them are ever coerced."

I stare at him for a long moment, afraid to believe what I'm hearing. I'm so scared to trust it, but Viktor is looking at me with that deep, intense gaze, holding mine in a way that tells me that he means everything he's saying, that it's not a trick or a lie. Somewhere between our fight and now, he's seen what I've been trying to tell him all along. He's right that it shouldn't have taken so much for him to understand—but he does now. I'm certain of it, looking into his eyes, this man that I've come to know so well no matter how hard I've fought against it.

I want him. I want *this, us,* our marriage. I want everything we could be together, and the very last reason that I had to fight against it has just been wiped away.

"Do you really mean it?" I whisper. "Truly?"

Viktor nods, his gaze never leaving mine. "I love you, Caterina," he murmurs. "And no matter what I have to change in order to be with you, I will."

He reaches for me again then, pulling me into his arms, and this time I go willingly. "I love you too," I whisper as his mouth comes down onto mine, claiming me in a searing kiss as he spills me back onto the pillows, his hands roving over my body as I feel him rise against my thigh, hot and hard and eager for round two.

"I love you," he groans against my lips. "*Lyubov moya.* My love. My wife."

"And I love you."

I kiss him back, fierce and hot, and I whisper it against his lips again and again as he slides into me, claiming me for his own.

I love you, I love you, I love you.

I love you.

* * *

THE NEXT MORNING, in the hotel's lobby, we part ways. Luca and Sofia are returning with Viktor, Max, Levin, and I to Manhattan. We stand there with Liam and Sasha, discussing what happens next.

"I haven't forgotten what you asked of me," Viktor says to Max, glancing at him. "Nor will I forget how you stood beside me in that fight. Luca and I have talked briefly, but we'll talk more once we're in Manhattan, and I'll do what I can. You can stay at our home with us until it's all settled."

"Thank you," Max says sincerely. "It's all I can ask."

"I'm headed back to Boston," Liam says, looking at Viktor. "But as soon as I settle a few things there, I'm going to begin looking into what happened to Ana." His gaze flicks to Sofia, who is pale again at the mention of her friend, her lips pressed tightly together. "I'm going to find her," he says quietly. "I promise. No matter what it takes."

"I'll give you access to the files I have on my old clients," Viktor tells him. "Come to Manhattan as soon as you can. If this Frenchman is someone I've sold to in the past, we'll find him."

Liam nods. "Thank you. I'll come as soon as I can."

Viktor glances at Sasha then, who is standing nervously to one side, stealing glances at Max every few moments. "I've done you a great disservice," he says quietly. "And I want to apologize to you, sincerely, though I know it can't undo all that you've suffered. I want to make it right. If you don't want to, there's no need for you to return to New York with us. I'll set you up here in Moscow if you want to stay, pay for an apartment for you, and cover whatever you need or want. If it's school, I'll pay for that as well. I know that it's not enough," he says, looking at her directly. "But I want to do what I can."

Sasha hesitates, and I can see the indecision on her face. She looks towards the large window of the hotel lobby, the view of Moscow just beyond it, the grey skies and streets, the colorful domes of St. Basil's cathedral rising up in the distance. I can see the longing in her eyes for just a moment, the desire to stay here, in the place where she was born, the place that she was stolen away from.

And then she looks back towards Max, and I see something else in her eyes.

Something that I know can never, ever work. Not with him.

I open my mouth to say something, tell her that she should stay, start a new life here. But something in her face stops me.

It needs to be her choice. No one else's. Even if it's the wrong decision in the end, even if it breaks her heart, it will be her choice.

Max looks over then, as if feeling her eyes on him, and their gazes lock for a moment. He looks away almost immediately, but I can see the decision settle on Sasha's face, and she takes a deep breath.

"I'll come back to Manhattan," she says quietly. "I want to stay with Anika and Yelena. I'm sure Caterina could use the help sometimes.

And I've grown very attached to them. I'd like to be their nanny, of sorts. If you'll have me," she adds, looking nervously at Viktor and me.

"If that's what you want," I say gently, and Viktor nods.

"It's your choice," he says firmly, echoing the thoughts in my head.

Sasha glances at Max, then back at us.

"I'm coming back with you."

* * *

VIKTOR and I take seats towards the back of the plane, a little distance away from the others. We both feel the need to have a moment to ourselves, and he reaches for my hand almost as soon as we sit down, his fingers lacing through mine. "Luca, Levin, and I talked more this morning," he says quietly. "There are investments we're looking into in Manhattan. Sex clubs and dungeons, nothing as elegant as you might have hoped," he says with a laugh. "But it's a good investment and one that I know. And besides that—"

He pauses, and I see a flicker of nervousness cross his face before he continues. "Levin has a contact with the syndicate that he once worked for. They need someone to train spies and assassins for their organization, and Levin would be an excellent choice for that, and to help me run it."

I blink at him, taking it all in. It's more than he's ever told me about anything involving his business. I know what he's doing—trying to include me, to make this the equal partnership that I now know we both want. I remember Sofia telling me about the things Luca talks to her about, how much they share, and I feel a swell of warmth in my chest as I squeeze Viktor's hand.

"Assassins and spies?" I raise an eyebrow. "I'd have a hard time believing it if it were anyone but you. I've never heard of such a thing. But if that's what you want to do, I support you."

"Is it enough?" Viktor looks at me, and I can see the worry plainly in his eyes now. "Is this what you want, Cat?"

I nod, holding his gaze with mine as I lean up to kiss him softly. "It is," I murmur. "And most of all, I want you."

"I'm glad to hear that." He reaches into his jacket then, and I gasp softly when I see what he pulls out.

It's a black velvet box, and I can hardly believe what I'm seeing as he opens it.

Nestled inside is an engagement ring, a blood-red oval ruby flanked by round diamonds on a yellow gold band. It looks gorgeous, like an antique unearthed from some ancient castle, and I stare at Viktor as he slides it out of the box and holds it out to me.

"I saw this when I bought our wedding bands," he says softly. "I had no idea then what this marriage would become. I wouldn't have believed anyone if they had told me. But I'm grateful that it did, Caterina. I'm grateful for everything that you've done for me. You've made me a better man—not different, just better."

He takes a breath, the ring still hovering above my hand. "I can't change entirely, Cat. I am still the man you married, the *Ussuri*, the man who can do what you saw in that room in the mountains and not flinch. But I swear to you, I will never again take a woman away from her home and force her into a situation in which she has no choice. That part of my life, I'm done with. I may be a bloody man still, as we all are. But I will be a better one, for you. For our daughters. For our family."

Slowly, he slides the ring onto my finger. It's a perfect fit, and it shimmers in the sunlight coming through the window of the plane, gleaming like blood on my outstretched hand. Blood and light reflected on my skin.

"Caterina, will you marry me?"

I look up at him, this man that I love, my Viktor, and I nod.

There was never any answer but the one that I say out loud, a breath against his lips as he leans down to kiss me.

"*Yes.*"

When he finally pulls away, I hold onto his hand, my heart beating hard in my chest all over again.

"I have something for you too," I say quietly, and I move his hand down to my stomach, pressing it against my still-flat belly.

Viktor stares at me in astonishment. "Caterina—"

"I took a test this morning while you were downstairs. I don't know why—missing my period could have been stress. I'd thought it was. But I just had a feeling, and Sasha went out to get me one." I look up at him, my eyes shining. "I counted back, and I'm sure of the timing. It lines up with just before I was abducted in Moscow. Our baby—" I swallow hard, blinking back tears. "Our baby survived everything, Viktor. It's a boy, I'm sure of it. An heir for your new endeavors, just the way you wanted."

"Caterina." He breathes my name, his hands pressed against my face as he brings my mouth up to his, kissing me fiercely. "I don't care if it's a boy or a girl," he whispers against my lips. "All I care about is that we're going to have a child together, a new member of our family. That's all that matters to me."

I feel tears spring to my eyes as he kisses me again, his forehead pressed against mine. We kiss like that for a long time, hands clasped together, the ring warm against my skin as we breathe each other in.

When we split apart at long last, I lean back in the seat, still holding Viktor's hand as I look out the window. There are changes ahead of us, a new life, and new challenges. But all I care about, right now, is that we're headed home.

Home to New York and our new future.

"I love you," I whisper, looking up at Viktor, and he smiles down at me, his face shining with all the love he has for me in return.

"I love you too," he murmurs, raising my hand to his lips and kissing it, just above the ring on my left finger.

"My Caterina. My beloved bride."

***

I HOPE you enjoyed Beloved Bride! Ana's story is just beginning. You can order here. Please continue to read for a sneak peek.

IRISH SAVIOR

ANA

Pain. All I know is pain, half-sensible, twisted into a position that no one should hold for this long, every muscle in my body aching.

Voices, someone is saying my name.

Hands, undoing the ropes. Bringing me down, the blessed feeling of being free, and then the rush of blood to all the places where my circulation couldn't reach, sending new waves of pain over me, through me, until I would scream with it if I could make a sound.

More hands, lifting me, carrying me. The feel of cool leather under my cheek, the smell of an expensive car. Cold air, and then the car moves around corners and over bumpy roads until I want to be sick, but I don't have the strength.

I don't think I'll have the strength ever again.

I wish I could just die.

The hands again, lifting me out of the car. Up, up stairs, more leather against my arms and legs, those hands settling me into a seat. My eyes focusing just long enough to see a strange, handsome face hovering over mine, and a rich, thick accent speaking to me.

"We'll be home soon," he says.

I don't know how to tell him that I no longer have a home. My apartment is gone. My life is gone. But my lips and tongue still aren't working, my body paralyzed, and I slump back into the seat as someone pulls a soft blanket over me. It feels better than anything has in a long time, soft and warm like cashmere, and I want to tell whoever it is that they shouldn't, that he'll be angry.

Alexei.

I don't want to make him angry.

The roar of an engine, the feeling of lifting, soaring, and then the exhaustion of it all creeps over me, and my head falls to one side as my eyelids slide shut again.

Am I falling asleep, or am I dying?

I can't bring myself to care.

* * *

THE SOUND of birds is what wakes me. I open my eyes slowly, blinking away the last of sleep as I struggle to wake up all the way. My face feels puffy, my eyes dry and sticky, and my tongue is stuck to the roof of my mouth, which feels as if it's been stuffed with cotton.

I don't know where I am.

There were no birds at the mountain chalet. At least, I'm pretty sure that there weren't. Alexei didn't let us out to see.

Alexei. Fear rises up in me, hot and sharp, and I feel like I'm going to throw up. I push myself upright, feeling pain shoot through me as I wrap my arms around my stomach, trying not to be sick. I'm not even sure if I can stand up, and I don't want to be sick all over the bed.

My eyes focus a little more, taking in more of my surroundings, anything to distract myself. *This is nothing like the room at the chalet*, I realize, reaching out with one hand to smooth it over the bedspread. It's a floral chintz, blue and white, and there are pillows to match, tossed on a wing chair by the window. I turn slowly, pressing my hand against the pillow I'd slept on, and my hand sinks into it.

Down. Luxurious and soft. Another one next to it, as if I might need two.

Slowly, I take in the rest of the room. There is a wide bay window open to let in a warm spring breeze and birdsong. Sheer lace curtains flutter at the windows, a soft throw blanket that looks like cashmere over the back of the wing chair. On the other wall, I see a wooden wardrobe that looks antique, the surface is worn down to a dark sheen with brass hardware. Everything in the smallish room looks old, but in a way that seems intentional, rather than shabby, down to the framing around the door and the antique knob. There's another door directly across from the bed, and as I lean forward, I can peer around it just enough to see that it's a small bathroom with an iron clawfoot tub.

Where the fuck am I? My heart starts to pound in my chest, anxiety rising up hot and thick, and I clutch the blankets around my hips, trying not to panic. I can feel a spiral coming on, the fear clutching at my throat, and I force myself to push back the blankets, swinging my legs over the edge of the bed.

After being forced into the pointe shoes that Alexei had made me wear, my feet are even more painful than usual. They cramp the instant I try to stand up on them. Still, I force myself to do it anyway, holding onto the bedside table and then the wall as I move towards the window, suddenly desperate to see out of it.

I'll know where I am then, maybe. There will be some clue. And if nothing else, at least I'll feel the sunshine on my face. It's been so long.

The breeze coming in is warm, nothing like the bitingly cold wind in the mountains of Russia. I'm far from there, wherever I am, and I breathe in for a moment, the smells of a city reaching my nose. It's not the scent of an American city, though, thick with exhaust and smog. Instead, I just smell sunshine, fresh bread, coffee wafting from somewhere below. My stomach rumbles, and I press my hand to it, looking out across the rows of apartment buildings that look hundreds of years old, like something out of a history book, like nothing I've ever seen before.

And in the distance, faintly, the shape of the Eiffel Tower.

I blink, once, and then once more. *I'm hallucinating. I'm dreaming.* I pinch my cheeks, slap my face, anything to wake myself up. But when I look again, it's still there.

What the fuck is happening?

The sound of the doorknob turning jolts me out of my freshly spiraling thoughts. I spin as quickly as I can, gripping the edge of the windowsill to steady myself as the door opens, terrified that it's going to be Alexei on the other side of it.

But it's not.

It's a man I've never seen before, strikingly handsome, with messy dark hair and piercing blue eyes, wearing silk pajama pants and a silk dressing gown over that. He looks at me as if it's not at all surprising that I'm here or that he is. I realize with a start that he has a breakfast tray in his hands with a covered plate on it, a glass of orange juice that looks freshly squeezed, and small glass pots of jam and syrup.

The smell wafts towards me, eggs and something made of sweet batter, and my stomach rumbles again, turning over painfully. I don't let go of the windowsill, though, shrinking back as he sets the tray on the bed and turns to face me.

"Good morning," the man says casually in English, but his voice is so thickly accented that there's no doubt that he's as French as the city outside my window.

I'm dreaming. I must be. Or I've gone mad.

"Did you sleep well, Anastasia?"

I stare at him, my stomach dropping to my toes as my mind races, trying to make sense of it all. *How the fuck does he know my name?*

"Who are you?" I blurt out, feeling the windowsill biting into my hands, the pain in my feet shooting up into my calves. But I don't move. I can't. I'm frozen in place with panic, my eyes flicking to the door as a possible means of escape, even though I know I'll never make it.

The man smiles at me. "Of course," he says, his voice smooth and rich as melted chocolate. "How rude of me." He makes a small bow at the waist with a flourish, and I stare at him, certain now that I've gone entirely insane.

"My name is Alexandre Sartre," he says as he looks up at me, straightening.

"A—Alexandre?" I can't wrap my mouth around his last name, not right now.

"Yes, that's right." He smiles pleasantly. "Alexandre Sartre."

"What am I doing here?" My voice is shaking, and I swallow hard. "I want to go home."

His smile falters a little. "I'm afraid that's quite impossible, Anastasia."

I blink at him, feeling my hands start to tremble too. "Why—why is that?"

"Well, Anastasia, it's quite simple." The smile returns to Alexandre's face, his lips parting to show gleaming white teeth.

"You're here because I bought you, Anastasia Ivanova." He steps away from the bed and walks towards me, his fingers slipping under my chin and tilting it up so that I'm forced to look into his brilliant blue eyes.

"You're very beautiful," he murmurs. "And you're mine now."

* * *

Ana's story is just beginning. You can order here.

Printed in Great Britain
by Amazon